GW00400103

BERLIN:
CAUGHT
IN THE
MOUSETRAP

BERLIN: CAUGHT IN THE MOUSETRAP

Paul Grant

© **Paul Grant 2017**

All rights reserved
ISBN: 9781521532386

Paul Grant has asserted his rights under the Copyright, Designs and Patents Act, 1988, to be identified as the author of this work.

This novel is a work of fiction and, except in the case of historical fact, any resemblance to actual persons, living or dead, is purely coincidental.

<u>Thanks</u>

I would like to thank Hilary Johnson for her advice when starting out on the road to writing my first book. She pointed me in the right direction when I clearly needed it. I would also like to thank Caroline Upcher, who provided tremendous insight and patience reading many different drafts of my work.

My partner, Hayley, has used her precious time to read numerous drafts and provided lots of practical advice. As always, I am truly grateful to her.

PROLOGUE

It had been a long day. The job of renovating the large house on the outskirts of Garbsen was not a problem in itself; it was the client, or more to the point, the client's wife, who was the problem. Her constant nagging about when the job would be finished, obsessed if it would be ready for her son's wedding, was making it more of a chore than it should have been. It would be ready a month earlier than Klaus had actually agreed upon if his calculations were correct, and they usually were. Not only that, he'd negotiated a healthy bonus if indeed it was finished early.

So it was with particular pleasure that evening, that Klaus Schultz was able to kick up his feet and let the dulcet tones of one of the red wines Ulrich had brought back from his latest trip wash over him. He snuggled down in his armchair, closing his eyes, allowing the wine to draw out the stresses of the day. He allowed a small grin to form on his face, feeling particularly grateful for the small comforts his humble abode brought him. He felt Maria's hands on his shoulders. As she started to rub, he let out a slow groan.

'Just a bit lower. That's the spot,' he managed.

Klaus believed some people didn't have the right priorities in life, but then again his own experiences had sharpened his perspective.

3

After five minutes or so of expert manipulation, Maria kissed him on the top of the head. Klaus mumbled his thanks. He felt his eyes dipping slightly as the warmth of the fire enveloped him. His leg jolted, hard, the remnants of past traumas still with him, if nonetheless waning gradually with time. He was toying with the idea of turning in for the night, but not seriously intending to move from a position of such comfort. The shrill ring of the telephone made him jump. He'd only had the thing installed for business and he certainly didn't expect calls at this time of night. Only the thought it could have been Eva or Ulrich made him answer it.

'Schultz.' He knew he sounded craggy and short and didn't particularly care.

Maria mouthed, 'Who is it?'

Klaus shrugged.

There was a momentary silence on the other end before the person bothered to answer.

'Klaus Schultz, you old warrior.' The voice was Russian-accented German. Klaus knew that well from the past.

'Who is this?'

'Come, come, Schultz. You can't tell me you don't recognise the voice?'

Klaus immediately felt cold in spite of the fire. The bitter chill of Kolyma prickled his spine. He had now placed the voice, and it wasn't welcome.

'What do you want, Burzin?'

He chuckled, 'It was always "What do you want, Burzin?" At least give me some credit. After all, when have I ever let you down?'

Klaus thought about it for a moment, and then conceded he was probably right, but didn't actually say so. He was still too annoyed at the interruption of his peace, especially by a man who was part of the system that now made him strive and treasure such comforts.

4

'A man could get really offended by such an affront. Try to relax a little, Klaus. Not everybody is out to get you.' He was shouting slightly above the noise of the street behind him. He was calling from a busy city; Klaus could imagine where.

'I was relaxing before you called. Now, what do you want?'

There was another delay. By now, Klaus knew Burzin was taking a long drag on a cigarette, like he had always done. It was his oxygen.

'I have some information which could be of interest to you.'

'What could you have to say that is of interest to me? We are in two completely different worlds, Burzin. Unless you know something about a building contract I might get my hands on?'

'Not quite, Klaus. Not quite. It is, however, some important information Ulrich could use. It would do his career the world of good.'

Burzin had hit a sore point. Klaus didn't like his son's chosen career one bit, but he couldn't help his curiosity being pricked. After all, what father wouldn't want to help his son advance up the ladder, even if he wasn't entirely comfortable with what he was doing?

'Of course, there'll be nothing in this for you?'

'Naturally, I would gain something, but nothing in life is free, as the Americans say.'

That didn't make Klaus feel any better. He disliked Americans nearly as much as he did the Russians.

'So why not give the information to Ulrich. Why involve me?'

'No, that's not the way it's done.' He was laughing again. 'We don't communicate with each other in such a crude way. Besides, I wanted you to be aware how important this information is.'

Klaus' mind had started to tick now. There was a reason for everything with these people. No act completed without giving a message or having an effect on somebody somewhere down the line. As Burzin had hoped, whatever it was, it was now gnawing away at Klaus, gripping his stomach, bothering him.

'Important to me?'

'Yes, personally.' Burzin had recognised the tension in his voice.

'Do I need a pen or something?' Klaus knew it was an idiotic question as soon as it came out, but these people had a way of turning anger into desperation in a matter of seconds. Klaus had been there before.

'There will be a package on the second floor scaffolding of that place you're renovating, opposite that hideous bathroom window you've just fitted today. It's all in there.'

Klaus felt sick. It was the detail that told him that after all this time they were still watching his every move, checking for any small matter they could exploit.

'And what am I supposed to do with this information?'

A cigarette was in his mouth again. 'You'll work it out. If there's one thing I admired you for, it was your ability to stick at it. After all, not many survive what you survived.'

Klaus nearly found himself thanking Burzin, then his anger returned.

'I don't think I'm your man. I am just a builder. Find somebody else.'

Klaus was about to put down the phone, but Burzin got in first, 'This is about *your* happiness, Klaus.'

'You're being obtuse again.'

'This information affects everybody in the Russian sector of Berlin.' There was another long pause, but it could have been to allow the point to sink in this time. Either way, it had grabbed Klaus' attention.

'Yes, Klaus, that means your daughter, Eva, and that lovely little granddaughter of yours. Tanja, isn't it?'

There was a click and the line went dead.

***

The next morning Klaus was on site earlier than usual. The late night call had unsettled him. He hated the shady world into which he'd been thrust after his belated return from Russia. Back then it had been a case of necessity, survival. He felt responsibility, guilt even, for his son's recruitment back in '53. He hated the fact that one of his oldest comrades had dragged Ulrich into the same shady world. Since then, he had known what Ulrich had been doing, for whom he had been working, but Klaus knew better than to ask the details. He didn't want to know, not that Ulrich would tell him anyway. Working with his hands most of the day helped him forget. Keeping his brain occupied during the times he wasn't on site, with company accounts, making sure the suppliers were paid and making sure he had a backlog of clients, dulled the past. Burzin's call had brought all the memories, and the pain, back. The problem was Burzin knew his weak spot. People like that always did.

It was just before seven. Thankfully, the client had decided to stay at his wife's sister's for a few weeks whilst they dealt with the roof on the large extension. It wasn't only that, or even the beautiful, early summer morning that brought him to the site half an hour earlier than his partner. He had slept fitfully thinking about the package Burzin had spoken of. What was so important to the people of Berlin, precisely those in the Soviet sectors, that word had to be passed in this manner? He knew why he had been chosen. Burzin was well aware what Ulrich did. He also knew Klaus' link with Markus Schram. It was informal enough for the KGB to leak information to the other side. Unwittingly, he would be the go-between.

Klaus felt the dew on his hands as he climbed the wooden ladder to the upper level of the scaffolding. Other than the dull thud of his boots on the boards, the morning birdsong was the only sound. He stopped opposite the bathroom window he and his partner, Ulf Danneman, had fitted the day before. Burzin was right; the stained glass was hideous, an unnecessary excess. He shrugged. It seemed to be the way of the world these days, but as long as he wasn't footing the bill, who was he to argue?

He got down onto his knees and reached over the edge of the scaffolding board in front of the window. He ran his hand along the outside of the kicker board for the length of the window, but couldn't feel anything. Having already checked the level below, he was beginning to wonder if Burzin had sent him on a wild goose chase. But he knew Burzin better than that. He pulled his hand back through and accidentally knocked the bucket they'd used for sand and cement to bed in the window the day before. Not only did he notice Ulf hadn't bothered to clean it, but as he'd disturbed it, something behind it had pushed the bucket towards him. He quickly reached around the back of the bucket and found an oilskin document holder, similar to the type used on ships to keep maps dry. The package was light and could have contained no more than a few sheets of paper. Klaus felt his heart quicken. Now that he was holding Burzin's document, he felt overwhelmed, even scared. It made him glance around to ensure nobody was watching him. Like it or not, he was part of the game now.

Klaus' natural disgust for Burzin and his ilk would normally have told him not to get involved in this matter anymore than he had to. That meant handing the package over, but no more than that. If he was to read the contents, he became truly involved. That would make things different.

He wandered back to his van, throwing the package in the open window and hauling himself into the cab after it. He wound the window closed, the secretive behaviour in evidence again; as much as he hated it, he couldn't help himself. Perhaps that was the reason he found himself breaking the seal on the package and the same reason he felt his hand inside once it was open. Deep down, he knew the reason he was so interested was the words Burzin had used. They had been the words rattling around in his head all night. 'This information affects everybody in the Russian sector, Klaus.' The words were vague, but personal to Klaus, enough to make him worry.

The document he held in his hand was typed, official looking. He quickly realised it was the minutes for a meeting. The heading was marked "Operation Rose." The participants' names were vaguely familiar to him: Honecker, Verner, Stoph, Mielke, Maron. They had been discussing some kind of large scale building project. There were detailed manifests of building materials, concrete blocks, posts, sand and cement, even barbed wire. These materials, in very large volumes, he noted, were to be stored in different locations around Berlin, and when Klaus looked at the name places in detail, Lichtenberg, Pankow, Friedrichshain, Treptow, he realised they were all in the Soviet sector.

When he turned the second page, he could see the project had a military element to it. It discussed numbers of Vopos, People's Police, Kampfgruppen, Militia, and NVA, the People's Army, and their different district postings. It was clear this was an East German government document and that no doubt explained how Burzin had come by it. Klaus' mind had started to tick over. Why would so many military personnel be needed for a building project? Why was there such a volume of barbed wire and coils?

Now engrossed, he turned to the third page. There was more detailed planning about the build-up to the operation. There were instructions to the Grepos, the Border Police, in how to spot and deal with "Border Crossers". There were to be intensified checks from first July at all S-Bahn stations close to the sector borders. People with luggage and extra baggage were to be dealt with by confiscation of identification. Klaus' mind returned to the source of his fear, his daughter Eva and the baby. They were still in Berlin, the Soviet sector, and Burzin knew it.

He could feel a sick tension building in his stomach. The document detailed support that could be expected from "friendly forces". I wonder if they knew one of the friendly force had leaked their documents. As he read on, it was clear the people in the meeting didn't yet have the authorisation for the final measure to be put in place, whatever that happened to be. Klaus was feeling confused, anxious. He couldn't put his finger on exactly why, but when he turned the next page, he knew.

The fifth page contained only a map. Without the context, he probably wouldn't have given it a second glance. With all the build-up of materials and men, with Burzin handing him the documents, leaking them from East Berlin, he now knew what he was looking at. There was a bold line running through the centre of the map, hand-drawn and crude. Klaus' mouth was dry and he felt sick.

A sharp tap on the window nearly made him jump out of his skin. Klaus dropped some of the papers in shock. He turned to see Ulf's beaming face staring back at him.

He fumbled with the window, eventually yanking it down, glad for the fresh air.

'You look like you've seen a ghost,' Ulf said, still smiling.

'I think I just have,' Klaus said.

Ulf looked in at all the papers, 'What have I told you about always looking at bills and stuff? They'll get sorted. You worry too much.'

Klaus was about to say something, then thought better of it. If only things were that simple.

***

It had been a long day, and Klaus had been distracted. Ulf had even commented on it. For once, he couldn't listen to Ulf's little anecdotes about his friends at the local bar. Normally, they kept him entertained for hours whilst they worked, but today had been different. He'd not eaten at lunch time and didn't feel like it now at the end of the working day. Normally, his appetite after a long, hard day in the open air was voracious. All day the content of the documents had been gnawing away at him. He knew that somebody had to do something about what was planned. Somebody had to stop it. The only thing that had kept him going was the thought he'd be picking Ulrich up from the train station that evening. He'd know how to handle things. He was smart like that.

The train from Munich was half an hour late. It gave him the chance to buy a beer and a würst and finish neither. His mind was on Berlin, on Eva and the baby. Klaus was not happy about her choice of partner. He felt the American journalist, Kaymer, arrogant and full of himself. He could only see trouble in it for his daughter. He shook his head trying to push the thoughts from his mind. He watched the people on the concourse come and go, saying their farewells, carting their heavy bags behind them. He was so lost in it all, he missed Ulrich standing in front of him, his blond fringe combed back perfectly, bag perched easily over his shoulder.

'Is that woman still giving you a hard time about the colour of the roof tiles?' he asked.

'What?' Klaus said.

'Well, you look like you've got the weight of the world on your shoulders.'

'Sorry, son, I was miles away.' Klaus gave Ulrich a hug and instinctively took his bag from him.

'So, what's up?' Ulrich said.

'Come on, we can talk about it in the van,' Klaus said, looking around nervously.

By the time they were back at the van, they were talking normally about Klaus' job, the train journey, what they might do at the weekend; in fact, anything but Ulrich's job.

In the privacy of the van cab, above the growling of the heavy diesel engine, Ulrich tried again, 'So what's up, Pap? It looks to me like it's much more than just a bit of business.'

'You could say that.' Klaus pressed down on the clutch and pushed the van into gear using the stick at the side of the steering wheel column. 'I had a call last night. You remember the Russian, Burzin?'

The surprise in Ulrich's voice wasn't hard to detect, 'The one that helped get me out in '53?'

Klaus nodded. 'He wanted to pass on a package.' He didn't take his eyes off the road. 'The document is under the invoices at next to you.'

'Pass on a package? To me?' Ulrich asked.

'You, Markus. Who knows?'

'You know I can't talk about the job,' Ulrich said defensively at the mention of Markus Schram's name.

'I didn't ask you to, Uli. Just read the document.'

He didn't need to turn toward Ulrich to know his mind was ticking. Clearly, he didn't expect something like this on his homecoming. Twenty-four hours before, Klaus hadn't expected it either.

Ulrich rifled through the papers and started to read. He let out a low whistle, 'Mielke? Do you know who this man is?'

'No, but I assume he's part of the East German government.'

'They all are, but he's head of State Security,' Ulrich said.

'I'd gathered he wasn't one of the cleaners. Never mind who. What about the subject?' Klaus said.

'Some kind of planning, border measures. They probably want to close the border. It's not a big surprise; they do it from time to time,' Ulrich said.

'From time to time?' Klaus said. He leant over and started to point at the paper. 'Look at the supplies, Ulrich. You were a builder. Look at the equipment manifests, the quantities. It looks like a pretty permanent closure to me, like they want to build a bloody wall.'

Ulrich was quiet now. Klaus glanced at him to check his expression. Ulrich was looking down at the map.

'Well, are you going to say something?' Klaus asked.

Ulrich put the papers back where he found them. 'I think they're fake, Dad.'

He wasn't sure if he'd heard him correctly. He pulled the van over, wrenching at the hand brake. Klaus turned to look at Ulrich, 'Fake?'

12

'It's not that unusual. They spread misinformation all the time. It's part of the game.'

Klaus shook his head. He always had difficulty understanding how the minds of the spying fraternity operated. Now his own son had caught the bug.

'Uli, your sister and your niece are caught in that mousetrap of a city, and all you can do is sit there and blithely say it's not real. How can you be so sure? I mean, why would they bother going to those lengths?'

'Why would Burzin want us to know? What will he gain from it? I'm telling you, Dad, they just want us running up a blind alley. It's a common tactic.'

'I don't see it. More to the point, I know Burzin. I'm sure he stands to gain from you having this information, but if I know him, it's more to do with getting one over on one of his rivals in the NKVD. He doesn't do things without good reason.'

'It's the KGB now,' Ulrich said.

'What?'

'It doesn't matter. What I mean is, what better reason to lead us up the wrong path?' Ulrich said.

'You're thinking about it too much, Uli. I'm telling you, this is real.'

'How can you be so sure?'

He was about to reply, but he couldn't. He didn't have a logical answer. He just sensed it, a gut feeling. Klaus recalled Burzin's feud with Dobrovsky, the man who consigned him to the gold mines of Kolyma after the war. It was only Burzin who had sprung Ulrich from Hohenschönhausen prison and, as much as Klaus didn't like him, Burzin was the only reason the both of them were alive to this day.

They made the rest of the journey home in silence. Klaus hadn't expected this response. He couldn't believe Ulrich was so sure, especially when his sister's freedom was at stake. Klaus was still brooding as he pulled up outside his house. If he hadn't been so distracted, he might have noticed his front door slightly ajar.

As it was, it took Ulrich to say something. 'Dad, the door...'

Ulrich jumped down from the cab and went to investigate. Klaus followed slowly, not quite believing he'd forgotten to shut his front door that morning, wondering where Maria was. As Klaus reached the door, he turned to the right to see the devastation in his living room. The whole place had been turned over; even the lining of his favourite fireside chair had been ripped out. It was the chair he'd been so comfortable in immediately prior to Burzin's call. He walked round the place in a state of shock. The kitchen was in chaos, drawers upended, cutlery strewn over the floor. The bedrooms were no different. Everything had been searched methodically, obsessively, as if somebody was looking for something. He had a good idea what that might be.

He returned to the living room to find a shocked looking Ulrich, his eyes wide open, struggling to take in the devastation.

Klaus rested wearily on the upturned chair to gather his thoughts. He looked transfixed into the ashes of last night's fire.

'So, Uli, do you still believe they're fake?'

CHAPTER 1

TUESDAY, 8th AUGUST 1961,
EAST BERLIN

Sitting on the cramped S-Bahn train, Eva's mind was focused on her father's pleas. He'd been at her the whole summer to get out of the eastern sectors. Everyone knew something would happen, but not exactly what. Deep down, she felt her dad just wanted her to move to West Germany with the rest of the family, where he could keep a protective eye on her. It wasn't that simple, though. Berlin was all she knew. More to the point, this was her life and she was determined to live it how, and where, she saw fit.

To take her mind off the difficult things, she looked around the carriage at her fellow passengers. The westbound train was full. Sitting opposite Eva on the wooden bench was a stressed looking young mother. Her skin was clammy and dark rings circled her sad looking eyes. Her husband, at least so Eva assumed, was sitting next to her with his knees close to his chest, as his feet rested on an oversized suitcase. His attention was focused on his two children. Next to Eva was a boy of around five in short trousers, and a pretty younger girl with the look of her mother, without the stress. Her dark pigtails swished to and fro as she chatted intently to the doll in her hands.

It was at this point that Eva started to feel apprehensive. No matter how many times she'd made this journey from the eastern to the western sectors of Berlin, she couldn't help feeling the same way. As the train crawled towards Potsdamer Platz station, the final stop before the western sectors, she took in the familial scene around her. She knew the relative peace was about to be broken.

Eva could only feel sympathy for the young mother in front of her. She was, after all, trying to do the best for her family. However, it was obvious what they were doing. The way the entire family was travelling together, and with large suitcases; it was a dead giveaway. The family were leaving East Germany by the only route open to them. Eva could see it, and sadly, in Eva's eyes at least, the Vopos, the East German policemen, would also see it.

As the train eventually ground to a halt, Eva could see the Vopos massed on the platform like a green swarm waiting to descend on the train. A murmur rippled up and down the carriage. The door of the carriage slid back, making the woman in front of Eva jump. The Vopos entered from either end calling for all identification to be readied. It was a barked order. If anybody wanted to get off, there was no way out without passing them. Eva saw the young mother glance nervously up and down the carriage, then turn and look with sheer horror at her husband. He squeezed her hand and turned his attention to his children. Aside from the young girl's innocent chatter, the carriage had fallen silent. Eva focused on the contented young girl next to her; she had done nothing to deserve this.

The Vopos made their way down the train. Already a number of people had been thrown off, unable to provide a convincing explanation for their journey to the western sector. The passengers not yet checked by the Vopos were becoming increasingly apprehensive. It wasn't surprising looking at the growing number of passengers on the platform who had been denied the right to travel. Eva knew they would have their identity cards taken from them.

Among the clicking of opening suitcases and the scraping of the policeman's boots on the wooden carriage floor, there were the harshly delivered questions fired from the fierce looking lieutenant leading the Vopos. They were getting closer to where Eva was sitting. The young mother opposite Eva started to get up only for the man to quickly drag her back down. Eva closed her eyes with dread; it wasn't the time to draw attention.

'You! Where are you going?' The officer was pointing accusingly at the father.

'We're going…to…see my aunt…'

'Speak up, man.'

'I said we're going to see my aunt in Spandau for a few days.' His voice croaked with nerves.

The Vopo's eyes narrowed.

'A few days? With the whole family?' He mocked the man as he turned to joke with his men. 'What do you think, boys? Another case of *Republikflucht*?' Eva had seen this kind of behaviour from the Vopos many times before and it still made her feel sick.

The man started to protest. 'Please, we're just visiting family…'

'Quiet! I wasn't talking to you.' The officer's eyes dropped to the large case on the floor. 'Open it.'

'What?'

'I said, open the case. Are you deaf?'

Eva could see the policeman was enjoying the man's suffering. Everyone had a job to do, but to make the man suffer in such a way was unforgivable. She saw the man's hands visibly shaking as he flipped the catches on the case. The lid sprang open to reveal an inside crammed with clothes, medicines, and toiletries. The whole carriage was now focused on the scene. Even the little girl had stopped talking.

The Vopo bent down, seemingly enjoying the theatre of the moment. He quickly flicked through the contents of the case.

'There are enough clothes in here for a month,' he said.

'I am travelling with all my family,' the man explained.

'So I see,' the Vopo said. He pointed to a similar case on the rack above. 'And this one?'

At this point, Eva wanted dearly to claim the case as hers. She felt sorry for the family, but in the end, she was doing exactly the same thing as them. She had her own small case and was ferrying supplies to West Berlin. No matter how much it riled her, she had no choice but to keep quiet; otherwise, she would be in the firing line.

The man admitted quietly, 'It's ours.'

'Of course it is,' the officer said, like he had won a satisfying victory. 'Get your things; this is your last stop.'

'What? I don't understand...' the man said. His wife started to whimper.

'You're trying to leave the country illegally and you're under arrest. Now, get off the train!'

It was at this point the wife flung herself at the feet of the policeman and started to beg. 'Please, we are only going to visit an aunt.' She clawed at his arm.

'I've had enough of this.' He turned to his men. 'Get them off the train!'

Two younger policemen stepped forward, grabbing the man and woman roughly, and started to drag them down the carriage. The lieutenant turned his attention to the children who, witnessing their parents' treatment, had started to cry. The boy took one look at the policeman and decided to run after his parents. The girl, clearly upset by the ordeal, was rooted to her seat. Eva felt like she couldn't sit back and watch any longer. As the officer went to grab the girl, her doll fell to the carriage floor and the wails turned to screams; that was the last straw for Eva.

'That's enough!' She grabbed the Vopo's forearm, surprising herself by the strength of her grip. The officer appeared shocked by Eva's response.

'She's only a child, can't you see that? Why can't you leave these people alone and stop harassing them?' The Vopo looked uncomfortable for a moment.

He soon regained his authority, however. 'These people are breaking the law. I am doing my job, madam.'

'Your job? Is it your job to manhandle innocent children?' By now the girl had pushed herself against Eva's legs for protection. The Vopo was now the only policeman remaining in the carriage and mutterings of support were growing to angry grumbles. Eva could see he was assessing his next move very carefully. Everyone was waiting for his reaction.

He took a deep breath, and looking like he was being forced to do something alien to his nature, slowly held out his hand to the girl. Not surprisingly, the girl pushed herself closer to Eva. For a few seconds the scene resembled a stand-off.

No matter how sorry she felt for the girl, Eva knew the best place for her was with her parents, even if it meant a trip to the police station for the whole family.

Eva gave the Vopo a long, cold stare, then she bent down to pick up the girl's doll and gently handed it to her. 'Now can you go with the man? For me? He will take you to your mummy and...' Eva flashed another look at the officer, '...I promise he won't hurt you.' She softly wiped a tear from the girl's cheek as one final act of persuasion. The girl reluctantly let go of Eva, and with her doll close to her chest in one hand, she took the hand of the Vopo with the other.

Eva watched with a heavy heart as the girl toddled along behind the policeman and off down the carriage. She worried about the girl's future. In fact, she worried for all their futures.

CHAPTER 2

TUESDAY, 8th AUGUST 1961,
WEST BERLIN

I came to the Leydicke bar to ponder the big things. Today was a case in point. Peering into those fine bubbles of that light Berlin pilsner was helping me focus; maybe the drinking of it helped, too. Something serious was about happen in Berlin. Everyone sensed it. It was clear Ulbricht, East Germany's canny leader, would have to close the hatch on East Berlin soon. It couldn't go on. I wanted the story. Whenever and however it came, I wanted that scoop. It wasn't only about my professional life, though. There was a personal edge to it. Eva and my daughter, Tanja, were living in the eastern sectors. I agreed with her old man - she needed to be out of that rotting apartment she called home. That said, if there was one thing I'd learned in my time with Eva, it was best to let her come to her own decision.

The beer was great in Berlin, but it never lasted long enough. I nodded to the barman that a refill was in order. He folded his newspaper with the haste of a tortoise and, eventually, poured me another. As I watched the froth growing on the head of the beer, I wondered about my next move. I had a few leads, but I was missing something and it was gnawing away at me. I decided this was my last beer, even before I was dragged from my thoughts.

'Jack!' The slap of the newspaper on the bar next to me woke me up. Judging by the reaction of the barman, I must have had a lousy look on my face.

'The phone!' He opened his eyes wide to emphasise the final part of my journey back from outer space.

I got off the bar stool, and then stopped. 'It isn't an Ami, is it?' I asked, paranoid that my boss at the newspaper had managed to track me down.

'Give me some credit. I know the score by now.'

I smiled. A good journalist needed a barman like Dirk Hausmann. 'He said he had some important information.'

The phone booth seemed older than the pub itself. I was surprised somebody wasn't passing smoke signals outside the window.

'You Kaymer?' The accent was thick, with a hint of Russian.

'Might be.'

The voice on the other end of the line hesitated, like he was having an argument with himself. Eventually the need to spill the beans won the day.

'What you're looking for is in the warehouse of the meat factory in Lichtenberg.'

It wasn't the first anonymous call in the last few days. It seemed my name had preceded me and every crank in Berlin wanted to pass on something vital. The fact these kind of people knew how to find me always worried me slightly. On the other side of the coin, a good journalist needs a fast relay of information. This call was different to the previous ones in so much as there was at least some detail about where I should be looking.

'And what will I find there, my friend?'

The line was already dead. It was another mystery, but this one was just the way I liked them: something to get my teeth into.

I took my seat back at the bar.

'Not going red on us?' Dirk asked.

Dirk Hausmann was in his fifties. He was unusually slim and wiry considering the temptation of the alcohol in front of him all day long, but then again I was judging him by my standards.

'What?' I asked, emerging from my daydream.

'The Russian on the phone.'

'Hmm. Interesting, Dirk. It might just be interesting for once,' I said, before taking my final swig.

All these phone calls were leading to something. The gnawing feeling was growing into a full-fledged bite. I'd already decided to check the tip out. I hated going over into the eastern sector, all regimented and dreary as it was. I wasn't exactly on the invitation list to the House of Ministries after some of my previous articles. There was only one western journalist based in East Berlin, and that was the wet behind the ears kid they had working for Reuters. Whatever the case, before long, I knew I'd be scouring around Lichtenburg looking for a bloody meat factory. Shit, it sounded depressing before I even got there.

In the meantime, I needed to check one particular contact. One who had provided me with good information for some big stories in the past. He might be able to give me something more concrete before I got my hands dirty in East Berlin.

CHAPTER 3

TUESDAY, 8th AUGUST 1961,
WEST BERLIN

Matt Collins and me went way back. Those days in Korea had been a nightmare. The dead bodies, the blood and guts; when you go through things like that together, you never lose touch. When you get together again, it's like you've never been apart. For us, that gap had been about five years. A few months ago, Matt had turned up in Berlin in the State Department. Since then we'd enjoyed some good nights together and I'd enjoyed the benefit of some good intelligence. As well as an old buddy, Matt was a damned useful contact for any journalist to have.

He was already in the bar at Kempinski's when I arrived. He was quite small in stature, but lean nonetheless. His slicked back dark hair fell in with his immaculate grey suit. He had always been clean shaven, even amongst the flying bullets of the Korean war.

'Old habits die hard, Matt,' I said.

He looked confused.

'You're in a place like Kempinski's and you're sat up at the bar like it's a dirty saloon.'

'Yeah, something like that. How are you doing, Jack? Stirred any more shit up lately?'

'You'll hear about it when I do.'

'I'm sure I will.' He smiled and took a drink from his glass. 'Whisky?'

'Why not?'

I was never one to turn down hard liquor even if it was early in the afternoon. I looked around the foyer. Kempinski's was the kind of place that dripped with money. Even the waiters looked like they had plenty; then again, I wouldn't have minded their tips. The place made me feel uncomfortable for a number of reasons, not least that my boss was more likely to track me down here.

'So what brings you to the Ku'damm? It's not your usual stomping ground,'

'Can you tell I feel edgy?' I grimaced and took a stool next to him while the bartender made a meal of pouring a Jack Daniels on the rocks. I was half expecting a paper umbrella in the glass.

He smiled. 'So what are you working on, Jack? What am I going to be reading about tomorrow?'

'Not much, but my nose tells me something big is going down.'

'Well, things are certainly hotting up. Ulbricht's turning the screw and the birds are flying the nest in their turn. The refugee camps are full to bursting over here. Do you know one thousand four hundred people checked into Marienfelde yesterday? That's equivalent to half a million on annual figures. He can't let that go on much longer.'

The mention of Marienfelde reminded me of something I should have done days ago. Ackermann had set me up a meeting with the director at the refugee camp, the largest in West Berlin. It was another dull chore I'd not got round to yet.

'Everyone's saying that, but what's going to give?'

'I don't know, Jack. My sources are saying it'll be autumn before anything's done, but it's not what I hear from Brandt's boys.' Willy Brandt was the mayor of West Berlin.

This was where my ears pricked up. 'Oh yeah, what have you heard?'

Matt took a sip of whisky and smiled. 'Am I giving you another tip here, Jack? Do you ever do any work yourself?'

'Not if I can help it. Come on, spill the beans.'

'Well, the guy's a bit of a renegade in the parliament. Even the Berliners say he's a nut, but he's been right before about things. He says they're going to close the border.'

'Shit, Matt, that's not news.'

'It is if he says it's going to be this weekend.'

That stopped me in my tracks. This piece of news definitely deserved a drink, so I took a long swig on the whisky. 'That's *very* precise,' I said, suddenly talking quietly.

'That's the word. I'll leave you to dig out the rest, pal.' He downed his drink, got up and slapped me on the back.

'Thanks for the drink,' he said as he left.

'Hey.'

He waved before I got a chance to argue. I shrugged and paid the tab. The information, even if incomplete, was worth a whisky for an old friend, even at Kempinski's ridiculous prices.

As I got to the main door of the foyer, one of the concierges was by my side.

'Excuse me, sir. Sir, there's a call for you.'

'What, me?'

He pointed helpfully to the desk and escorted me over like I had no choice in the matter.

I picked up the phone.

'Kaymer?' It was my boss, Ackermann.

'Chief, I was going to call you…'

'That's crap, Kaymer. I've had the director's secretary on from Marienfelde.' There was a delay. I didn't need to see Ackermann to know he was pumping on a fat Cuban cigar on the other end of the line. It certainly wasn't a pause for me to talk.

'You know what she told me, Kaymer?' It was a rhetorical question. 'She told me you've not been up there yet. Now, I'm asking myself why not. You've not had to do any work to get this interview. It's all been set up for you, Kaymer. What more can you ask for?'

'I've had a few personal issues, boss.'

'Don't cry on me, Kaymer. I don't know what you're up to, but I need a human story from Berlin. America needs to know about the refugees. Would you kindly get your butt over there and drop whatever other spurious leads you're following. Don't think I don't know you, Jack.'

For all his bluster, Ackermann was right.

The constant buzzing coming from the phone was a strong indication that the conversation was over.

CHAPTER 4

TUESDAY, 8ᵗʰ AUGUST 1961,
WEST BERLIN

I cranked the Karmann-Ghia to life and headed for the Mehringdamm. The Marienfelde refugee centre had been opened at the time of the workers' uprising in June 1953. At that time, it was needed more than ever due to the massive influx of people from East Berlin. In the aftermath of the uprising, the clamp down on the population resulted in the centre being full to bursting point. Eight years later, once again, the place was stretching its 3000 capacity. Even though I'd heard all the stories about the numbers of refugees pouring into West Berlin, I didn't really expect what I witnessed when I arrived at the camp.

Nestled in the southern part of the Schöneberg district in the US sector, the grounds of Marienfelde stretched up to the border of the Soviet zone. When I arrived there, the queues were immense, snaking up and down and around; there seemed to be people for miles. If it took two weeks to place each person in West Germany, and with over a thousand a day arriving at the camp, it didn't take Einstein to work out the camp would be well over its intended capacity.

Considering the vast numbers of people, there was an eerie silence about the place. Normally, with families, so many children in a small space, you would have expected noise—talking, laughter, babies crying—but apart from the odd murmur and the sound of the occasional announcement, the place was silent. It was weird and not what I had expected.

As I approached the main entrance, I could see the only windows the building had were small and above head height. I suppose it prevented the curious from peering in. Above the single door in crude white letters was the word *Notaufnahmelage,* Emergency Reception Camp. I fought my way through the crowds to the front door area. I was stopped on at least two occasions by harassed looking door staff telling me the area was *verboten*; like everything else in Germany, it seemed.

When I eventually gained access to the Administration building, my progress was once again blocked by officialdom, this time in the shape of the director's secretary. She had wispy grey hair and she moved around the place in small, ponderous shuffles, much like a crab. Come to think of it, her large saucepan glasses made her eyes look just like a crab's. Maybe she could read my mind.

'I am sorry, the director cannot see anybody. He's far too busy.' Her manner put my back up immediately. There's something about being the boss's secretary that makes them think they have more power than the bosses themselves.

'Actually, I have an appointment. Jack Kaymer, Newsweek.' I smiled my most sarcastic smile. It didn't do me any good.

'Kaymer? That name rings a bell.' But apparently it wasn't opening any doors. 'Yes, I remember, you were due two days ago and didn't bother to show.' Her nose went up and down as she inspected me, and then it twitched. Probably her alcohol radar was kicking in.

'That's right. I was reassigned at the last minute.'

'Yes, it smells like it.'

I didn't have time for this delay. I wanted to get Ackermann's piece out of the way so I could concentrate on the bigger fish. 'Listen, lady, just do your job.'

Her lips pursed. 'He's on a call at the moment with the mayor. He hasn't time for people who don't keep appointments.'

Our little spat was just about to step up a notch, when a tall man, seemingly deep in thought, stepped out of the office marked "Director". I didn't miss my chance to cut out the dragon.

'Jack Kaymer, Newsweek.' I thrust out my hand for him to shake. 'Sorry about the delay in getting here. Willy Brandt insisted on an interview before he went off electioneering.'

The man sucked on the end of his glasses for a moment, then took my hand and pumped it enthusiastically. 'You know Herr Brandt was here only three weeks ago? Come in, Mr Kaymer. Hildegard, fetch some coffee, will you?'

I followed him towards his office, but couldn't resist another sarcastic smile in Hildegard's direction. It's really childish when women in their fifties stick out their tongue, but she did it anyway.

His office was pretty basic. There were a couple of plaques on the wall, a table, a couple of wooden chairs and a stack of papers. That was about it. There was a pile of framed photographs in the corner, which he obviously hadn't had the chance to put up yet. Hildegard must have been right about him being busy.

'Helmut Festag, director of this show, Mr Kaymer. What can I do for you?'

Under the slightly stressed exterior, he seemed at ease, even friendly. His hair, or what was left of it at his temples, was dark brown with tinges of grey. His bald pate was slightly tanned, suggesting to me maybe he had time for the odd holiday. Now that his thick glasses were back on his nose, I thought he had the look of Phil Silvers.

'Maybe you should think of it the other way around. A bit of publicity in my magazine might help you get some of the resources you need. I can't imagine it's easy looking after that lot out there.'

He looked me up and down for a moment, as if he was assessing my offer.

'I suppose when you put it like that, you might be right, Herr Kaymer. Only this morning, I had to make an appeal on RIAS for all doctors and nurses to come and help. Just one extra shift would do a lot of good. You can't imagine how many people we have to deal with.'

'Well, there you go. Why don't you take me through the process of what happens when a refugee turns up here?' I was trying to sound as enthusiastic as he was, but it was difficult.

'Look, Herr Kaymer, I can give you a rough idea, but I wouldn't want you to print too much detail. It would be like a handbook to our friends in East Berlin. You understand?'

'Sure.' It sounded like paranoia to me, but I suppose they had their reasons.

'We start by giving everybody a number,' he said. 'In fact, the date and then a serial number, number one from midnight, and so on.'

'That sounds more like the culture of the country the refugees are trying to escape. You don't use names.'

'No, you have to be very careful. Many people are scared to talk when they arrive here. They've been living under a very oppressive regime and just because they've travelled a few kilometres, it doesn't make them feel anything has changed.'

I must have looked confused because he felt the need to explain further.

'No matter how hard we try to sift out the spies from East Berlin, they will still be here. People need protection, and if we're shouting out their names every two minutes, it doesn't need a rocket scientist to know who's fled the Republic.'

'Quite clever,' I nodded. I was starting to understand the need for security and the reason for all the silence outside. It was times like these I felt privileged to be an American. We took these liberties for granted. In a way, I was glad I had come here, but I wasn't sure the full story was going to be found in the director's office.

'And necessary, Mr Kaymer.'

'Ok. So what then?'

'First, it's the Allied registration, then the doctors for health screening. We put them up in our apartment blocks. We have modern living quarters for three thousand people. Normally each refugee has four square meters of space, but under present circumstances, we are struggling to maintain that.'

'How long do they normally stay?'

'Usually a couple of weeks, less sometimes. Enough time to check out they are who they say they are and find them a place in West Germany, which the Admissions office deals with. Then there are some preliminary examinations and the acceptance boards, which are panels of three normally. If they have a trade, this helps speed things up.' The director nodded his head like I should understand.

'You can see Ulbricht's point then? It might look like you're stealing his skilled workers?' I said it with a smile, but I couldn't resist it.

'These people are free to come here or not. We don't drag them here. As you have seen for yourself, we have more people than we can handle.'

'Sure, but you've solved the shortage of skilled engineers in West Germany overnight.'

'I think Ulbricht did that himself, Mr Kaymer.'

That was one to him, but there was something that was bothering me about the guy, the office, the whole thing. To say he was busy, his phone hadn't rung once since we'd been in there. There were some papers, but it looked decidedly unlived in. I couldn't help thinking that there was more to him than met the eye.

'You said you had to sift the people?'

Festag nodded.

Hildegard chose that moment to stomp into the room clattering coffee cups. The director was served coffee with an adoring smile. Mine, however, was thrown in my direction like a grenade without the pin.

With the interruption over, I continued. 'How exactly do you do that? I mean, if you are looking for spies, it must be difficult.'

31

Festag's eyes narrowed a little bit. Not much, but maybe enough for him to start thinking this journalist was going a little too far. 'I am not sure I understand you, Mr Kaymer.'

'Well, it takes one to know one, doesn't it?'

I was playing games with him, but I knew I wasn't getting everything from the man. Festag turned his head to one side like he understood me, but was pretending not to, so I spelled it out.

'Security services, spies from West Germany. Surely you have to have them on site to spot things from the other side?'

'That's not necessary. Our people are highly trained.' He looked at his watch in an irritated manner, which told me he was feeling the pressure for the first time.

'It would only be expected, Mr Festag. Ulbricht is a slippery fish…'

'I am not sure I like where this is going.' He was on the phone calling Hildegard. 'My meeting with Mr Kaymer is over. Please show him out.' She was at the door quicker than a dog that had heard the leash being rattled.

'You sure you don't want me to repeat that appeal for doctors and nurses?' I asked, a virtual picture of innocence.

'Thank you. That won't be necessary. Good day, Mr Kaymer.'

With that, the meeting was over and the Rottweiler was showing me the door with her teeth.

With the meeting with the director finished quicker than anticipated, and with my overactive curiosity pricked, I thought I'd have a dig around and see what was going on. I'd got half a story; I might as well finish it off with something real. I couldn't repeat some of the lines I'd picked up in the meeting with the director; that would have been professional suicide, but it was fun while it lasted. Besides, I had to find something I could actually put in the article.

I thought if anybody were to provide the story, it would be the people themselves. There had to be some interesting angles among them. I found my way to a canteen and managed to scrounge a cup of coffee or whatever it was they were serving. The makeshift building was crammed with people whispering and shuffling around. I wasn't surprised nobody was saying anything; the black and white warning signs were everywhere:

"Be careful: during conversations (danger of spies)
With invitations (danger of kidnapping)
In what is written in correspondence with the Eastern zone."

With that epitaph, it was hardly likely to be a talking shop. So I took my cup outside and sat on a wall in the sunshine. It wasn't over warm for the beginning of August, but when the sun did break through, it was pleasant enough. One or two others had the same idea. A couple, five years or so younger than me, were huddled together in silence.

'Quiet place, isn't it?' I said with a smile.

The suspicious stares I received for my efforts told me this wasn't going to be easy. I suppose what Festag had said was true; the people were careful who they spoke to. I was about to the bottom of my coffee cup and ready to call it a day, when a voice at my shoulder made me take notice.

'What's wrong, Yank? Nobody want to talk?'

I turned round to see a kid of fifteen, maybe sixteen, sucking on an ice-lolly. Now, my German was pretty good and I wasn't the archetypal American in Berlin, but evidently I stood out.

'Is it that obvious?'

'Might as well be JFK himself sat there.' He was very sure of himself.

'Where's your family?' I asked, wondering if there was a story in there.

'Around somewhere. I prefer to strike out on my own,' he said.

'A man after my own heart. Where are you from, kid?'

'Friedrichshain. Well, I was anyway, not for much longer.'

'A one way ticket then?' Friedrichshain was in the eastern sector.

He shrugged. 'Looks like it. Not for a bit yet, though. I've only just arrived. It'll take a few days to sort things out.'

He seemed to know all the ropes. 'So why did you leave?'

'Seemed like the right thing to do. My dad's a train driver. He said he could earn more in the West. Anyway, no one likes to be tied down and if that's what's coming…'

'Should you be telling me all this?' I pointed to one of the signs.

The boy just laughed. 'You stand out too much to be a spy.'

It seemed I was losing a lot of the verbal arguments today.

I looked at the boy as he flicked his hair out of his eyes nonchalantly. He was a smart type and had a lot of answers. I thought he might be useful. I wondered how well he knew East Berlin.

'You said you're from Friedrichshain? How well do you know Berlin?'

'What sort of question is that? 'Course I know Berlin.'

My mind was ticking over like a journalist, but not necessarily like a human being. Maybe this kid could be really useful.

'Do you want to earn some pocket money?' I said.

His eyes narrowed. 'Pocket money is for kids. I take dollars or cigarettes.'

I should have known. These kids had grown up with four occupying armies; they were nothing if not streetwise. I nodded and smiled. 'Ok, I am sure we can cut a deal.'

The kid came down from the grass and sat on the wall. It seemed he wanted to be eye to eye if a deal was to be done.

'What you got in mind?' He said it like James Cagney planning a bank raid. I thought to myself, could I really ask a kid to do what I wanted? I could see Eva at my shoulder shaking her head.

But I wasn't about to give up, especially when my instinct was working overtime.

'How well do you know Lichtenberg?'

CHAPTER 5

TUESDAY, 8th AUGUST 1961,
EAST BERLIN

The official letter from Lichtenberg Town Hall didn't really say much, but it didn't need to. Eva had been invited to "discuss her work arrangements". She knew exactly what that meant. This was another part of the war the authorities were waging on the public who were forced, or chose, to cross the sector border to go to work or to study. She'd considered not attending, but deep down Eva felt this might be an opportunity to get some things off her chest.

She sat in the waiting room among other men and women. They were clearly Grenzgänger (border crossers) with jobs in West Berlin. Some of them were still in the work overalls of mechanics, chef's whites, and waitress uniforms. Eva glanced anxiously at the clock on the wall; her appointment time was fifty minutes ago and she would be late to collect Tanja. She knew the delay was all part of the game; they liked to cause as much inconvenience as possible.

Eva didn't care now because she knew she wouldn't be in East Berlin much longer. She'd heard what her dad had to say on it all and, in a way, he was right. All this pressure was leading to something. That said, it didn't mean she would move to West Germany, as her father wanted. She would make her life with Jack and Tanja in West Berlin. That would be hard for her father to hear; she knew her father hated

Jack, more because of what he represented rather than who he was. Whatever her dad thought about Jack, it wouldn't sway Eva's decision.

She stared at the framed picture of Walter Ulbricht on the wall. His goatee beard seemed to be styled on Lenin. For Eva, and many others, it was a point of ridicule, providing Berliners an easy nickname for him. In a perverse kind of way, she was looking forward to this meeting. The opportunity to fight back against Ulbricht and his like had been a long time coming and she wasn't going to miss it for an hour or so.

A severe looking woman in her fifties eventually called Eva's name. She was directed into a large hall, which Eva knew was used for public meetings. She'd been dragged along by her brother Ulrich in the early days after the war. He didn't repeat the same mistake after one or two.

There were three of them sitting at a table on the stage. Above the stage was a huge red banner in white lettering that proclaimed: "Socialism is triumphing. We are the stronger!" Eva raised her eyebrows; she, along with a waiting room full of people outside, remained unconvinced. There was a single chair on the lower, audience level in front of them. Nobody invited her to, as they were busy ignoring her presence, but Eva took the seat anyway.

The old man in the middle peered down his nose at Eva like he was hugely disappointed by something.

'Eva Schultz, I presume?'

'Correct,' Eva said in a voice that sounded stronger than she actually felt.

'Normally I would ask you to sit down, but it appears you've already taken that upon yourself.'

Eva didn't say anything. She wasn't to be intimidated at this early stage in proceedings.

'Firstly, the question of your job in West Berlin…'

'You mean my studies, not my job. I'm a junior doctor…'

'Quiet!' the attack dog barked. 'When we want you to say something, we'll ask. What you are doing in West Berlin is irrelevant. The fact you are crossing the border to do it, is.'

'You must stop your work there immediately,' the thickset man blurted out.

'What?' Eva was incredulous.

'What my colleague is saying is, you are denying Democratic Germany the services of a good doctor. You should find a position in East Berlin.'

Eva couldn't help letting out a laugh.

That only wound up them up. 'This is intolerable. This country has provided your education and you brazenly decamp to West Berlin and give the warmongers the benefit of it. You're nothing but a disgrace!'

Eva felt herself starting to boil. Who were these people to say this to her? Didn't they know what had happened?

'You have four weeks,' the old man said like the decision was taken.

'Four weeks? Four weeks to do what?' Eva asked.

'To find a position here, in the eastern sectors. You will sign today to indicate your commitment.' He waved a piece of paper in the air, like they had it all planned out.

'I'll do no such thing.'

It was the turn of the men at the table to appear shocked.

'It would be wise do as we ask, Schultz. There's coming a time very soon when it won't be possible to do a job in West Berlin anyway. You may as well get a headstart on all the others and find a job here,' the older man said.

Their condescending manner made Eva even angrier; she preferred the threatening approach. She wouldn't be told what to do by anybody, least of all a bunch of bullying party officials. She knew their type and wasn't scared of them. She hadn't forgotten the treatment of the little girl on the train. She'd had enough.

'Did any of you idiots take the time to read my file?' She pointed at the papers in front of them.

'How dare you?' the old man blustered.

Eva continued anyway, 'If you had, you would realise that you people blocked my application to study medicine at Charité hospital. Yes, because you arrested my brother because he had the temerity to complain about the shitty pay and conditions in 1953. Not that I, personally, have done anything here except live a quiet life.' Eva was jabbing her finger at them now, but she still wasn't done. 'Even though I was at the top of my class you denied me a position at Humboldt, forcing me to go to West Berlin to study. So you can demand all you like, you can bully and threaten, but I've heard it all before. I won't give up what I love doing for anybody.'

The strength of Eva's verbal assault led them to cower for a moment, but the well-dressed man eventually found his voice. 'Eva, may I call you Eva?'

She stared back at him defiantly.

'I know all about your past. You see, things are changing in East Berlin and the signing of the peace treaty will bring a different, but brighter future. Citizens of East Berlin will not need to work in West Berlin. It is not part of our...vision.'

The words were less provocative, but they still meant the same to Eva. 'It doesn't matter to me how you dress it up; I don't share your vision, along with the thousands deserting your sinking ship. Signing a peace treaty will make no difference to them or me.'

There were only two of them in the conversation now. The man sat up and rested his well-manicured hand on the table and Eva noticed his cufflink shining in the light momentarily. 'Oh, it does matter to them and it will to you.' His tone suddenly hardened. 'Now, whether you like it or not, maybe not today, or within the four weeks my comrade suggested, you will get another job in East Berlin.'

Eva was shaking her head. 'Not a chance.' She stopped suddenly and felt her eyes widen at his next words.

'I am sure that job will not be as a doctor either. You see, if I have it my way, when the treaty is signed, you'll be packed off to some farm in the back of beyond and you'll never see a hospital again, not as a doctor anyway. Very soon, Eva Schultz, we will be able to do what we want with people like you.'

There was a real tension now. The man's mask had slipped. Underneath the seemingly pleasant façade was a face uglier than the two sitting next to him; at least they were transparent. Whatever the case, Eva wasn't quite finished yet.

She shook her head once more and looked down towards the floor, regaining her composure. She started quietly, 'So this is what it has come to? It's not enough that you've ridden roughshod over the real workers in the last fifteen years, slowly working to death anybody that dared to disagree. Now you want to send your female doctors off to work on the land like a Hessian milkmaid?' She was shouting now. 'Well, you can do what you like because I won't be here.'

Eva got up from the chair and started to walk to the exit.

The old man started to bluster. 'Just one more thing, young lady.'

Eva turned at the door, still seething.

'You are the only resident in the apartment in Lichtenburg. Is that correct?'

Eva was confused at the change in subject. She shrugged her shoulders, past caring.

'By the regulations against Grenzgänger of July first, you are now liable for the rent, electricity, and gas in *West* Marks, not East Marks…backdated to first July. That will be all.'

CHAPTER 6

TUESDAY, 8th AUGUST 1961,
EAST BERLIN

I had it all planned out in my head. I knew what I wanted. I loved Eva and I wanted her and Tanja with me and out of the eastern sectors, out of danger. Eva was fiercely independent, but I knew I had to take the bull by the horns and tell her she was coming to live with me. Her father wouldn't like it, but I wasn't concerned about him. Eva was the one who could dig her heels in. That's not to say I didn't have my own faults. On occasions, my drive for the next story got in the way of my personal life. Tonight, I had to focus.

There were only cursory glances at my identification as I passed through the sector border at Checkpoint Charlie. The fact I had Allied plates, thanks to a dodgy US sergeant I knew at Andrews barracks, aided my smooth passage. On the front seat next to me was a soft toy rabbit for Tanja, some flowers for Eva, and a camera. The camera was for something else. With everything ready in mind, and presents in hand, I felt that even I couldn't mess this one up.

I felt like things were finally falling into place in my life. There was even the chance of a good story flitting about in the background. Well, maybe it shared the foreground in my mind, but a leopard can't change its spots overnight. Even the rotting old staircase up to Eva's apartment didn't seem as abhorrent as normal. She would soon be out of the place for good and then none of us would have to come back here again. That time couldn't come soon enough for me.

After all my planning, I knew there was something wrong as soon as I walked through the door. Baby Tanja was normal, happy as always, especially when she'd just been fed. It seemed to give her extra beans, and the rabbit was accepted with squeals of delight. Eva, however, was on edge. From the minute I arrived, I couldn't seem to do anything right; the bunny was nice, but Eva wanted to wash it before, like all things, it ended up in Tanja's mouth. The flowers were pretty, but needed to be cut at the stems, even though I thought I was being helpful by putting them straight into a vase. The camera had been put down in the wrong place; anyway, why did I have a camera? I am quite thick skinned, but sometimes you feel like you are being picked on. I almost wondered if she was in cahoots with Ackermann, but that would have been verging on paranoia. Enough was enough.

'Can I ask what's wrong?'

'Nothing's wrong.' She wouldn't sit still. I followed her into the kitchen where she was now cutting the flowers. She put them down, pushed past me, and went to pick up Tanja. I wasn't very good at reading signals. I was the type who preferred to be told something straight.

She fussed around the baby for a while, a little too much if you ask me. I mean, it was as if she was doing it for something to do. I only wanted to get out what I had to say, but I felt knocked out of my stride now.

'I'll put Tanja to bed,' Eva said with nervous edge in her voice.

'Here, let me. I don't get to do it much.' This time Eva passed her over with a tense smile. She was being really strange.

As I watched Tanja go through her routine of rolling around in her sheets and kicking her feet in the air (I knew she did that even if I wasn't there every night), I looked around the room. To say it was ropey didn't insult the place anywhere near enough. Most of the plaster had cracked and fallen off the walls. It smelled damp. She needed to be out of here, away from it, with me in West Berlin. She was happy, of course; she didn't know any better. But to grow up here wasn't a life she was going to live. No way.

With Tanja settled, my motivation to raise the subject of her and Eva moving to West Berlin increased. Even journalists have emotions sometimes.

Back in the living room, if that's what you could call an old chair with a settee facing it, Eva was sitting in the chair.

'She's settled down now, even if she's done a tour of the cot first.' It was my feeble attempt at a joke. Eva ignored it and took a deep breath like she was about to swim twenty yards underwater. Then she said quickly, 'Sit down, Jack. I want to talk to you about something.'

When she said it, my heart sank. I was worried. This must have been what the pantomime had been about. I sat down opposite her and waited. And then, I waited. In fact, I felt like I was waiting for her to swim the twenty yards and get her breath back. In the end, I'd had enough. I had something to say as well and I'd been waiting all day.

'Look, Eva, there's something I want to say, too.'

Her eyes widened, like I'd shocked her. I carried on anyway. Now that I was in the mood, I wasn't turning back.

'I want you and Tanja to come and live with me.'

'What?'

I thought she might fight it, but I wasn't giving in. 'I'll not take "no" for an answer. You can't stay here anymore. Tanja can't stay here anymore.'

Eva wasn't saying much. Well, not much that made sense. 'Yes, I mean...well…I wanted to ask you…'

I shook my head, a bit perplexed. I'd expected a reaction, maybe a few things thrown at me, but not indecision. This wasn't her.

Then as soon as it was there, it was gone. 'Oh, Jack,' she whimpered, then threw her arms around me. To say I was surprised was an understatement. She let go and then looked at me. 'Do you mean it? Do you really mean it?'

'Yes, of course.' It wasn't the time to go into the mental torture I'd been through to get to that decision; it could well have been misinterpreted.

'I have been stressed by my dad going on about things here. He was pushing me to go and live near them. I know he doesn't like you...'

'Don't worry, I know he's not keen on me, but that's no reason to stay here.'

'Jack, that's just great!'

Her excitement was that of a small child at Christmas. I had my own mixture of emotions. Relief it was finally resolved. I was angry at her father. What he didn't realise was that, by making her choose between me and West Germany, he had actually been delaying her exit from East Berlin.

Anyway, I was caught up in the moment. I grabbed her shoulders and looked her in the eye. 'Eva, I want you both with me.'

'Jack, this is wonderful. We can stay in Berlin, we can all be together, and I can finish my studies.'

'Yes.' I nodded, happy like I'd never really felt before.

'When, Jack? Can we do it tomorrow?'

'Well, I have to clean up the apartment first. It's hardly ready for Tanja yet. Give me a couple of days?'

'A couple of days?' Her voice was flat. I'd ruined the moment like only I could.

'Ok. Look, let me see what I can do. Don't worry, I'll sort it as quickly as I can.'

'Sorry, it's fine. I just want to be away from here now, Jack. I can't stay in this place anymore. I went to that meeting at the town hall today. They're bastards, Jack.'

I wanted to hear more about it, but Eva brushed it aside. She just gave me that look that told me it might be my lucky night. In fact, it was the same look that brought Tanja into the world. I couldn't get enough of Eva. She was the kind who was noticed wherever she went, lighting up the place. It wasn't only about sex, but for me, it was a nice part of it. And now, with the deal seemingly sealed for the two of them to come and live with me, it seemed the most natural thing in the world that we would fall into bed. I had no complaints about that.

***

I lay looking at the cracked ceiling in the afterglow. Eva was letting out satisfied sighs, but I wasn't so full of myself to think they were about anything other than the fact she was moving out of this dingy apartment. It seemed my concerns about Eva being reluctant to leave had been unfounded. I didn't blame her either; the place was one step up from the sewer. It made me itch just thinking about it.

I looked at my watch. In all the excitement, I'd forgotten about the meeting.

'Do you have to be somewhere?' Eva's voice had turned stern in the blink of an eye.

The check of the watch had been a mistake, but the story was important.

'Look, I've got some business to deal with.'

'Tonight?' She sounded annoyed. It seemed it wasn't expected, or welcome, for that matter.

Eva took a deep breath, as if to intensify her disappointment in me. 'We've just decided to live together, to spend the first night of our lives together. Normal people celebrate, but not bloody Jack Kaymer. No, he wants to go out to work.'

I had a feeling it was the timing she was mad about. The joy of a few moments ago had evaporated like a Nazi party membership card after the war.

'I won't be long…'

44

'Jack, just go, will you?'

I was a bit worried I'd messed it up, but it didn't sound too terminal. After all, the story was important.

Eva hadn't finished. 'If you're not back to get us by Thursday, we'll be gone to my father's.'

'Don't worry, I'll be back before...'

She waved away my assurances. I went towards the door, not forgetting to pick up the camera. Eva had one parting shot.

'And if we go to my father's, Jack, it'll be for good.'

***

With my head still buzzing from what had happened at Eva's, I had to get myself focused on work. The kid was waiting for me as I appeared on the street from the apartment block.

'You're late,' he said.

'I had business to take care of. You sound just like my boss.'

'The name's Gerd. So, where are we going?'

Even as a hardened journalist, I'd had second thoughts about using Gerd, taking him from the safety of Marienfelde and his family. Using him as my guide around East Berlin was ranging from slightly to very irresponsible. But when the negotiations started, I could tell he knew exactly what he was doing. I knew I was dealing with a businessman. So we'd agreed to a time and a place, and here we were, not quite in the dead of the night, but not far from it.

'You're keen, kid.'

'Well, if there's money to be earned, Mr Kaymer...'

'Call me Jack.'

'I prefer to stick with Mr Kaymer, if that's okay. This is business.'

I had a feeling Gerd was about to teach me a thing or two.

'So where's it to be?' he said with all the confidence of a Berlin taxi driver, bored with the mundane runs to see the Reichstag.

I passed him the camera. He took it without question.

'We're looking for a meat factory.'

'Ok.' He started off without hesitation. I caught up with him, wondering if this was a wise idea. Here I was running around Berlin, following a kid who'd only just graduated into long trousers, especially as I'd left my personal life in the balance back at Eva's.

'You know the place?' There must have been surprise in my voice.

'Sure, it's near the bakery.'

'Right.' Now I sounded unsure.

That's when Gerd turned to me. 'Look, Mr Kaymer, if we're going to be business partners, you have to trust me. I not only know the place, my cousin used to work there. We had a sideline in rationed meat that wasn't rationed, if you know what I mean. So I know the place like the back of my hand. I assume as a journalist you are looking for evidence of something?' He held up the camera. 'Just one thing, I don't think it will be wise to go flashing this thing around at this time of night. Now, are you ready?'

His fringe was pushed back from his eyes for further dramatic effect and I was well and truly put in my place.

It was dark now and getting on for midnight. After passing over the rail lines, rather than using the bridge, at Gerd's insistence, we were cutting through the streets of Lichtenberg like a slalom skier. It was my nose that told me we were somewhere close to the target before Gerd actually announced it. The smell was a cross between an overflowing latrine and a pig farm.

'Ok, the main gate is up there on the right,' he said.

'Something tells me we're not going in that way.'

Gerd flashed a smile. 'At last, you're catching on Mr Kaymer. Follow me and keep quiet.'

I was getting used to being ordered around. I wondered if the kid wanted a job running a newspaper, but figured he might be a harder taskmaster than Ackerman, once he got to know the ropes. Judging by his performance so far, that wouldn't take very long.

We made it to a high back wall, the top of which was covered in broken glass. Conveniently, there was a glass free area, which Gerd seemed to locate with consummate ease. I watched as he expertly clambered over with the camera hanging from his back. It reminded me of going over the top in Korea, only this time the excitement wasn't tinged with the fear of copping a bullet in the mouth, only something more unsavoury, judging by the odour.

After a laboured effort getting over the wall, we found ourselves against a pre-fab concrete building. The site seemed quiet. Maybe there wasn't a night shift after all, but then again, I suppose a country without potatoes was more than likely a country without meat.

We started out across an exposed area between buildings and I was just starting to enjoy myself. However, before I was able to get giddy, I ended up face down on the floor, covered in something not so nice. Gerd had tripped me up. Still, it was a good job he had; I lifted my head to see most of the forecourt shrouded in the light coming from the canteen. A man dressed in a grubby looking cap, and an even grubbier looking rubber apron, went off in the other direction, smoking a cigarette. If I was an East Berliner, I would be glad if the meat coming out of this place was scarce.

That scare over, we were off again and, after two minutes dodging from truck to building, Gerd pointed to the warehouse. 'It covers three adjoined old buildings, usually empty, except for old machinery from the factory,' he said.

We heard the scraping of boots in the distance and we made for the back of a battered old truck that didn't look like it had made a delivery in ten years. A guard walked towards us looking particularly disinterested in his work. It was a warm still night and the glow of his cigarette soon gave way to the smell of harsh tobacco. It dragged at my throat like it had been swept from the floor. Satisfied with his cursory inspection, the guard flicked his cigarette aimlessly towards the truck and headed off over the courtyard. By the sudden spring in his step, I guessed the canteen beckoned.

'Kampfgruppen,' Gerd said.

'Militia?'

Gerd nodded and already had a tool of some kind out of his pocket. He worked quickly on the door and we were inside in seconds. The first thing that struck me about the interior was that it was full. We climbed up and over the concrete posts partially blocking the door. When we were on top, in spite of the darkness, we were able to see everything. I let out a low whistle, which brought dark, reproachful looks from Gerd, but I couldn't help it. Each post was around eight feet in length, and whilst not being able to put an exact figure on it, thousands wouldn't have been an understatement.

'Now why would a meat factory need so many concrete posts? And a guard, come to think of it?'

'I know why it needs a guard,' he laughed.

'I won't ask.'

'Best not. Shall we check out the next one?' he said, thinking quicker on his feet than me. A rusty door linked the two warehouses with a "Close this door" sign on it. The next area was more revealing than the first. The number of coils of barbed wire looked impressive. I checked one of the labels and they were from a company in England, each containing around 200 yards. It was difficult to imagine a country that couldn't grow enough food to feed its population, could afford to buy enough wire to fence in the Grand Canyon.

I'd seen enough. The intention of the East German authorities was clear to me. On this scale, I was convinced the borders were going to be sealed off, and by the looks of it, it was going to be at least a semi-permanent operation. Whoever was giving out the anonymous tips had proved to be spot on.

'Come on, kid, let's go!'

'You don't want to see the last one?' He still seemed untouched by the possible dangers.

'No, let's go. My nostrils are burning'

Gerd flashed a smile and we were out of there. We dodged the lax guard, and in five minutes were clear of the factory. He found us a quiet place next to the railway line where we could talk. I peeled off the money and laid it in his hand. He eyed it suspiciously before stuffing it in his pocket.

'Ok. You up for some more work?'

He nodded eagerly, the feel of the notes on his palm no doubt still fresh in his memory.

'With the camera you have, I need some pictures of what we've seen tonight. It's important they're good pictures and payment depends very much on the quality of the photos.'

'This sounds dangerous.' It was strange coming from a kid who'd not flinched at the risks so far, but I knew it was part of the negotiation.

'I thought you'd be the guy who could manage this sort of thing without a problem?'

I knew I was playing him and, to be honest, I felt a twinge of guilt. I was starting to like the kid, so I did worry for his safety. Somehow, I suspected, he'd been up to far worse than this in the past few years.

'It would be no problem for me. The problem for you is that you couldn't get anybody else to do it. Twenty dollars.'

'Dollars?'

'I figure those materials are for building something in Berlin. Maybe a fence along the border? My feeling is it won't do much for the value of the East Mark or for West Marks, for that matter. I think dollars would be the safer option.'

I was flabbergasted by the front of the kid, which made me wait a moment. Gerd took that as an indication he may have undersold himself.

'Up front.' He cracked a smile.

I shook my head. 'Here's what we're going to do. I'm going to give you fifty West Marks now, because that's what I have in my wallet.' Gerd pulled a face.

'With good quality photos and confidentiality, that's very important, Gerd, then I'll stump up another 150 West Marks on delivery.'

'I'll take the 50. Make it 200 on delivery and it's a deal.'

We shook on it.

'I'll show you how to use the camera.'

'No need. I know someone who runs a shop over the border. I know how to use modern cameras.' He looked it over disdainfully. 'Even if this isn't one of those.'

Nothing was surprising me about Gerd. He'd delivered so far, so I had no reason to doubt his word.

'I'll meet you tomorrow night at seven on the Ku'damm, near the zoo station steps. Ditch the camera if you get caught.'

He just laughed. 'Don't worry about me, Mr Kaymer. I'll be fine.'

Somehow I knew he was right. 'Come on, I'll give you a lift back to Marienfelde. We'll have to hide you in the back. What will you tell your parents?'

He just gave me that look again. The look that said I'd said the wrong thing. That had happened more than once tonight, and not only with Gerd.

'You just worry about getting us over the border, Mr Kaymer. The rest is my business.'

CHAPTER 7

WEDNESDAY, 9th AUGUST 1961,
WEST BERLIN

They took me from the street in broad daylight. I was so surprised I didn't struggle or call out to alert anyone. Not that the depressed looking Wednesday morning shoppers would have batted an eyelid if I had. I knew who had taken me. The abduction was clean and professional; there was one man either side of me in the back, one in the front to take care of the doors, or something else if things got out of hand, and the smooth getaway driver. To top it off, inside the car, the aroma was of sweat, cheap coffee, and cigarettes; it was the smell of a stakeout. They'd clearly been watching me for some time and, when I was whisked through the Heinrich Heine Strasse checkpoint without the hint of an identity card check, I knew I was in the hands of East German State Security.

The man to my left had a round head sunk into his round shoulders. He could have been Max Schmeling's son, but ten kilos heavier. His companion, the other piece of bread, with me acting as the compact sandwich filling, was taller. His legs were raised from the seat and he looked like he was giving the driver a good knee in the back. He had a specific nose. It should have been long, thin, and pointed like his legs, but it wasn't. Somebody had connected well with it in the past.

51

Eventually I found my voice from somewhere. 'In case you clowns didn't realise, I'm an American citizen.' There was nothing, not even a flicker from my companions.

'Hey! I'm talking to you.' I turned to my left until I was level with his ear hairs. Judging by the lack of response, it seemed to me there was more intellectual thought going on inside a goldfish bowl. It was only when I started to struggle that I had a response. It wasn't exactly the one I was hoping for, but at least the blow to the ribs told me I wasn't the only human in the car.

'Shut it!' The one with the flat nose growled, following it with another pointed elbow to my ribs. I was obviously being taken to see the organ grinder and by the look of the monkeys, it wasn't going to be a welcoming experience.

Sitting with my arms tied behind me in the back of a car with an American football front line for company made me feel like a processed sardine. It had crossed my mind what the East German Security Services might want with an American journalist, and I suspected I wouldn't have long to find out.

It had taken no more than fifteen minutes, but already we were deep in the grimy bowels of East Berlin. We slowed to a halt and a pair of rotting wooden gates opened to quickly reveal a cobbled courtyard. We were off the streets and the view wasn't any better from my perspective. I was hauled from the car with all the tenderness that might be afforded a sack of coal. My last glimpse of the blue sky left me wondering when I might see it again.

As I tried to walk, I had my round-shouldered companion for company at my front and another behind, who I assumed was the other one with the nose, by the way he maintained the playful insistence on jabbing my ribs when it appeared I might be slowing down. We were soon descending a rusty looking flight of steps and I had the impression this wasn't a place the paintbrush saw too often. As we entered a small cell area, judging by the peeling iron doors, the smell was an unhealthy mixture of sweat, puke, and fear; the latter no doubt causing the former two. As if to prove my point, at the second Flatnose lovingly pushed me through an open cell door, another guard was busy swilling unknown human emissions from the floor with a pail of fetid water.

As the door swung shut behind me, I had to pinch myself that I was actually in such a place, having so recently breathed the free air of West Berlin. To reinforce my unease, I heard an involuntary scream emanating from close by. Not being the naïve type, I had a good idea what this place was all about. It was the main reason I didn't want Tanja to end up living here. Fortunately, if you discounted my current predicament, I hadn't yet sampled what life was really like in day-to-day East Berlin. I had a feeling I was about to. It was time to think quickly if I was to extricate myself from this mess.

***

By the time they came for me, the pain in my ribs had dulled to a mere throb. I knew it couldn't have been that long, as my nostrils still hadn't got used to the burning sensation that had been attacking them since I arrived. The place smelled almost as bad as the meat factory, and that was saying something.

The one with the flat nose greeted me with a grunt a hog would have been proud of and lifted me bodily to my feet. Outside the cell, the floor had been cleaned of its dubious contents, but the stench remained. After being escorted along a myriad of corridors with grey painted walls and worn lino, I came face to face with the organ grinder. I recognised his ample grey uniform as that of the State Security, which, whilst confirming my suspicions, didn't reassure me. The man filled the uniform, and then some. He looked to be in his late forties, but there were so many jowls hanging over his collar it was impossible to be sure. His hair was black and greased back like he'd just dipped it in a vat of beeswax. He sat examining me with his face partially hidden by his hands, which were held in an arc, as if he was holding a ball. His fingers, as thick as Krackauer sausages, were touching at the tips.

He nodded towards a small stool opposite him. 'Take a seat, Herr Kaymer. We have a lot to discuss.'

'Thanks, but I'd rather stand.' It wasn't the time to be dictated to.

He shrugged. 'I hope you weren't treated too roughly on your way here. I am Major Weber.'

'Don't worry yourself. It's not every day kind men give you a free taxi ride around Berlin,' I said.

'Yes, that was slightly dramatic, but we thought it was time we had a little chat.'

'You could've just called me like anyone else.'

'Quite, but that would not have conveyed the seriousness of your situation.'

I narrowed my eyes at him, trying to understand what my situation actually was. The major didn't wait for an invitation to tell me.

'We have reason to believe you are planning another derogatory article about Democratic Germany.'

So that's what this was all about. I'd been abducted off the street because they were worried about one of my articles. As a journalist, that made me feel quite proud. I felt myself starting to relax a little. 'I fail to see what business that might be of yours, and come to think of it, why you feel it's a good idea to snatch a US citizen from the streets of West Berlin if, as you say, your country is so democratic.'

The major let out a gruff, deep throated chuckle. 'It's our business, Herr Kaymer, because things are a little sensitive at the moment. We wouldn't want you causing any problems within our populace by stirring up false allegations. In fact, we would prefer it if you didn't publish this article.'

I was starting to understand what was going on here. It also meant whatever I had seen, and whatever I had deduced as a result, was very likely true.

'So you think by holding me here I won't be able to tell the world what you're up to?'

I had him just where I wanted him and I was loving every minute.

'Well, Herr Kaymer, it would be difficult to publish your story from an East German prison cell.' He chuckled again. So did his chins.

'You might be right…' I paused, enjoying my moment. 'But it just might be the case that I did what all good, professional journalists do when they're in my situation.'

Weber started to shuffle awkwardly on his chair, which led it to squawk in complaint.

'What might that be, Herr Kaymer?'

'I posted a copy of the article to someone for safekeeping.' I wasn't lying. 'If I'm not in a certain bar in West Berlin in…' I stopped to look at my watch, '…twelve hours, the article will be published anyway.'

His portly smile turned to a grimace. 'It's a shame you are not willing to cooperate with us, Herr Kaymer. If you allow your article to be published, it would be very irresponsible.' His eyes examined me, like they were looking for the place to administer the fatal poison. 'Maybe some more time alone to think will help?'

The one with the flat nose re-entered the room in a flash as if he had been listening at the door all along.

Weber barked, 'Take the prisoner back to his cell.'

I smirked at the organ grinder. Even if back in the cesspit of a cell was the last place I wanted to be, I knew I had won this particular battle.

CHAPTER 8

WEDNESDAY, 9th AUGUST 1961, EAST GERMANY

It had been a four a.m. start for Hans Erdmann, but he didn't care. Out here in Pätz, 40 kilometers to the south of Berlin, he felt content. He was a million miles from all the intrigues and politics of the capital and that suited him just fine. Spread out here, among the lakes from Potsdam to Alt Glienecke on the southern approaches to Berlin, there were up to 40,000 armed men, all primed and ready to go. It wouldn't be long now.

He'd taken breakfast with his men, listening to their banter. Any soldier worth his salt knew something was coming. All the training and drilling was obviously leading to something and, as they enjoyed their breakfast, there was a buzz about the camp. Whilst Hans was happy here, amongst his comrades, he did have concerns about the exact nature of the operation they were being prepared for.

His old friend and colleague, Bernie Schwarzer, joined him at the makeshift camping table, mess cup in hand.

'Good to see you, chief. Do you have a minute?'

'Sure.'

Bernie flicked his head to one side to indicate they required some solitude.

Hans took the hint. 'Let's take a walk.'

Bernie had been with the regiment putting the men through their paces over the last few days. Hans envied him being here, away from the city. Bernie was a sergeant and not an officer like him, but to Hans, there were other ties, stronger than mere rank. When Hans had been a young, raw recruit to the panzer grenadiers in 1943, his life expectancy had been short. At that point, the war had already turned and the long hot summer in the dust and heat of the massive tank battles around Kursk had been his baptism. Without Bernie Schwarzer to show him the ropes, he was convinced he wouldn't have survived. Some things, some shared experiences, transcended rank.

When they were out of earshot, Hans said, 'What's up then, Bernie?'

'Goltz has been on the phone.' Goltz was Hans' quartermaster back at HQ in Treptow. As soon as Bernie said it, Hans knew immediately there was trouble brewing.

'More missing supplies?' Hans said.

Bernie nodded his head with a severe look on his face. 'Weapons this time.'

'Weapons? Bernie, this is getting serious.'

'Ten Kalashnikovs, to be precise.'

Since the end of the war the two of them had always been together in some way. They even reposted to Berlin together after the death of his wife, Monika. Hans stopped and stared out over the lake. There were small wisps of early morning mist seemingly held there by the surface of the water. He felt like somebody had a hold of him and was squeezing hard on his nether regions.

'Someone is after me, Bernie.'

Bernie nodded sullenly.

The two of them had watched with a mixture of horror and resignation at the retirement, and redeployment to obscure postings, of their old comrades. Admittedly, many were older than Hans, but it was the same people he and Sergeant Schwarzer had survived the tough times with, the ones they resonated with. They were military men, non-politicals. East Germany was changing. Now, they both knew it was Hans' turn.

Hans was a soldier to the core. Even if he didn't always agree with the tough decisions the leaders of East Germany had taken since the war, he'd followed his orders. He hadn't particularly enjoyed the part he had played in helping Russian soldiers put down the Workers Uprising in 1953, or the tough policing job his regiment was forced to make during the collectivisation of the farms, but he did it, nonetheless. For that loyalty, he had been duly rewarded with a rapid rise up the ranks to his current position of colonel in the Volksarmee, the People's Army. His subsequent transfer to the capital had brought him a standard of living few others in East Berlin enjoyed. The Army was all he had in his life since Monika's untimely death. However, over the years, for a number of reasons, doubts had started to grow in his mind.

'So what do we do, Chief?' Bernie asked.

'I've already hauled Goltz in over the previous supplies. He clammed up like someone had stuck a mortar pipe up his backside. He was scared, Bernie. Someone has got to him.'

Since his move to Berlin, his job had become increasingly political. He wasn't satisfied sitting in endless meetings at the centre of intrigue. He hated dealing with the slippery politicians. He preferred men who said what they wanted straight out. The sharks of the regime knew it too. Hans found it difficult to hide his true feelings, but he knew he had to do his best.

'We could have Goltz followed,' Bernie said hopefully.

'No, Bernie, you're not a spy. You keep doing your job out here. I will deal with it.'

Hans would find a way to deal with it, just like he'd found a way to survive all these years.

'I'll call you if you're needed before the weekend.'

'The weekend?' Bernie asked.

'I have got a meeting later back in Berlin.' Hans paused, putting his hand to his chin in a pensive pose.

'We're about to find out what all the training exercises have been for.'

CHAPTER 9

WEDNESDAY, 9th AUGUST 1961,
EAST BERLIN

So this was it. The reason for the prolonged heightened state of alert, and the explanation why his headquarters at Treptow had been taking constant deliveries of concrete blocks, fence posts, and barbed wire since the beginning of July, was about to be revealed. Hans had smiled to himself when he'd received the invitation to the old Health Ministry building on Wilhelmstrasse. The wily old fox Ulbricht was up to his old tricks: throw people off the scent by holding the most important meeting in East Germany's short history at an obscure building, well away from the Central Committee Headquarters.

Honecker stood up to address his audience. Hans was among other military, police, and political officials straining at the bit to find out what it was all about. Honecker cut an unusual figure in his brown cheesecloth suit and dark horn-rimmed glasses, seemingly lost in the sea of military uniforms around him. He was clearly, however, the leader of this project. The FDJ youth leader had been carefully handpicked by Ulbricht.

He started his speech with the usual platitudes and indoctrination that seemed to have become the norm these days. It was one of the many reasons Hans continued to lose faith. Eventually, Honecker got to the figures, the justification for the action he was about to reveal.

People were flooding over the border at an alarming, unsustainable rate, lured there by dubious means, if Honecker was to be believed. Something had to be done and he was about to reveal exactly what and when.

Honecker was right to be worried, because the figures were damning. Hans' country was haemorrhaging 1500 people a day. These people were not only street cleaners or labourers, although no doubt they were in the number; there were doctors, nurses, and teachers, too. During the previous week, the director of the Volkspolizei Hospital had left for West Berlin complaining of political interference and lack of supplies. "A traitor to medical science and his patients," Honecker had referred to him. "A doctor at his wit's end," RIAS called him. It depended upon where one's political views lay. Many of the HO department stores had been forced to close at lunchtime for four consecutive days due to the number of defecting staff. The figures were compelling; Hans didn't doubt East Germany would be on its knees unless something was done soon.

The audience of fifty of the most senior members of the East German government and military listened intently to the facts and figures. Karl Maron, the interior minister, was sitting in the front row, next to a slouched Mielke, head of the Stasi. Hans' own boss, Xavier Marks, was with them, one of them. There was no doubt he was an up and coming star to the people in power. To Hans he was nothing but an upstart, sliding up and down the House of Ministries' corridors, without actually doing anything worthwhile.

Just as Honecker had whipped up expectations with all his facts and figures, he called a break in proceedings so attendees could discuss matters with their comrades. Hans felt like shouting at him to get on with it and put everyone out of their misery, but he knew how much Ulbricht and his cronies loved the drama.

No sooner had he grabbed a cup of the morose, weak looking excuse for coffee, than Xavier Marks was on his shoulder.

'A word, Erdmann.' He flicked his head in the direction of a quiet corner of the old corridor. Hans had to wonder why, considering there were ten other similar secretive, whispered conversations going on around the room. The drama of the situation was taking hold.

Xavier Marks was deputy to Interior Minister Karl Maron. Hans did have a nominal ranking superior, a general who was about to be put out to grass, but he knew the politicals of East Berlin held the power, and Xavier Marks was definitely one of the latter. Not tainted by running off to Moscow and reappearing suddenly after the war, Marks was part of the new breed. In his early forties, he'd been a student during the war. Marks was someone who wouldn't think twice about leaving the footprint of his expensive looking shoes on your forehead. The suit matched the shoes, costly and not from East Berlin; a cut like that only came from the western sectors. Hans knew some things about Marks which made him despise the man, and the enmity appeared mutual. Marks hated the military types and it was the main reason Hans' old comrades were disappearing from their positions at such speed.

'I hear you've been having a few problems at the barracks, Erdmann.'

Marks didn't mince his words and he smiled, seemingly enjoying the fact. To Marks, Hans knew he was another name to tick off the old school list to make way for younger, more politically reliable replacements. But Hans had dealt with bigger men than Marks.

'Yes, Deputy Minister.' Hans spat the words out like he had drunk too much of the poison they were passing as coffee. 'The lack of space due to all the concrete posts is giving my quartermaster a major headache.'

Marks' eyes narrowed. 'Yes, well all that will be explained in due time, Erdmann. I was talking about the missing supplies.'

'Missing supplies? You must be misinformed, Deputy Minister.'

'Oh, I had it on good authority.'

Hans looked at him wondering how he was so well informed, unless he was in on the whole thing, of course.

'I'd be surprised if a deputy minister knew about missing supplies before a colonel who was responsible for Treptow barracks.' Hans was starting to enjoy himself. 'That would strike me as very strange indeed.'

Marks looked angry and adjusted the collar of his expensive silk shirt. Before he could reply, Honecker was waving them back into the meeting room, but it didn't stop Marks hissing, 'Just watch your back, Erdmann.'

Hans retook his seat towards the rear of the room. In spite of his confident outward demeanour, he was worried. Marks had left him feeling uneasy, if only for the reason it finally confirmed his suspicions: He knew for certain the missing supplies were an effort to discredit him. He knew Marks was behind it; it was just a question of who else was involved.

At the front, Honecker's little drama was reaching its denouement. A young NVA soldier had joined Honecker in front of a large board. The sheet covering the board was inexorably removed. The fact that Honecker wasn't quite tall enough to flick the sheet over the corner of the board, and a man from the audience had to assist him, only added to the delay.

The sheet eventually dropped to the floor, revealing a map of Berlin and its surrounding areas.

'This,' Honecker pointed dramatically at the map, 'is what it's all about, comrades. Operation Rose, the sealing off of West Berlin.'

Hans stared openmouthed for a moment. The people around him gasped audibly, some smiled nervously, one man even clapped. On the map, West Berlin appeared strange. It was now an island, or an ugly wart, a blot on the landscape of the DDR, in Honecker's words. To others, many thousands by the increasing defection rate, West Berlin was an oasis.

Whatever the case, there was one feeling building inside Hans Erdmann. It was one he was fighting to keep down, like bile rising in his throat.

Disgust.

CHAPTER 10

WEDNESDAY, 9th AUGUST 1961,
EAST BERLIN

I was more nervous by the time they came for me again, as, I am certain, was Weber's intention. I needed to get out of this place. I was desperate to take Eva and Tanja to West Berlin before they sealed the border. On top of that, I'd missed my meeting with Gerd to collect the photos, and I needed them for the story. Before I got back to that pokey little room, I had a word with myself to cut the games short.

This time Weber was not alone. Seated next to him was an older, sterner looking character. He was short, without a hair on his head apart from bushy white eyebrows. It was then I noticed his uniform. I wasn't a military expert, but it was Russian, and a high ranking Russian, to boot. To add to that, Weber looked nervous, sweating profusely under his overworked jacket. The atmosphere felt a whole different.

'Please.' Weber extended his arm in the direction of the chair.

This time I sat down without a smart comment. I felt the Russian sizing me up. I looked back at him, determined not to blink. It was almost as if Weber wasn't in the room.

Weber cleared his throat nervously. 'This is General Dobrovsky...'

I raised my eyebrows at the "General" part.

'...of the KGB,' Weber completed the introduction.

Now I knew I had a scoop on my hands. If they'd sent a general in KGB to talk to me, it must have been important.

'May I be direct with you?' the Russian asked.

'It's how we prefer it back home.'

'Likewise,' the general growled. 'Let us suppose you know what is planned here in Berlin.'

'I'm no building surveyor, but by the look of all that material, I would hazard a guess at a big fence, or a wall of some kind.'

The general didn't say a word, nor did he flinch. I wondered if he played poker.

I raised the stakes. 'It looks as if it would be permanent to me. Imagine a wall right down the middle of Berlin. It would be quite a story. Especially after goatee said, what was it? I should remember, I was at the press conference earlier in the summer. Oh yes, that was it, "Nobody has any intention of building a wall." '

I was getting into this. I could hear Ackerman's excitement when he read the story.

Weber nervously jumped in. 'So let's say you're right. To break such a story…' Dobrovsky's head turned slowly towards him and administered what could only be described as a "death stare." Under his glare, Weber's final words trailed off, 'For this story, words alone would not be…'

'Enough!' I finished his sentence with glee. 'You know what, Weber, you could get a job as a journalist. I'm genuinely impressed,' I said, almost warmly.

Dobrovsky had heard enough. He turned back to me, 'Where's the film, Kaymer?'

'I can't imagine what you mean,' I said, all innocence.

Dobrovsky's gloves were off now. 'It's not at your apartment.'

I winced. 'I hope you cleaned up afterwards, General.' I was only half joking. Things were getting a little too close to home.

'Trust me, Kaymer, we'll find it or you'll give it to us.' He raised his white bush-like eyebrows to reinforce the point.

I was starting to feel some discomfort. Dobrovsky had provided a harder, more steel-like approach to proceedings. It was time for a change of tack. 'Look, you and I know you can't keep me here much longer. Only if you are planning on doing it, can you get on with it? I've got some sleep to catch up on back in my cell.'

'You're right, Kaymer.' Dobrovsky smiled for the first time. It didn't make me feel any warmer towards him. 'We can't keep you much longer and nor will we.'

'Somebody from the State Department giving you pressure to release me?'

'You have friends in high places, Kaymer. In fact, we'll be handing you over to one of your countrymen shortly. But before we do that, there are some conditions to your release.'

'Conditions?' I said, a little too quickly.

'You'll be released on the condition you don't return to East Berlin. We will be escorting you to the border to ensure you leave. You'll not be welcome back in the Soviet sector.'

It all seemed too easy. I shrugged. I could live with that, given the fact East Berlin and me didn't exactly agree with each other. I made a move to get up.

'And, of course,' Dobrovsky went on, 'you won't publish your story.'

I snorted. 'I'm afraid that's not possible. It's like taking the food from the mouth of my daughter.'

Disconcertingly, this didn't seem to register with Dobrovsky. He was still acting like he had a royal flush close to his chest.

As if by magic, Flatnose reappeared in the doorway.

'My comrade here will take you to the place where you're to be handed over. I can't say it's been a pleasure to meet you, Kaymer.'

To him the meeting was done.

'You'll not stop me publishing, General. The whole world will know what you're up to.'

He just shrugged.

I was in the doorway now, feeling like an unsuccessful salesman being unceremoniously shown the exit.

It was then I found out just how good Dobrovsky's hand was.

'As a citizen of the United States, Kaymer, we could never keep you here, not for long anyway. However…' His words hung in the air. '…Eva Schultz would be an entirely different story.'

CHAPTER 11

WEDNESDAY, 9th AUGUST 1961,
EAST BERLIN

As Eva returned from her shift in West Berlin, she noticed increased activity at the border S-Bahn station. She felt the anxiety rise in her. She still hadn't completely shaken off her anger after the meeting with the authorities at the town hall. She had had enough now and couldn't wait to get the move to Jack's place done. She knew he wouldn't let her and Tanja down, but he did have to understand his priorities. Jack let work get in the way of things too much. It was something she hoped would change in time.

As she made her way through the courtyard of her apartment block, Eva was so caught up in her own thoughts that she didn't see the boy approaching.

'You're Jack's missus, right?'

Eva looked up in surprise. He was no more than sixteen years old, but he still had his hair styled like James Dean, swept across at the front. Most of his clothes looked well-worn, apart from the expensive looking leather jacket. The boy pulled a face, possibly in response to the puzzled look etched on Eva's face. 'Are you Jack's wife or not, lady?'

'I'm sorry, should I know you?'

The boy looked nervously over his shoulder. 'I work for Jack Kaymer. I was under the impression you and him were together.'

'Yes, I suppose so. What do you want?' Eva said warily.

'Can we talk somewhere quieter?' He continued to look nervous, although Eva could see he was trying to look tough in the jacket.

'I'm in a hurry. Is it important?' she said.

'It's very important to Herr Kaymer.'

Eva sighed. She was already late. She didn't particularly like the look of the boy, but there was something in what he said that intrigued her. She didn't know a great deal about Jack's work, but if the boy had come here to search her out, she reasoned it must be important.

'Ok. Five minutes. Walk with me.'

They left the courtyard away from prying eyes. In front of them on the road was a Police paddy wagon. The boy quickly took control, grabbing Eva's arm and steering her away from the van and on down the street.

Eva looked at him with mounting concern and said, 'So what can I do for you?'

His voice was clipped and business-like. 'It's best you don't know my name. I am working for Jack, as I said. We were supposed to meet earlier, but he didn't turn up.'

'Well, I'm sure he's just busy...'

'No, you don't understand. What I did for him...' He looked over his shoulder again, 'What I have for him, he really needs for his work.'

'Why all the secrecy?' Eva asked.

The boy was starting to get impatient. 'Look, lady, we had a deal. He didn't turn up and he owes me money...'

'Oh, I see. That's what this is all about. Well, you'll get nothing from me. Jack's business is his business.' Eva started to head back towards the apartment.

'Wait!' The boy was around in front of her, blocking her path.

'Hey! What is this?' Eva said, starting to get annoyed.

He put up his hands in a placatory manner. 'Ok. Ok. I'll be straight with you, but you mustn't repeat this to anybody, for your own good.'

'I'm waiting,' Eva said, with growing impatience.

'I have a film. It contains photographs of certain materials…'

'This doesn't make sense. What are you talking about?'

'Look, they are going to build a fence or wall. I have pictures of the stuff they'll use: a mountain of posts and barbed wire. Your husband, Jack, is going to break the story.'

'A wall?' Eva said in a high pitch.

'Yes! Can you keep your voice down?'

Eva was confused. It wouldn't surprise her if it were true. It was obvious there was something coming due to all the measures on the border, but a wall sounded far-fetched.

'Even if what you say is true, I still have no money to pay you,' Eva said eventually.

The boy looked down to the floor. 'You don't have any money? Nothing at all? Not even back at the apartment?'

'A few Marks, that's all.'

The boy turned up his nose. 'Ok. I'll give you the film. I don't want to carry it around with me, but tell Herr Kaymer the price just doubled and I'm keeping hold of the camera as a guarantee.'

Eva shrugged, unsure what to say in response. 'If that's what you want to do, but you'll have to speak to him about the money.'

He grabbed her hand and stuffed a small black case into it.

'Don't worry, when I see him, I will.' The boy looked in her eyes and nodded. 'Take care, lady.'

With that, he rushed off down the street.

***

We were not yet back in West Berlin. I only had Flatnose for company in the back of the car and I was so mad at Dobrovsky's threats, I was ready to take him on. I was in the process of wondering if the heel of

71

my shoe could make my companion's nose any flatter than it was already, when we reached the sector border on the Oberbaumbrücke.

Leaning on the bonnet of the black Buick was Matt Collins. I jumped out of the car quickly, thankful to see a friendly face. It was lucky for my guard that Matt was there, otherwise God knows what I would have done. I heard the engine gun behind me and the East Germans were back over the border from where they came.

Matt was holding out both arms for an explanation. 'When I got a call from a friend at the CIA, why did I know it was going to be about you?'

I didn't say anything. I just stormed around the car and got in the passenger seat. Matt joined me in the front.

'Thanks for coming, Matt. Don't mention it.' He turned towards me. 'Care to tell me what the hell's going on, Jack?'

I stared out of the windscreen over the bridge back into the eastern sectors. 'Later, we don't have time right now.'

'I get called out of a meeting to be informed you're a prisoner of the Stasi and told to collect you, and you don't have time to explain?'

He was becoming incredulous, but I didn't care. There was only one thing on my mind. 'Are you going to drive or what?' I fired back.

He just shook his head and turned the key in the ignition.

'Good. Now drive into Kreuzberg and then double back towards Friedrichstrasse. We're going back to East Berlin,' I said.

Matt stopped and turned to me. 'Jack, as I understand, you gave them assurances. You're not supposed to go back there. There's no way I'm taking you back there in a car with Allied plates. That's asking for more trouble than you're already in.'

'Fuck the assurances, Matt, this is important.'

'No way.' He folded his arms. 'I'm going nowhere until you give me an explanation. This is about that story you sent me, isn't it?'

I turned on him, 'They arrested me, Matt, because I know they're planning to build a wall. I found a whole bloody warehouse full of barbed wire and concrete blocks. They're going to split the city in two.'

'I read the copy you mailed me. So, now tell me why we're going back there,' was Matt's sarcastic response.

'We have to go back because, even though they let me go, they threatened me to keep me quiet.'

'How can they threaten you, Jack? You're an American citizen?'

'Don't be so fucking naïve, Matt. They don't give a shit about liberty and human rights. They abducted me off the street in West Berlin, for Christ's sake. And now…' I felt my voice crack. Emotion. It surprised me, but it was there and Matt heard it too.

'Ok. Ok, buddy. Where are we heading?'

'Lichtenburg. I just hope we're not too late.'

***

Klaus Schultz's train was on the final approach into Friedrichstrasse station. It felt strange to be back in Berlin again. He recalled the time when he returned from his last leave from the Eastern Front in November 1942. He'd arrived at the now bomb-ruined Anhalter station. Those were the last ten days he had spent with his wife and family in the following twelve years. His life in Russian captivity had been hard. He felt a shiver at the thought of being cut off from Eva again. Now, he had a granddaughter to think about as well.

Even though Ulrich had shared Burzin's documents with his bosses at the BND, the West German Security Service, they had seemingly done nothing about it. Klaus had even met with his old comrade Markus, now an agent for the BND, to push the point. To Klaus, if the documents were genuine, it was clear the East Germans were planning to close all access to West Berlin from the east. Why the hell didn't they want to believe it? Why the hell hadn't they done anything about it in the last couple of months? Were the West Germans happy to let it happen? Had they informed the Americans? What were they going to do about it?

He'd seen all the commentaries in the newspapers and listened avidly to news about the situation in Berlin. He could feel things reaching a boiling point. In the end, whatever the superpowers and governments may or may not do, one fact remained: If they closed the border, his daughter and granddaughter were living in East Berlin. Klaus had to take things into his own hands and do something. He was determined to bring Eva and Tanja back to West Germany before it was too late. Maria had warned him not to interfere between Eva and the American, but Klaus couldn't sit back and do nothing. Anyway, as far he was concerned, the American, Kaymer, was trouble. He was more interested in his career than Eva.

Klaus wasn't going to be separated from his family again. He wasted no time in heading for the U-Bahn to Lichtenberg and Eva's apartment.

***

Now that she was back in the courtyard, Eva couldn't resist looking down at the black, plastic film case in her hand. It was small enough to hide in her palm. She was aware of the nature of the film's contents, if what the boy had said was true. If it did prove the authorities were going to put up a wall, it would be political dynamite. If it became public knowledge, a few checks at the border wouldn't stop the stampede that would certainly follow. After her experience at the town hall, it wouldn't surprise her in the slightest. The very fact Ulbricht had said only a few months ago that it wasn't their intention, said everything to Eva. As she ascended the wooden staircase to the apartment, she had the overwhelming urge to take Tanja and get out of East Berlin now.

As she reached the apartment door, it was ajar. She thought maybe Helmi, her mother's old friend, had taken Tanja for a walk and was just putting the pram away. Eva heard Tanja crying as she went through the door; maybe her teeth were bothering her again. In the living room, Helmi was trying to calm the baby down. She saw the strain on Helmi's face and instantly knew that Tanja wasn't the cause. Helmi quickly put a finger to her lips and pointed towards the bedroom, mouthing the words: 'You have to go, quickly.'

It was then Eva heard the sound of wardrobes and drawers being emptied.

'Stasi! Go!' Helmi mouthed again.

Eva suddenly remembered the police van she'd seen outside on the street. Surely, it wasn't meant for her. Normally, she would've taken Helmi's advice, but the events of the day, the town hall officials, the guard on the train, all made her react differently. She didn't feel like running from anyone, quite the opposite. Eva wanted to know who was ransacking her room, and why. Helmi half whispered, half squealed, 'No!' But it was too late.

Eva forced open the bedroom door, hitting an obstruction at the back of it with a dull thump, bringing a yelp of pain from one of the men.

'Just what the hell do you think you're doing?' Eva demanded.

The man who was searching the wardrobe stopped. 'Eva Schultz? You must come with us. You're under arrest.' The other man was rubbing his head furiously. It seemed he had been searching the small cabinet behind the door when Eva had opened it. She didn't care.

'Under arrest? For what?' Eva held Tanja in one arm with the other planted firmly on her hip.

'Reasons of national security.' He grabbed at her free arm and Tanja started to scream.

'How dare you?' Eva kicked him hard in the shins. That left both of the men nursing injuries and Eva scowling at them.

'Get out of my bedroom,' she ordered. Maybe it was the sheer anger in her voice, maybe it was her general reaction to the search, but the two men meekly left the bedroom.

Eva followed them into the living room. 'Now what the hell is going on here?'

'Please hand your child to the lady here. You are under arrest.' The man showed his identification, slowly regaining his composure.

Eva suddenly remembered the case in the palm of her hand. She couldn't believe all this was due to the film; it would have been too fast. More probably it was due to her behaviour at the town hall earlier in the day. She had to do something with it quickly. She looked anxiously around the room. She could pass it to Helmi when she handed Tanja over, but they would surely see. Anyway, she didn't want to bring Helmi any trouble.

'We have to go now, Fräulein Schultz.'

Eva was starting to panic. What could she do? It was then Tanja dropped her rabbit to the floor. Eva kissed Tanja on the head and handed her over to Helmi. Without thinking, she bent down and picked up Tanja's rabbit. Already the stitching had come loose even though it was only a few days old. Since Jack had bought it, Tanja hadn't let go of it. In fact, Eva had only managed to wash it when she'd been asleep. The loose seam was Eva's opportunity to stuff the plastic case inside. She did it quickly and handed the rabbit to Tanja in one movement.

The two policemen were not waiting any longer, and with the baby now out of her arms, they grabbed hold of Eva. She started to struggle, but realistically she had little choice but to go with them. She didn't want to upset Tanja more by causing further commotion. Helmi looked on, openmouthed.

'Take care of Tanja for me and tell Jack what happened,' Eva called out.

The last view Eva had of the living room was Helmi holding Tanja. Her baby's arms were outstretched towards Eva, her eyes pleading for her mother's touch. Eva tried to suppress her emotions. At least she knew Tanja would be safe, which was more than she could say for herself.

CHAPTER 12

WEDNESDAY, 9th AUGUST 1961,
EAST BERLIN

Sprinting through the courtyard, I feared the worst. I was up the mouldy steps in a few bounds. The door to Eva's apartment was wide open and I could hear a baby's cries.

As I made it into the small living room, Helmi had Tanja on her knee and was trying to soothe her.

'Where is she, Helmi?' I asked with desperation.

Helmi's face was full of concern.

'Tell me I'm not too late,' I pleaded.

'I am sorry, Jack. They've just taken her,' Helmi said.

'No!' I howled.

The room was spinning. I let myself slump into the worn chair. I closed my eyes, my head in my hands.

'Who took her, Helmi?' It was a stupid question. I knew the answer before I asked. I needed some reassurance I hadn't been such an idiot, but I had the feeling it wouldn't be forthcoming.

'The Stasi.'

I winced. Confirmation was difficult to hear. Eventually, I came to my senses and took my daughter from her. I held her close to my chest and she quieted for a moment.

'What did they want?' I cringed, not really wanting to know the answer, not wanting to know this was really all my doing.

'I don't know, Jack. They were looking for something. That's all I know.'

I looked around the place, noticing the disorder for the first time.

'What's this all about, Jack? What are you going to do?' Helmi asked.

I stared back at Helmi, helpless. I guessed they were looking for the film, although I'd no idea why they thought it would be with Eva. I thought I'd been smart, making a copy of the story. I thought I'd had all the angles covered. I was naïve enough to believe I could outfox Weber, Dobrovsky, and the like. I hadn't thought it through properly. It was my fault Eva had been arrested.

***

Close to Eva's apartment, Klaus didn't fail to notice the gleaming new Buick parked by the kerbside. Neither did he fail to miss the slick dressed, if worried looking man standing over it. He was out of place in Lichtenberg.

As he made his way through the courtyard, he recalled his reconciliation with his daughter when he returned from Soviet captivity. She was full of confidence and strongly defensive of her mother. He didn't blame Eva for that. Klaus had made a mess of his reunion with Maria. He tried to push the thought from his mind. It was one of the reasons he was determined to act now. He wasn't going to repeat mistakes of the past.

At the door of Eva's apartment, he heard voices through the open door. As he approached the living room, he recognised Helmi's voice.

'What's it all about, Jack? What are you going to do?' she said.

Klaus dropped his bag by the living room door. The apartment looked like it had been ransacked.

'Klaus!' Helmi said, getting up to greet him. 'I didn't know you were coming.'

Helmi was one of Maria's oldest friends. He wasn't surprised she was at the apartment helping Eva.

'I had to come, Helmi. It's a long story. Where is she? What the hell happened here?' Klaus said.

'Oh, Klaus! The Stasi have been here…' Helmi paused, seemingly not wanting to say. 'They took her. Not more than ten minutes ago.'

Klaus turned his attention to the man in the chair holding his granddaughter. Kaymer hadn't said a word. So much so, he hadn't even looked at Klaus.

'Arrested? What, *now*?' Klaus felt his heart sink. He knew what was coming. If they sealed off the border and Eva was in prison, even if only for a few days, there would be little he could do. He couldn't believe it had come down to ten minutes. He was mad he hadn't been here earlier.

He turned to Jack, 'Is somebody going to tell me what's going on here?' His voice was louder and Tanja started to cry again. 'Kaymer, is this your doing?'

He didn't know that much about the American, but he didn't like what he did know. Something didn't feel right. Klaus could sense Kaymer didn't want to say too much.

'Herr Schultz…I don't know what to say,' Kaymer barely managed.

'That makes a bloody change,' Klaus fired back.

Tanja's crying became louder and Kaymer stood up to try and soothe her. Klaus felt himself maddening, impatient at the lack of answers. He was barely aware he'd not even greeted his granddaughter.

'Come on, Kaymer, what's going on?' Klaus was shouting now.

Helmi intervened, 'Klaus, maybe this is not the time. Tanja is getting upset.'

'Yes, sorry,' said Klaus, remembering himself. 'Would you mind taking her for a moment?'

Helmi took Tanja and withdrew out of the firing line.

'Look, Herr Schultz, this is my fault. It's all my fault,' Kaymer said.

'I am waiting.'

'It's a long story…'

Klaus exploded, 'My daughter has been arrested. She could be stuck in this forsaken place forever and you tell me it's a long story.'

Kaymer looked puzzled for a moment. 'You said "could be stuck here"…?'

'Never mind that now. Why the hell has she been arrested? What have you been up to?'

Kaymer took a deep breath. 'I've upset the East German authorities with one of my stories. They arrested me. They knew they couldn't hold me…so, they took Eva instead.'

Klaus looked at the American, considering whether he should knock his head off. He was mad at him, no doubt, but he, more than anybody, understood the way the East Germans and Russians worked. Deep down, he was also mad at himself for not having come here sooner.

'Well, we have to get her out and quickly,' Klaus said, almost to himself.

'I know.'

Klaus couldn't help getting riled again, 'No, you bloody well don't know. You see, that's the problem with you Amis. You think you know about Berlin, but you don't. You cause all the shit and leave us to deal with it.'

'Now, just a minute. It wasn't the Americans who started the war. We're dealing with the mess you people put yourself in…'

Klaus was about to respond in kind when Helmi shouted, 'Enough! Just listen to you both. This is going to get us nowhere.' Tanja's crying started to intensify. 'Don't you think you should concentrate on getting Eva out instead of blaming each other for something that cannot be changed?'

Klaus felt suitably chastened. He'd only been thinking about his own anger.

'Sure, Helmi, you're right,' Jack said apologetically. 'I just hope we're in time.'

Klaus narrowed his eyes, 'What do you mean, "in time"?'

'That's the story, Herr Schultz. They're going to close the border.'

'Yes, that's what everybody thinks,' said Klaus. 'How can you be sure?'

'I have seen warehouses full of materials, concrete posts, barbed wire, blocks. Enough for a wall through the city,' Kaymer explained.

'So the papers *were* real,' Klaus said, almost to himself.

'What papers?'

'Ah, it's a long story,' Klaus said.

Jack raised his eyebrows at him.

'I can explain, of course, but later. We need to focus on getting Eva out.'

'We do, Herr Schultz, and quickly. As far as my sources are concerned, they will seal the border this weekend.'

CHAPTER 13

WEDNESDAY, 9th AUGUST 1961,
WEST BERLIN

He'd given me an earache all the way back to my apartment in
Schöneberg. I didn't need to hear just how much I'd messed up. I didn't
know it would turn out like this. I should have realised they wouldn't
stand back and let me continue to publish the articles. The Stasi always
found your weakness in the end. They'd found mine, and Klaus Schultz
was hammering the point home to me with all the subtlety of a
sledgehammer cracking a nut.

As we got to the apartment, Eva's father wasn't about to give up
his analysis of my usefulness.

'You intended to bring my granddaughter to live here?' Klaus said.

He looked scornfully at the bombsite that was my living room. I'd
forgotten what Dobrovsky had said about searching my place.

I couldn't resist a retaliatory dig, 'If you hadn't realised, Herr
Schultz, the Stasi called here, too.'

To be honest, the place hadn't been much tidier before Weber's
men had called without invitation, but it got Eva's father off my back
for at least thirty-seconds.

'Yeah, they're handy like that,' he conceded, but it wasn't long
before the next shot across my bows. 'Though I don't suppose the Stasi

emptied your beer bottles for you,' he said, flicking one of the numerous bottles disdainfully with his boot.

This was going to be a long afternoon; I didn't need an oversensitive gut to work that one out. We needed to call a truce and focus our resources, but I wasn't sure if Klaus was ready for that. He was tetchy at best, prone to bouts of outright anger at worst, but I wasn't really surprised about that. His physical appearance wasn't what you would imagine that of a man who had been held captive in a Gulag for all those years. He looked relatively fit, his face healthy and flush, although that could have been the anger. He was built of strong stuff for someone into his fifties. It was time to break down some barriers if I was to get him off my back, let alone on my side.

'Look, Klaus...you don't mind if I call you Klaus?'

He was sitting on the couch now, with Tanja on his knee. He stared back at me, or should I say, through me, giving no indication if it was okay or not. Tanja was snuffling one of the ears of the rabbit under her nose with her thumb in her mouth. Her saucer-like blue eyes stared back at me, too. Two generations of the Schultz family were eyeballing me. I felt like a gladiator about to receive the thumbs down from the emperor and his little princess.

I took a deep breath and ploughed on, 'Klaus, I know I've messed up here.'

Neither pair of eyes flickered at that assessment.

'Before I followed the tip-off from my source, I'd already agreed with Eva that she would come and live with me here.'

Klaus' eyes started to roll around the room, no doubt taking in the state of the place. I needed to step things up, as my start hadn't been a good one.

'I love your daughter, Klaus. No matter what you might think of me, and what I've done, that's the truth. Now, I know I've made mistakes, but I was trying to do my job. These people are ruthless and will stop at nothing to build their so called socialist paradise. I feel I have to try and stop them. I wanted to try and stop them. Is that such a bad thing?'

He was staring at me again. He looked like he was weighing things up before he eventually answered. 'Believe me, you won't stop these people. East Germans, Russians, the whole system. You cannot fight it. You just have to conform or get yourself and your family away from it, somewhere they cannot be affected by it. There is nobody that knows that more than me, Jack.'

There was real meaning in his voice. Eva had told me about Klaus' time in Siberia, but I wondered how much this man would really open up and tell the full story, even to his own daughter.

'Getting the true story out there is my job, Klaus. I am paid to expose the truth.'

'It all sounds very idealistic. Then again, I suppose I am an old cynic,' he said. A small smile broke on his face. If I didn't feel so bad inside, I might have got the flags out.

'So, they've taken Eva for a reason. I assume they are trying to blackmail you.'

I nodded. He knew the game.

'So what do you have that they want?'

'A film. Photographs of all the materials. Warehouses full of barbed wire and concrete posts, I told you about.'

'It's simple then. You give them the film and we get Eva out,' Klaus said.

I rubbed my chin. 'That's the problem. I have to go and get the film.'

'You don't have it?' Klaus asked, incredulous.

'I missed my meeting to pick it up because I was in a Stasi cell,' I explained.

'Well, what the hell are you doing sitting here? Go and get the bloody thing!'

CHAPTER 14

It was late in the evening when I arrived back at Marienfelde in my hunt for Gerd Braun. The kid had the film and I needed it to bargain for Eva's release, but it appeared I wasn't going to get my hands on it anytime soon; it seemed, as much as the staff there would tell me, Gerd had already set off for the airport for his relocation to West Germany. I could have shouted and wailed, not least at the thought of Eva's angry father waiting back at the apartment for some news. My last choice was to contact Matt Collins and see what he could do to help.

By now my bank of favours with Matt was well and truly in the red. After fetching me from East Berlin with my tail between my legs, here I was, once again, with the metaphorical begging bowl. I needed Gerd's new address, and quickly. The only way I could get that was through secret channels. In essence, I was asking Matt to set up a meeting with one of his CIA contacts at the refugee centre. At least, that's who I assumed he was. Matt would never tell me that outright, but when he said "our man at the centre", I guessed that was the case.

The seething mass of people outside the camp had not abated; if anything it was worse than at any time since I'd been there. If you asked me, given what I knew, they weren't bad judges to be fleeing East Berlin. I could imagine that if my story had been published the place would have been literally overrun. Now, fortunately for the already overworked staff at the centre, I had other priorities.

This time I headed straight for the administration office, thus bypassing the heavies on the front door. I was directed to the Allied Screening Office. Since my discussion with Matt, I'd learned the whole front office operation was in Allied hands. The staff were clearly all German, but working for the Allies nonetheless. It was mainly American, but the British and French had their own piece of the action, which meant each applicant had to jump through the three hoops before they were accepted into West Germany. Gerd and his family had passed those checks. I just hoped Matt's contact could tell me where in the Federal Republic they had been placed, otherwise I was on another wild goose chase.

At the American office, I was asked to wait by a young, polite, and very pretty secretary. I wondered if my nemesis Hildegard had been fired since our spat a few days earlier, but that was probably wishful thinking on my part. The five minutes I waited seemed like an age. I was trying not to focus too much on Eva's fate because each time I did, my stomach was providing its very own Titanic moment. I could have killed for a beer.

The good-looking secretary took me to an unmanned office where I was asked to wait. The person I needed to see had left for the evening, but was on his way back to the camp. Unfortunately, that gave me time to pore over the events of the last couple of days. I felt like a loser for many reasons, least of all for the incessant dressing down I'd received from Eva's father. I couldn't work him out. He clearly had his issues, but whatever the case, I wanted him on my side in the quest to get Eva out, rather than against me. At least I felt we'd eventually reached an understanding of sorts.

After a wait of around half an hour, a man with dark, backswept hair and thick horn-rimmed glasses entered carrying some papers. Since our last meeting hadn't ended so well, I was worried whether what I had said to Helmut Festag then, and the way I'd said it, would count against me.

My mouth was hanging open as I took his hand, and for the first time in my life I could honestly say I was lost for words.

'You look surprised, Herr Kaymer?'

I was busy recalling my thoughts, from our first meeting, that something hadn't been right. My instinct had been correct.

'You could say that. I didn't expect the director of Marienfelde Refugee Centre to be working for the CIA.'

He winced. 'We don't mention organisations too much around here. The fact is, Herr Kaymer, you weren't very far off the mark in your comments about spies at your last meeting, but there are very good reasons for that. And, of course, this part of our discussion is off the record.'

I nodded in understanding, knowing I needed his help this time.

'Look,' I said, changing the subject quickly, 'I apologise if I was a bit rude before, it's just there have been a lot of strange things going on lately. My interest is in a Gerd Braun, 15 or 16 years old. He can only have left here earlier today.'

Festag nodded. 'Can I ask you why you need to know?'

'It's complicated.'

'We have to think about security and the integrity of Marienfelde,' he said by way of explanation. He actually said it like I should understand what he meant, but catching on took me a moment.

'Oh, no, this is purely personal, I can assure you. I owe the boy a favour. It does not involve a story I intend to publish.' It really hurt me when I said it, even if it was true.

Festag nodded slowly, as if he didn't really believe me. 'Well, this is a favour for a colleague more than you, Herr Kaymer. However, I'm sure if you misuse this information, you will have to answer to your countrymen, not to me.'

It was a strange feeling, being threatened—even if it was only implied—with my own country's security service, by a German, in the German language. Given the circumstances, and our previous meeting, I understood his reticence. Either way, there wasn't much to add to that; we both knew where we stood.

Eventually, he turned over the papers in front of him and started to talk. 'The boy and his family have been relocated to a small town on the Rhine, Urmitz in Rheinland-Pflaz. Here is the address.' He slid a piece of paper across the table.

I picked up the paper and pocketed it before he could change his mind. 'Thanks.'

He looked at his watch. 'Unfortunately, you have just missed them. They were on a flight out of Templehof a couple hours ago.'

I rolled my eyes. I would have to be on the first flight in the morning. I must have looked ready to leave.

'Before you go, Herr Kaymer, if I might ask a small favour?'

I wasn't sure if it was it just me, but all meetings I'd had recently seemed to have a sting in their tail.

He pushed another piece of paper towards me, this time in one certain thrust. 'As I didn't see the article in your newspaper yet, I assume you've yet to complete it. These are a list of items and resources we require. Please see to it that we get some much needed exposure.' He smiled.

'Sure,' I said, fearing it could have been a whole lot worse.

In the end, nothing was free in Berlin.

***

Ever since Festag told me where Gerd and his family had gone to live, something had been bothering me. I'd tried to imagine Urmitz, a small town or village sitting on the banks of the Rhine. It sounded idyllic, if you were about to retire, that is. One thing was for certain, it was a million miles from the hustle bustle of a city like Berlin, which is why it came as no great surprise to me, when I walked into my front room, to find Gerd Braun, as large as life, sitting on my couch.

'Well, well. The fresh air by the Rhine just doesn't seem to suit some people,' I said.

Gerd shrugged. 'It sounded boring. Anyway, I still have some unfinished business here.'

In a way, I felt sorry for the kid that he couldn't let go of Berlin. On the other hand, it saved me a lot of time, as now I didn't have to rush off to West Germany. At this stage, I could've kissed him.

I couldn't say that about Klaus Schultz, however. He had managed to settle Tanja in her cot, but he didn't have the same disposition as his granddaughter, judging by the steam coming from his ears.

'Kaymer, a word!'

He pulled me away from Gerd towards the window.

'*This* is your contact? He's only a boy.' He was half whispering, but I'd no doubt Gerd could hear every word.

'I admit he's young, Klaus, but he knows his stuff.'

His look was one of desperation crossed with outright disapproval. 'He has the film?'

'Sure, he has it. And at the moment, Klaus, you're holding us up.'

Klaus didn't look convinced, but evidently I'd placated him with my confidence, because he moved aside. I had every faith in Gerd.

'I have to say I'm not too disappointed you stayed in Berlin,' I said.

'Don't get too excited. Once you've paid me what you owe me, I'm on my way,' Gerd said, eyeing Klaus warily.

I was a little disappointed. Gerd was like a breath of fresh air around the place. There was, however, no time for sentimentality.

'Two hundred Marks we said, right?' I asked.

'So your wife didn't tell you the price doubled?'

'My wife? You mean Eva?' I asked.

I could see Klaus' eyes widen as he followed the exchange like a game of ping-pong.

'I don't know her name, Herr Kaymer,' Gerd said, as he flicked the fringe off his forehead, only for it to instantly flop down again. 'I just took her the film when you didn't turn up as planned. All the photos you need will be on it. 400 Marks is cheap if you ask me.'

I must have looked like I disagreed because he'd started to negotiate again, but I wasn't thinking about the money.

'She didn't tell you then? I think an extra two hundred is fair considering you didn't keep your end of the bargain. A man has overheads, you know,' he said.

'You gave her the film?' At this stage I had slumped low into the armchair and felt myself sinking further.

'Of course I gave her the film. It was the next best thing; you weren't there, so I gave it to her. Do you know how dangerous it was walking around East Berlin with it?'

I was quiet now. I rubbed my face. I was starting to imagine the pain and cruelty that Eva must have been going through, especially if they'd found it. If they did have it, I had nothing to bargain with. In fact, Weber would be laughing at me. I closed my eyes to think.

Klaus turned to Gerd, 'Am I hearing this correctly? Did you say you gave the film to Eva?'

Klaus didn't wait for the answer and instead rounded on me. 'Is that what he just said?' He threw his arms up in the air in exasperation.

'Hey, if this is a trick so you don't have to pay me, then it's a lousy rotten one,' Gerd said.

If that's what he was thinking, Gerd had evidently dealt with some shifty characters in the past. Judging by Klaus' reaction, I suppose it wasn't a surprise. He had done his job, though, even if it hadn't turned out as I had hoped. I reached into my wallet and pulled out its contents and handed it over to the boy without checking the amount.

He nodded, satisfied. 'I should think so too.'

'You're still going to pay him?' Klaus hissed.

Gerd quickly counted the notes, whilst I was back among my thoughts. When he'd finished, he looked at me. 'There's 600 Marks here.'

'Take it. Use it for your new life,' I said.

'Thanks,' he said sheepishly. We were both quiet now.

'Anyway, what's he so excited about?' Gerd said, nodding in Klaus' direction.

I thought Klaus was finally going to explode. 'He doesn't know, Klaus. Give the kid a break,' I said.

'Know what?' said Gerd.

'They arrested Eva,' I barely whispered.

'Oh, I thought the van had been following me, but it must have been for her. Outside the apartment, I mean.'

'The van?' I asked.

'The paddy wagon on the street.'

'What did you do with the film, boy?' Klaus asked impatiently.

Gerd narrowed his eyes, 'I am not a boy, Mr.' He turned to me, 'Can you get this guy off my back? Who is he, anyway?'

'*I* am Eva's father,' Klaus said, barely holding back his anger.

'Ok. I get it.' Gerd held his hands defensively. 'Let's just calm down for a moment, should we?' He slipped the notes into his back pocket in one swift motion.

He was clicking his tongue on his bottom lip. 'She struck me as a smart type,' he said after a while.

'She is, but even that doesn't help you when the Stasi come calling,' I said.

'Yes, but what I mean is, she would have managed to hide the film somewhere. In the apartment, near the apartment, wherever.'

I liked his thinking. I could see Klaus did, too, as he was listening intently for the first time. Maybe we were just grasping at straws, but the kid's manner was infectious, and right now I was willing to grab hold of any crumb of comfort, no matter how small.

'So what do you have in mind?'

I had an idea what was coming. Gerd smiled. 'For a fee, I'd be prepared to check over her apartment.'

Klaus' eyes were popping out his head, once again.

I wasn't surprised. 'What about the quiet life on the banks of the Rhine?'

'Not really me, is it?'

***

Eva Schultz took in her surroundings. To say the cell was basic and filthy didn't do it justice. The only permissible light came from a weak bulb above the door. It didn't help that the light casing was smeared in dirt. The bed, upon which she sat, was rusted, and the mattress had multiple stains. Directly opposite her, only an arms-length away, was a rank sink. Eva imagined the stains in the sink came from the dripping water, when it was running; she'd tried the tap, it wasn't anymore. There was a toilet bowl in the corner, but its only purpose was to fill the cell with a foul odour, which was turning her stomach.

Her journey there, and treatment since her arrival, hadn't been any better than the décor. She'd been kept in a single, cramped compartment in the paddy wagon. On entry to the prison, she'd been made to strip and had endured a brutal internal search, which had been administered by a tough looking woman with arms the size of a champion weightlifter. Eva's ill-fitting prison fatigues made her glad it was August and not January. All that had been done in less than an hour, or so she estimated; she didn't know exactly, because her watch had been taken from her. Since then, she had been left alone in her cell.

All the physical hardships, Eva Schultz could handle. She had not been a stranger to a difficult life growing up in wartime Berlin. In the tough aftermath of the war, she had been forced to grow up fast. It wasn't her harsh treatment that bothered her so much, it was being away from her daughter. In the year since Tanja had been born, Eva had not been separated from her for more than the length of her shift at the hospital. She had a horrible feeling it might be a long time before she saw Tanja's happy smiling face again, and it was this that Eva was having the most difficulty dealing with.

The sitting and waiting was getting to her. Was Tanja all right? She was sure Helmi would take care of her, at least. Then there was Jack. What would happen when he came to collect them at the weekend and she wasn't there? Would he just assume she'd left to go to her father's? She couldn't stop her mind turning over and over.

The place reminded her of Bautzen, the hell-like place where she had visited one of her friends in prison. Eva remembered the manner in which she had been treated, even though she was only a visitor. First, it was to get the information of where he was being held, then the way the guards mocked her and made derogatory remarks to her. She couldn't forget her friend's condition when she first saw him. He was like a skeleton after two years in that place. And now, the smell, the filth of her cell brought it all back to her. These thoughts were stuck in her mind when she heard the cell door opening.

***

The man sitting in front of Eva repulsed her. It wasn't his personal appearance, it was his uniform. He didn't need to speak for Eva to know what type of person he was; these were the people she'd fought just to get to see her friend in prison in the past. He was a major in the Stasi and it told Eva all she needed to know about her perilous position.

'Sit on your hands, Schultz,' the man barked. Eva was nudged roughly by the weightlifter who had reappeared, chaperoning her with a brutal hand whilst she was out of the cell.

Her surroundings hadn't improved much either. The room was all brown lino and patterns. She was seated in the corner on a rickety stool. Behind the major was a window, which provided Eva with a tantalising view of the city and freedom. Knowing the methods or the people who held her, Eva suspected that was exactly what it was supposed to do.

'Now Schultz, I am Major Weber and you know why you're here.' It was a statement not a question, but Eva shook her head anyway.

'You can't expect me to believe that?' he said sharply.

'I have no idea.'

He looked at her sternly. His eyes were close together, much like a shrew's. His dark hair was pressed flat to his wide head. 'Well, I'll not waste my time. We're looking for a photographic film, which we believe was given to you by Jack Kaymer. You know Kaymer very well, of course, as he is the father of your child.' He waited just long enough for the menace to be apparent. 'Tanja, isn't it?'

The mention of Tanja's name grabbed her attention and she answered a little too quickly. 'I don't know about any film.'

'You're sure about that?' he held up his finger dramatically. 'Before you answer, you should be aware that we don't have to have a reason to keep you here. It could be a short time or it could be a long time. It depends on how you cooperate.' He raised his eyebrows before he went on. 'I'm sure you'd like to see your daughter again.'

Eva was starting to lose some of her rustiness. Those hours alone in a cell had made her feel mentally tired, but now the hatred was building for the man in front of her.

'You have no right to do this.'

'You have an interesting little family, don't you? There are a lot of instances of you making a nuisance of yourself, Schultz. I hope you're not going to do the same thing here. I mean, it must be terrible for you being away from your child like this, not knowing what has happened to her? Now, where is the film?'

95

Eva hesitated. She knew it was the worst thing she could do, but the mention of Tanja, her surroundings, made her lose her track of thought.

'I told you, I don't know about any film.'

'You're lying.' He nodded to the guard next to her. The slap she felt across her face didn't hurt particularly, it was more the shock of it. She felt her cheek burning slightly, but her defiance was growing by the second. The guard hit her again, this time knocking her from the stool. As Eva was on the floor, the woman hit her twice more in the ribs with a rubber truncheon. She curled up, expecting more.

'Get up, Schultz.'

She slowly clambered back on to the stool. Weber was watching her closely, as she lifted up her head to look at him.

'Only the beginning, trust me. Now, where is it?'

Eva didn't know why, but she wasn't scared. She should have told him what he wanted to know, but she couldn't bring herself to cooperate. She hated this type of authority. This bullying was something she'd known all her life in one form or another. Since that morning at the town hall, she'd decided she wouldn't put up with it anymore. She drew up her chin and looked Weber directly in the eye.

'You want to know about the film?'

Weber sat forward like an expectant schoolboy next in the queue at the sweet shop counter.

'Go to hell,' Eva hissed.

CHAPTER 15

THURSDAY, 10th AUGUST 1961,
EAST BERLIN

Hans Erdmann sat at his desk staring at the two men in front of him. The younger one was of the Xavier Marks mould. He was well-dressed, not a politician by trade, but certainly by nature. He was good looking, but Hans didn't envy him that. One day, not so very long ago, and even now to a certain extent, he could claim the same. No, it was the dark, cold eyes that set the alarm bells ringing. The eyes and what he had to say when he finally opened his mouth.

'You see, Colonel Erdmann, when a commanding officer loses control of his barracks then we have a problem, and more to the point, you have a problem.'

Hans appeared unfazed, even if he was worried about this escalation in the situation. He shouldn't have been surprised; it was what Marks had suggested would happen.

'Exactly why would the Staatssicherheit be interested in a military matter, Herr Kampmann?'

'*Inspector* Kampmann. When supplies go missing—arms, we are led to believe—then it becomes a question of National Security. It would seem unreasonable the Volksarmee be asked to investigate its own problems. One might expect a…cover-up.' His smile was sour and ungenuine.

The inspector moved forward and perched himself casually on the edge of Hans' desk, seemingly as much as a statement of his power, as a need for comfort.

'I trust you have the necessary paperwork to undertake such an investigation?' Hans asked.

'You'd be correct to think that.' Kampmann produced some papers from his lined inside pocket and tossed them nonchalantly towards him.

Hans didn't move, only raising his eyebrows. It was clear the man had little military training by the way he showed such an arrogant attitude towards a senior military official, as Hans was. It was another trait of the new political breed he particularly hated. Without taking his eyes off him, Hans calmly reached forward and picked up the papers.

He took his time. In fact, he wasn't reading the words. In a way, it was a small act of defiance in the face of the inevitable. Hans knew he couldn't stop the investigation, but it was an attempt to buy a bit more time and to work out exactly how to deal with this. The one thing that did stand out on the paper was the name at the bottom. Erich Mielke's spidery signature sent a shiver down his spine; it couldn't have come from any higher unless Ulbricht himself had signed it. When Hans had finished, he carefully folded the letter and placed it back on the desk in front of him.

'Do you want to tell me anything before we start, Colonel Erdmann?'

'This investigation is coming at a very inconvenient time. My men are preparing for a major operation. You will have their cooperation, but you need to consider that whilst you are here, these barracks are under my command. Treptow is my domain, Herr Kampmann.'

'For now, Colonel Erdmann. For now.'

Kampmann turned to his older colleague, who until now had maintained his silence in the background. 'I will start with the Quartermaster. You can start in the guardhouse.'

With that, Kampmann left the office.

Hans looked at the older man and smiled. 'Take a seat, Georg. It must be, what, fifteen years?'

The man accepted the offer. 'More, Hans, I believe. Those were tough days,' he said with a growl.

'There were no tougher days than at the POW camp at Vorenzeh. Sometimes I wonder if losing the war was such a good idea.' Hans nodded in the direction of Kampmann's exit.

'Ah, he's only a boy. An excitable, dangerous one, but still a boy.' The man felt in his pocket for his cigarettes and Hans tossed a lighter across the table to him.

'So how does Georg Neumann end up in the Stasi? I wouldn't have thought it was your thing.'

Georg waved the plume of smoke from in front of his face and coughed deeply. 'It's not. You know I was in the Kripo before the war. I joined to catch murderers, but it didn't quite turn out as I expected. Besides, I'll be retiring soon.'

'Another one being pensioned off? It seems there soon won't be many of us old comrades left,' Hans said.

'It's not bad for me, but you're not so old. You have to learn to work with these people, Hans. You can't beat them,' Georg warned.

Hans dismissed his warning. 'Ach, I've fried bigger fish than Kampmann.'

Georg shook his head more vehemently. 'No, Hans, this is serious. I shouldn't be telling you this, but we got orders from the very top this morning. I don't know whom you've been upsetting, but you're going to have to call in some favours to dig yourself out of this hole.'

Hans had been thinking exactly that, but didn't say it. Georg was puffing happily on his cigarette. He wasn't exactly a picture of health. Even if he was just sixty, Hans wondered if he would be around to enjoy much of his retirement. He had certainly put on weight since he'd last seen him, but given the rations at the time, it wasn't surprising.

'Anyway, I better get on,' Georg said, looking for somewhere to stub out his cigarette.

Hans pushed forward an ashtray and held out his hand. Georg took it and looked into Hans' eyes. 'You know that if you need to tell me something, I'm sure I could help you, Hans. For old times' sake and all that.'

Hans thought for a moment. Georg Neumann had been a prisoner of the Russians just like him and Bernie. Back then, he wouldn't have doubted the sincerity of such an offer, but 1961 was a different time and Berlin was a different place. He felt he could only rely on himself for this one, or at least, those he trusted.

'Thanks, Georg, but it's under control.'

CHAPTER 16

Klaus Schultz wasn't about to let the boy go to Eva's apartment alone. Klaus could see he was smart, but he didn't exactly trust him, and certainly not with his daughter's liberty on the line. Klaus' doubts about Jack Kaymer hadn't gone away either. Klaus could see the brash American who had taken liberties with Eva's safety. The use of the young Gerd as a contact was reckless, too. That aside, Jack's idealism in pushing for the truth about the intentions of the East Germans, and the closure of the border, resonated with him. Klaus knew he meant well. Unfortunately, as he knew to his cost, goodwill meant nothing when it came to dealing with the East Germans and the Russians.

It was a cool morning as they crossed the sector border into East Berlin. Klaus knew he couldn't afford to be there for too long. His earlier visit to bring Eva back had simply been a quick retrieval mission, even if he had been thwarted due to Eva's arrest. Now, he was back again. It had been eight years since he had rescued Ulrich, but he still knew they would be on to him. Klaus knew the man who followed him from Stalingrad to Kolyma and back to Berlin wouldn't be far from his tail. Dobrovsky would never leave him alone.

As they reached Eva's door, Gerd whipped out some tools and started to get to work on the door. Klaus immediately placed a hand on Gerd's shoulder, 'There's no need for that.'

Klaus opened the door opposite and nodded for the boy to follow him.

'Helmi? It's Klaus, are you there?'

They heard a shout from the kitchen. 'In here.'

Klaus took in the smell of fresh bread and coffee, as Helmi met them at the living room door. 'Any news?' she asked.

Klaus shook his head.

'What are you doing back here?' Helmi asked.

'We need to get into Eva's place to look for something. Photographic film,' Klaus said.

Helmi nodded. 'I'll get the keys, but I warn you, they've been back searching the place.'

Klaus felt this was going to be a lost cause, especially if the professionals had been there, but at least they had to try, for Eva's sake.

'Are you sure the place is not being watched?' Helmi asked.

'Not from what we could see,' Gerd chipped in.

Helmi looked quizzically at Klaus.

Klaus shook his head. 'A friend of the American's.'

'They're probably relying on our Portierfrau keeping an eye open. It's not Ina Stinnes anymore, but you know the type; they miss nothing. We have to be careful.'

Klaus remembered the old block warden all too well. From Nazi to Stasi stool pigeon, there wasn't a great deal of difference.

'We should keep our chat limited when we're in the apartment; the place might be wired,' Klaus said.

Before entering, they agreed to a plan for who would search which room and then got to work.

The place was still a mess. Drawers had been emptied of contents, threadbare cushions littered the floor, and carcasses of stripped furniture were upturned. Klaus couldn't believe, if there was anything to find, that it wouldn't have been located already.

They searched for at least an hour. The place wasn't exactly large, so there were a limited number of places to hide things. Eventually, Klaus gestured to Helmi and Gerd that they should call off the search.

Back in Helmi's living room, Klaus couldn't help feeling they'd missed something obvious. He looked across at Gerd, who appeared deep in thought.

'Tell me, Helmi,' Gerd said like a seasoned detective, 'you were here when Eva was arrested?'

Helmi's eyes flashed to Klaus. She seemed uncomfortable with Gerd's familiarity. Klaus was growing accustomed to it.

'Yes…That's correct,' she eventually said.

Gerd continued unperturbed, 'It was Wednesday around noon?'

'How did you know that?'

'Just bear with me. When she came into the apartment, what *exactly* did Eva do?'

Klaus looked at the boy, wondering where he was going with his questions. He kept quiet, though; he was starting to understand just how resourceful Gerd was.

'Well, she went crashing into her bedroom shouting at the Stasi men.'

Klaus smiled. He couldn't help feeling pride in his daughter's strength in the face of adversity.

Gerd said, 'Did she have something in her hand, Helmi?'

'Not that I could see.'

'So what happened then?'

'They all came back into the living room. It's hard to think. It all happened so fast. Tanja was crying. It was all a bit chaotic,' she said.

'I understand. Did they just take Eva away?'

'No, Eva was holding Tanja and she passed her to me.'

Klaus joined in now, seeing the benefit of Gerd's line of thinking. 'Eva couldn't have given the film to Tanja. We've changed her since, so we'd have found it.'

'Wait!' Helmi said. 'She dropped the rabbit.'

'Eva?' Gerd said.

Helmi was talking quickly now, 'No. When Eva passed Tanja over to me, Tanja dropped the rabbit.'

'And?'

'It was the last thing Eva held before they took her. She picked it up and gave it back to Tanja. Then they took her away.' Helmi's voiced cracked.

'She hid it in the rabbit?' Klaus asked incredulously.

Gerd shrugged. 'It makes sense.'

Klaus was up off the couch, 'Come on, let's get back.'

Helmi looked bewildered for a moment. 'Hang on a minute! Why is this film so important?'

Klaus stopped himself. In his haste, he'd not told Helmi the full story. She was Maria's oldest friend.

'They're going to close the border, Helmi. We're not sure exactly when, but from the pictures we have and the information from Jack's contacts…' He paused for a second. '…it looks like they're going to do it soon and this time for good.'

'I see,' she said quietly.

'Don't wait. Soon you won't be able to leave even if you want to.'

'Ok, Klaus. Thanks for the warning.'

'Maria sends her love. I have to go.'

***

No sooner had Klaus stepped back onto the street, than two large men were either side of him. He went to run, but the men were having none of it. In a flash, they linked under his arms and marched him to the black sedan at the side of the road. Klaus only had time to glance to his left to see Gerd making his escape.

The back door was opened and Klaus was bundled into the car. He lurched for the door on the other side, but he was yanked back by a strong arm. He found himself sandwiched between the two heavies. He struggled to right himself. There was a fug of blue cigarette smoke in the car; the smell took Klaus back and he instantly shot a glance to the passenger seat.

'Klaus Schultz, it's been a long time.' The man who spoke didn't turn around. He just focused on the street in front of him and took a long drag on his cigarette.

'Burzin. I might have known,' Klaus eventually managed.

'Yes, it's me. Luckily for you, my friend,' Burzin said.

Klaus started to relax. At least he knew he wasn't being arrested.

'Do you really have to drag me off the street like that?'

'Better me than somebody else, Klaus.'

Klaus knew exactly who he meant.

'Well, what do you want? I am rather busy.'

'Always in a rush, Klaus. You should be relaxing in West Germany with that good wife of yours,' Burzin said.

'I was trying to until you brought me those bloody papers.'

Burzin lit a second fresh cigarette with the dying embers of the other.

'I was trying to help you, Klaus. Help you and your family.'

'You were trying to further your own ends, as usual. Anyway, the information didn't exactly do me much good, did it?' Klaus said sarcastically.

Burzin nodded. 'Quite. My little plan didn't work.'

'I gave them the papers, but they didn't believe it. Surprisingly, the BND doesn't trust you, Burzin.'

Burzin chuckled. 'No, they don't, but they should have more faith or at least, more sense. You will have gathered by now the papers are quite genuine.'

Klaus didn't answer. He knew they weren't fakes. He also knew the longer he wasted here, the longer Eva would be languishing in a Stasi cell. He hoped Gerd was heading straight for Jack's place.

'Your American friend has had some problems publishing the story, too,' Burzin said, letting the meaning of the words sink in.

'He's not my friend.' It was the only thing Klaus could think to say. Once again, Burzin was one step in front of him.

'You are in a spot of trouble, aren't you, Klaus?'

Klaus looked down and shook his head. He swore to himself he wouldn't end up in this position again. It had happened before in East Berlin back in '53, when he needed help to free Ulrich from the Stasi. Now he was in the same position again, only this time with Eva.

For the first time since he'd been in the car, Burzin turned to look at him. Klaus thought he must have had something serious to say, if he wasn't dragging on one of his cigarettes. He didn't disappoint.

'He's still here, Klaus. In East Berlin.'

Klaus felt his stomach lurch.

'You mean…?'

'Dobrovsky. That's right, Klaus.'

Burzin had him in the palm of his hand and was toying with him. He nodded. 'I am sorry, Klaus. He has Eva.'

***

Eva had been suitably punished for her earlier outburst. Almost immediately, she'd wished she hadn't done it. It must have been towards evening when she'd started to nod off, sitting on the bed, her knees to her chin, with her back resting against the wall. That's when the real torture had started. At first she wondered what was happening, because no sooner had she fallen asleep, than the guard had entered the cell to shake her awake. On that first occasion, Eva had risen to her feet, expecting to be taken for more questioning; she'd come to wish that had been the case.

And so it continued throughout the night, and for what seemed longer. It was five or six times they woke her up until, in the end, Eva got to her feet and thought that she would show them. She started to stride around purposefully, as much as she could in her small confines, determined to stay awake. She tried to think positively, that all would turn out well, that Tanja would be taken care of, that Helmi had told Jack she was here. Unfortunately, it had only lasted so long, because, in the end, inevitably, she had to sit down, and when she did the all-enveloping feeling of sleep soon followed.

On one occasion, Eva was awoken in her cell by a hand gently rocking her awake. She tried to focus through blurring eyes. As much as she tried to shake the drained feeling from her head, she found it impossible. She felt like she was going to be sick.

'Take your time, Eva.' She noticed the German was Russian accented.

Eventually, she managed to look up and take in the man standing in her cell. He was short in stature without a hair on his head. The gold braid stood out on his already ridiculously wide epaulets.

'What do you want?' Eva asked.

The man chuckled, 'I don't want anything, Eva. I just came to see you.'

Eva was confused, if slightly intrigued. She still couldn't help some indignation rising to the surface. 'I didn't know Weber was handing out visiting cards? Perhaps he could send one to my family?'

'That's very good, Eva. You should always try to retain your sense of humour through such…an ordeal.'

'Are you here for moral support or did you just pop in to wake me up?'

'Actually, I came to introduce myself to you,' he said. 'I am General Dobrovsky.'

'Should the name mean something to me?' Eva was struggling to hide her fear. There was something about this man that was troubling her.

'I know your father, Eva. We go way back.'

'I didn't see you at any family gatherings, so I assume you're not exactly a friend of my father's.'

'You're very smart, Eva. No, I wouldn't call us friends.'

The man turned and rapped on the door. It was quickly opened. As he stood in the doorway of her cell, Eva could see a manic smile on his face that made her shiver.

Then, he said, 'We do, however, have some catching up to do.'

***

Whilst Gerd and Klaus were in East Berlin, I had to deal with more practical matters. Diapers, creams, bottles, milk, baby food; the list was endless and I hadn't the first clue where to start looking for this lot. The temptation to run off to the Leydicke was almost overwhelming, but I remembered the promise I'd made myself, to at least try and be a good father. Even if the thought of a quiet beer or five was pulling me like a circus strongman, I couldn't let Eva and Tanja down.

If I'd been in the right place mentally, I might have noticed the man next to me inspecting the baby talc. I was momentarily distracted by the fact that I'd just dropped a pack of diapers on the floor, and the ribbon which held them together had come apart, sending them in all directions.

I sat Tanja down whilst I scrambled on the floor. She was giggling at me. Unfortunately, this wasn't an act to make her laugh.

'So this is Eva Schultz's daughter?'

I saw a pair of over shiny shoes and then looked up to see a man looking down at the scene.

'You look like you have your hands full, Herr Kaymer.'

The lack of sleep and the stress of Eva's arrest, coupled with the fact this stranger was stating the patently obvious, made me snap. 'Where did you gain such amazing powers of deduction?'

I could see my sarcasm was lost on him. He was around my age, wearing a light coloured jacket and what looked like a cheap suit underneath. A man dressed like that looking at baby products aroused my suspicions. I might be out of my depth, but he just looked out of place.

I gave up on the rest of the diapers and stood up to face him, pulling Tanja close to me. He had that know-all look I'd seen before somewhere.

'Frau Schultz is comfortable, Herr Kaymer. We thought you should know that.'

He had short-cropped hair and the bluest of eyes. Goebbels would have been proud of him, until he opened his mouth, at least. The fact that every "s" covered me in hiss and spit meant he would have been good for the propaganda photographs, but not for a movie career.

'If you've got her in my old penthouse suite, I hope you've fixed the toilet since I was last there.'

If Tanja hadn't been in my arms, I might have been tempted to shove a safety pin up his nose.

'Major Weber thought it was important you knew where she was and that you could help her, if you wanted to.'

I narrowed my eyes, more to show that I was annoyed than to give my position away. I thought keeping quiet was the best course of action.

'If you could see your way to delivering the film you discussed with Major Weber, he might look kindly on her situation.'

'Tell Weber he can go and whistle. I will publish the story with the photos tomorrow.'

The fact I was bluffing was neither here nor there; I was just plain angry. I was fuming, knowing they had Eva and that this guy had followed me here, accosting me whilst I was trying to buy supplies for my daughter. Deep down, I had a wicked vision of the beads of sweat forming on Weber's fat neck.

The walking lisp was quick with the threats. 'Major Weber thought that might be your reaction, so he told me to remind you that it might just make life very uncomfortable for your girlfriend. Is that what you want, Herr Kaymer?'

I swallowed hard and I think he saw it. In that particular instance, the horrible smells of that dingy cellblock flashed through my nostrils. It was strange how the smell had stayed with me, but they do say you can smell fear. In spite of my earlier thoughts about Weber, I was the one reduced to a cold sweat.

I looked daggers at the Aryan lisp. 'Tell Weber he'll have his film, but if she's harmed in any way… tell him I'll poison his food.'

I know it was childish, but it was all I could think of on the spur of the moment. It still made the man crack a smile, however. Seemingly, he knew Weber personally.

The man turned to walk away and I sent him on his way with a scowl. He was near the end of the aisle when Tanja dropped her rabbit. Strangely, the soft material made a hard sound as it hit the tiled floor.

Tanja's arms immediately reached out for it, like she'd lost the ability to breathe without it. As I picked it up, a black case rested on the floor.

I swallowed hard in realisation. I flashed a look to the end of the aisle, fearful somebody else would see the film. Fortunately, my Stasi friend had already gone.

**

The longer it went on, the more disoriented she became. Her thoughts were not following a logical pattern. After the positive feelings of earlier, she started to panic that bad things had happened to Tanja. Eva was anxious, anxious to get out. She kept telling herself that was exactly what Weber was trying to achieve, but it didn't always help. The mind was a powerful thing and, the longer she went without sleep, the more the lack of meaningful rest was becoming Eva Schultz's worst enemy.

Her head was spinning and her ears were ringing. As she sat, she wondered how long it would be before she told Weber all she knew. She eventually turned on her side, facing the wall, and fell asleep.

They came for her again. She was so groggy, at first they had to lift her up the stairs and down the corridor. Eva felt herself slump down into a chair. She managed to raise her head. It must have been early in the morning because the sun was dazzling her, as it shone low over Weber's left shoulder. She tried to shield her eyes. Weber continued to talk, but Eva had difficulty taking in what he was actually saying.

'So Eva, why do you think you're still here?'

She mumbled a reply.

'I didn't understand you. Maybe you can say it again?'

Eva felt her head slump to one side. She just wanted to go back to sleep. The shake from the guard came again, more gentle than before, but it still made her snap. 'For God's sake, leave me alone.'

'I'll tell you, shall I? You're still here because Jack Kaymer hasn't brought the film to us.'

Eva looked dazed for a moment, and thought to herself, *That isn't true.*

'You see, if he had, you would be free. He thinks more of his story than he does of you, Eva. The story is more important than you and Tanja.' Again, the mention of Tanja's name was like striking at an open nerve. It didn't go unnoticed.

He moved his chair around to be next to her. As he sat down next to her, the chair creaked in complaint.

'You would like to see your daughter, wouldn't you, Eva?'

Eva nodded. She couldn't help it. She missed her desperately. Weber went on, 'You could see her within a few hours, if you tell us where it is, Eva. It's very simple: the film, your freedom.'

He held out his hands with a smile, as if he were the most reasonable man in the world. Eva knew what he was doing. There were voices in her head shouting warnings at her, but there were others, getting louder, which told her to get it over with.

'How long will you wait for Jack, Eva? You can't trust this American.'

Her chin was wobbling now, she could feel it. She felt the tears in her eyes. They stung like soapy water. She knew she had to put an end to it.

Her mouth opened, but nothing came out, apart from a squeak.

'Get her some water!'

Eva grabbed the offered cup and gulped down its contents. It was fresh, not like the rust filled drops she'd been surviving on.

'Well, Eva, what is it to be?'

She'd had enough. She couldn't cope with it anymore. She knew Jack would've come if he could, but it was apparent to Eva, he hadn't found the film. Telling Weber was the only way out.

'What you're looking for….'

Suddenly, the room door was flung open. Weber was apoplectic at the untimely interruption.

'Get out, you blithering idiot! How dare you just barge in here?'

The guard stood firm. It took a brave man. 'I thought you would like to know immediately, Major.'

'Know what, man? Get over here and tell me,' Weber bawled.

In the four or five whispered seconds it took and with Eva's eyes now fully accustomed to the light, she saw a marked change in Weber's persona. The anger was replaced by a beaming smile.

'Splendid. Splendid.' He clapped his chunky hands together with a dull thud.

'Return the prisoner to her cell.'

Eva was dragged to her feet in a state of confusion. Evidently, her information was now surplus to requirements.

CHAPTER 17

I had showed Gerd the film and explained how I'd come across it on the supermarket floor. Their hunch about the rabbit had been right. Gerd also told me about Klaus being dragged into a car at the roadside. It didn't exactly surprise me. I had a feeling Klaus had been holding something back on me, but I didn't have time to think about it now. I left Tanja in Gerd's capable hands and headed off into East Berlin with the film.

It hadn't taken long to arrange to meet the Stasi. Once I'd told them I had something they needed and who I was, it seemed to open doors. It wasn't long before I was staring at Weber's over-filled chops again and I instantly went into battle mode. I was ready for the man who'd made me spend a night in this hellhole, the man responsible for imprisoning the mother of my child. This was personal now, not professional. I'd had to deal with many uncomfortable feelings in the last couple of days, not to mention an overfilled diaper or two. Weber was only another challenge in my shaky transformation from hard-bitten journalist to full-time father. Judging by the cold sweat on my palms, the transformation wasn't yet fully complete.

My obese friend was as jovial as ever. His laughter and size wouldn't have looked out of place at a medieval banquet. Needless to say, I didn't share his happiness.

'So here we are again, Herr Kaymer.' Weber rubbed his considerable hands together like he was trying to start a fire. I couldn't help wondering whether Eva would end up being the sacrifice, if I didn't get this right.

'Well, it's hardly a pleasure, is it? If this is my very last time at the Adlon, I won't be too disappointed.'

'Come, Herr Kaymer, surely it's not that bad.'

I raised my eyebrows, but held myself in check from offering my true feelings.

'So, you have the film?' Weber asked.

'There are some conditions before we get to that,' I said.

The furrow I'd seen before returned to Weber's brow. 'Conditions?'

'I want to see Eva first.' I looked him in the eye. 'To check she's unharmed.'

It was in that instant I felt something wasn't right. In fact, it was when Weber started to shuffle about, like somebody other than him was about to take the last würst on the plate.

'See her? I can assure you that won't be necessary. She's fit and well. The sooner we agree about the photos, the sooner we can discuss Fräulein Schultz's release.'

My journalistic nose told me I was onto something and I didn't like it one bit. He was being shifty for a reason and I couldn't help feeling it wasn't one I was going to like.

'I insist. I see her now, or we go no further.'

The strength in my voice belied my nervousness; after all, this was a game of bargaining on the one hand, but a deadly serious personal matter, on the other. I had delivered the statement in such a way that he couldn't mistake my resolve.

115

Weber pursed his lips like a poker player who'd been forced to make the call. The question was not what I had in my hand, but what he thought I had in my hand. 'Very well, but it will take some time to…prepare her.' He saw my face drop. 'I mean, she is sleeping. We have to wake her up and give her some food, you understand?'

He quickly pressed a buzzer and got up to leave, 'My colleague will take care of you until she is ready.'

'Just a minute, I want to see her now.'

There were a couple of explanations for his reticence to let me see Eva straight away, and neither were too nice to contemplate. Either he was happy to stall the process so the contents of the film became worthless, such as when the border was sealed anyway. Or, more worryingly, Eva was in a bad way.

'No, no I assure you, it'll be a couple of hours at the most. It's in our own interests to sort things out rapidly, Herr Kaymer. Believe me.'

I didn't believe him, but it was either trust Weber, much as that was against my nature, or make a deal without seeing Eva, and I wasn't prepared to do that. I needed to know, first of all, that she was there and that she was safe. My eyes were boring a hole in Weber's head. I was sure he knew what I was thinking.

***

Klaus made it back to Jack's apartment in double-quick time. He was desperate to know if they'd found the film. Originally, he had been worried about the border being closed before they got Eva out, but those worries now paled into insignificance, ever since his enforced rendezvous with Burzin and he'd learned Dobrovsky had Eva. Stalingrad seemed like such a long time ago, but Klaus knew Dobrovsky would still be out for revenge, even after all those years.

Gerd was on the couch, stretched out like everything was under control. That alone riled Klaus.

'Well?' Klaus said, appealing with his hands.

'Well, what?' Gerd said, coolly.

'Never mind, "well, what?" Where's Jack? Did you find the film?'

Gerd's relaxed demeanour didn't alter. 'Sure.'

Klaus wasn't in the mood for this. He walked forward, swiping Gerd's legs off the couch. Klaus was now close to Gerd, who was sitting upright in shock.

'Listen, boy, I don't have time to play around...'

'Hey, what's your problem?' Gerd said, defensively.

'My daughter is in a Stasi cell and I'm bloody worried, if you hadn't noticed. So when I ask you what happened, I don't expect you to be vague or lie there like you're swinging on a hammock.'

'Ok. Ok. Keep your hair on. What is your problem with me? I have done nothing but help Jack, you, and Eva.'

'Help or make money from?' Klaus fired back.

Gerd swayed his head from side to side. 'Yeah, admittedly I made a few dollars along the way, but if I'm honest...'

Klaus scoffed, 'Honest? Are you kidding?'

Gerd gave Klaus a hurt look, then continued, '...if I'm honest, I would have done it all for nothing.'

'Somehow, I doubt that,' Klaus said.

There was silence for a moment, whilst the air between them settled. Klaus knew he was being hard on the kid, but his emotions were doing the talking.

'Look, Gerd, I am sorry. I am anxious and you know why.'

'You're telling me,' Gerd said, with a raise of his eyebrows.

'Where's Tanja?' Klaus asked.

Gerd nodded towards the cot.

Klaus jumped up. Looking inside the cot, he could see his granddaughter looked content. She was sleeping through all the commotion, her mouth wide open, with the rabbit at her shoulder. Klaus was thankful she wasn't aware the danger her mother was in.

'Did you change her?' Klaus asked.

Gerd just nodded.

'What about milk? Did you feed her?'

Gerd looked at Klaus like he was growing tired of all the questions. 'Does she look unhappy to you?'

Klaus conceded he had a point.

'Now, if you'd sit down for two minutes, instead of jumping around all over the place, I can tell you what happened with Jack.'

Klaus thought Gerd was right. He looked relaxed because everything was under control, for him, at least.

He took a seat next to Gerd on the couch. 'Ok, go on.'

'Good,' Gerd began. 'Now, Jack found the film. It actually fell out of the rabbit when Tanja dropped it on the floor.'

Klaus felt some relief. 'Thank goodness for that.'

'Jack left with the film about two hours ago.'

'That's good. That's good,' Klaus said.

'I am sure we'll get a call anytime soon to tell us that Eva has been released and they are on their way back here.'

Klaus didn't feel as confident as Gerd about the outcome. Dobrovsky would use any reason to keep Eva there, and Jack as well, if necessary.

Gerd started to sense Klaus wasn't entirely satisfied. 'Is there something you're not telling us about all this?' he asked.

'What do you mean?'

'I don't know. You still look worried after everything I have told you, like you know there's something else going on. Who were the people at Eva's place?'

Gerd flicked the fringe out of his eyes and looked at Klaus like he was working things out, working Klaus out.

Klaus thought about telling Gerd the full story, but dismissed the idea. There wasn't time to go through the history now. Klaus doubted

Jack was up to the task of outwitting Dobrovsky and the Stasi. He felt he needed some insurance, a fall back plan to get Eva out.

'There's nothing. I'm just concerned, that's all,' Klaus said, distractedly.

Klaus felt the impending urge to act. He wasn't one for sitting around and waiting. He got up, throwing on his jacket. 'Listen, I have to go out. Take care of Tanja. I'll be back soon.'

'Hey, wait a minute! Where are you going? You can't just leave without telling me what's going on...'

Klaus was already out of the door.

***

It's difficult to say how I felt when the sight confronted me. I wouldn't say I didn't expect it, but I just held out all hope, it wouldn't be the case. I was never really the one for true emotional outbursts, except the odd rant now and again. But at that moment I felt different. It was like it defined how I really felt about Eva.

My overriding emotion, when the hairy chinned female guard pushed the cell door back, was one of pity. I saw a ball in light blue fatigues on the disgusting stained bed I remembered so well from my visit. I felt sorry for the poor sod who was in the cell, having been in the very same position not a few hours before. Then it hit me like somebody striking the gong at the start of a feature movie; that ball on the bed, seemingly wrapped up against the potential coming onslaught, was my Eva.

Before I knew it, I was on my knees next to her. As soon as I touched her, she reacted like I'd given her an electric shock, recoiling away from me.

'Eva, it's Jack. Talk to me.' It was about all I could manage before my voice was choked in emotion. She didn't appear to be in the state to

119

talk to anybody. I could only start to imagine what the bastards had done to her.

I cuddled her, trying to protect, surround her, but it wasn't easy from my awkward position kneeling by her bed. She must have been in a deep sleep, but judging by her scarred and bruised face, maybe it wasn't only that. Whatever I'd read into Weber's reluctance to let me see Eva, it paled into insignificance now that I'd seen her.

'It's me, Jack. Eva, say something.'

She opened her eyes with what seemed like Herculean effort. The whites of her eyes were pink and she was blinking furiously. Aside from the damage to her face, she had the appearance of a confused, lost child.

I cupped her cheek with my hand and this time she only pushed back slightly. 'What have they done to you?'

Her eyes narrowed like she recognised my voice for the first time. 'It's me, Eva. I've come to get you out.'

She tried to talk, but her lips were matted in blood and chapped with dryness. I put my finger to them; I didn't want her to talk, it looked too painful. I had to get her in the right frame of mind, offer her some hope, even if deep down, I didn't really feel like it.

'Eva, I am going to get you out of here. Then we'll get you back home so you can be with Tanja.'

'Tanja?' Eva said. It was her first recognisable word at least.

'Yes, she's with me. She's safe and well.'

She nodded like she understood it all for the first time.

'Now I need you to stay strong for me. Can you do that?'

Again, there was a dip of her head.

I hugged her close, but she winced in pain. The bruises on her face were evidently not the only ones she had. I wondered how somebody could reduce another human being to this in such a short space of time. There was a blockage in the centre of my chest and I had to do something to get it out.

'Eva, I've brought the film and I'm going to get you out. Do you understand what I'm saying?'

She nodded through the sobs.

'It won't be long, just so they can develop the photos and we can go. It's all arranged.' It wasn't yet, but it wasn't the time to split hairs.

She lifted her head off my chest and I looked into her sad, pitiful eyes. It was at that moment I knew I was really in love with Eva. Anybody can say the words, but moments like that drive it home. The woman I'd always known I had an intense physical attraction to, was now confirmed to me as something much stronger. I felt shallow because it had taken something like this to realise how important she was to me. It wasn't about the big stories anymore.

'You know that I love you, don't you?'

She cracked a smile, and I say that quite literally, as her lips looked dry enough to have been in the desert for a week. She looked at me and said, 'Are we going home to Tanja, Jack?' she managed.

'Soon. Very soon.'

As I cradled her head in my hand, the emotion that had been building up inside me was slowly giving way to anger. I now had to negotiate Eva's freedom with the man responsible for her current state.

***

It is not difficult to judge if the apology being offered is genuine or not. You feel it. You look the person in the eye and know if they mean it. We all make mistakes from time to time; God knows I've made my fair share of them in the past and no doubt will again in the future, but when you listen to an apology, it's a question of contrition and knowledge of the facts, which enable you to decide if what you are hearing is reasonable.

As I sat listening to the fawning Weber rumble on about how sorry he was for the "mistake" that had befallen Eva, and how those

121

responsible would be disciplined, I was starting to feel physically sick. I think I was still in shock at seeing her. Eva was normally so beautiful and strong, and now she appeared utterly exhausted and defeated. I knew the person sitting next to me was responsible for that transformation, so the more Weber went on, the more my shock was building into a dirty, uncontrollable anger.

'You see, Herr Kaymer, some people get a little bit carried away and become…heavy-handed. I really don't know how this happened, but you can be assured I will look into the matter and deal with those concerned very severely.'

'Like Eva,' I thought.

Needless to say I didn't buy a word of it. It was clear that what I had witnessed firsthand in the cells, and what I had seen with Eva since, was that Weber and his sort had a very deliberate way of dealing with their prisoners. All thoughts of the film were rapidly disappearing off into the sunset. My mind was now elsewhere, although there was no way I could pin it down. I certainly wasn't in the right place to make a cool-headed business decision.

'Herr Kaymer, really, I'm sorry about all this. Shall we get down to the real subject that brings us here?'

The red mist was descending over my eyelids and there was nothing I could do now to stop myself. I was totally gone. I did remember saying, 'You make me sick.' Sometime afterwards, probably mere seconds, my right hand shot out and attempted to encircle his blubber-covered neck. By the time my left hand had joined the right, I knew I'd completely lost it.

By now, Weber's eyes were bulging and I was aware he was scrambling around to reach the alarm to summon help. Frankly, I didn't care. I was kneeling on the desk in front of him to get better access in my task and would have happily killed him at that point. The fact Weber had eaten so much during his life probably saved him that day. It wasn't easy to get a good grip on such a wide rubber-like neck; I can certainly say I tried my best.

At some stage, I became aware of a number of hands roughly hauling me off Weber and carrying me bodily down a maze of corridors, alive with a rather concerned sounding alarm. By the time I was thrown headlong into a cell, very likely the one next to Eva, I realised things hadn't quite gone as they should have. Whatever the case, the simple truth was, at that very moment, it felt good.

CHAPTER 18

FRIDAY, 11th AUGUST 1961,
EAST BERLIN

The plan had been hatched. Hans Erdmann couldn't take all the credit. He'd had help. The help he would only ever call on when there was no other choice. The kind of help he knew he would have to repay. But that was for another day; now he had to focus. If the plan worked, it would probably only delay the inevitable. They would catch him out one day. He couldn't avoid that, but in the meantime, he had friends to take care of. It was something the likes of Xavier Marks and Kampmann would never understand. Just after nine that morning, as Inspector Kampmann crashed through his office door without so much as a knock, Hans had a feeling he'd have to rely on all his experience and training to come through this one unscathed.

Kampmann had a contented look. Hans' adjutant followed Kampmann into the office, full of apologies. 'I'm sorry, Colonel, I couldn't prevent him coming in.'

Hans took a deep breath. He waved away his adjutant, as if he wasn't worried by the intrusion. 'It's not your fault that some people have no manners, Corporal. Please close the door behind you.'

Thankfully, Kampmann was alone. 'Inspector Kampmann, to what do I owe this dubious pleasure?'

'Always a smart answer, Erdmann, but not for long.' He held up what looked like a stores report.

'Ah, yes, the missing supplies you've been turning my barracks upside down for. Well, what's the outcome of your *investigation*?' Hans said.

Kampmann smiled proudly then held himself upright as if he was about to read an announcement on Alexanderplatz. Hans looked towards the door for some salvation.

'The missing supplies are as follows: two cases of Karabiner S rifles, Lot numbers 2912 and 2913; two cases of AK-47 assault rifles, Lot numbers N272/423 and N272/424. Up to 6000 rounds of 7.62x39mm cartridges for said rifles. Not only that, Erdmann, but we also found a shambolic system of stock counting and a barracks in disarray. You will be suspended forthwith...'

'If, and it's a big "if", I am to be suspended, it will be something done by my commanding officer, not some upstart of an inspector...'

For the second time in a matter of minutes, the office door crashed open and one of Kampmann's underlings bundled into the room. Kampmann looked annoyed at being interrupted in the middle of his moment of glory.

He slapped the papers down on Hans' desk and snapped, 'What is it? You can't just come barging into an office like that.' Hans raised his eyebrows.

'A call from HQ, sir,' said the man, out of breath. 'I thought you'd like to know immediately.'

'Well, get on with it then.'

'The rifles and ammunition have been located at...'

'That's enough!' Kampmann said quickly. 'We don't want Colonel Erdmann here intervening with the course of our duties. Come here and tell me.'

As the man did, a smile broke out on Kampmann's face. 'Good. Good,' he said.

'Well, it appears we have the missing evidence now. You're right, of course, Colonel Erdmann, you'll be judged by your superiors and the people of the DDR, not by me. I'll just provide the ammunition, so to speak.'

Hans smiled at the poor joke. 'Just make sure they don't use it on you, Herr Kampmann.'

Kampmann was now more interested in locating the guns and ammunition, just as Hans had planned. 'Bring the car,' Kampmann ordered the man. 'And where the hell is Neumann?'

'Nobody's seen him in the last hour, Inspector,' the man said.

'Well, there's no time now. Remain here and inform him where we've gone.' Kampmann then turned to Hans. 'Don't get too comfortable. You'll be hearing from me very soon.'

Hans quietly pocketed the manifest Kampmann had left on his desk, and said to himself, with a smile, 'Happy hunting, Inspector Kampmann.'

***

Ten minutes after Kampmann had left the office, Hans' adjutant knocked and entered with Bernie Schwarzer and Georg Neumann following in his wake.

'I'm sorry, Georg, I could've sworn I'd seen something down there,' Bernie said, winking to Hans.

Georg Neumann grunted and took the offered seat. He didn't say anything until his cigarette was lit and well aglow. The usual plume of smoke mushroomed above his head and Georg sighed contentedly. 'You know what? I think all the years of denial in the camp have made me addicted to these things ever since,' he said.

Bernie laughed. 'Come on, Georg, you were smoking like a chimney when we met in France in 1940.'

'That doesn't count. Everyone smoked during the war,' he protested. 'It's much worse since the camps.'

'If your only suffering from the war, and its aftermath, is an addiction to cigarettes, then you've fared better than many others,' Hans said.

Georg grunted a begrudged agreement.

The phone on Hans' desk rang and he picked it up with some relief.

'Yes, he's here.' He handed the phone to Neumann. 'For you.'

'Neumann.'

There was a period of ten-seconds whilst he seemed to be listening.

'Who is this?' Neumann said. Then he held up the phone, as if whoever had been there, wasn't anymore. He sat down and rubbed his hair.

'Problem?' Hans asked.

Georg looked at Hans and then at Bernie. 'I don't know what's going on here, but since I arrived this morning, I have had the distinct impression I've been led by the nose.'

Both Hans and Bernie shrugged innocently.

Georg continued, 'And now, an anonymous tip-off has told me where I might find some missing items. Now, I'm not a young ambitious sort like Kampmann. I tend to look a gift horse in the mouth and wonder exactly what I'm getting myself into.' He raised his eyebrows at Hans.

Hans sat for a moment in deep thought. He wondered how much he could trust Georg Neumann. He knew him to be a good man and a fine comrade, but was worried about what all the political indoctrination might have done to him. He weighed up his options and eventually decided to go with his instinct.

'To be polite, your Inspector Kampmann is very keen. I suspect he's beside himself to impress his political masters.'

Georg said, 'An understatement, if ever there was one.'

'So you're not exactly friends?'

'Can't stand the prick,' Georg said. 'But don't mistake that for thinking I'm going to put my neck on the block for you, Hans Erdmann. You seem to do a good job of that yourself.'

'Nobody would expect that, Georg. But let's say that you find yourself in a situation where you can retire on a high. Solve an issue on the one hand and make Kampmann look an idiot on the other.'

'I'm listening.'

'You still have that important piece of paper with Mielke's signature on it?'

Neumann patted his breast pocket.

'Good, then here's what I propose...'

***

It had taken some time for Hans to receive the information, but when he did, he realised just how high the conspiracy against him had reached. The barracks at Bernau housed elite troops of the Felix Dzerzhinsky regiment. They were the hand-picked regiment of the regime, posted close to the Wandlitz compound, home to the leadership of the East German government. Hans knew his information was reliable; it came from a source he had worked with for a number of years. Eventually, Hans had managed to talk Georg Neumann around and convince him that his plan was in both their interests.

Georg Neumann led a squad of men with them to make arrests, if necessary. Hans stayed quietly in the background, praying things went the way he had planned. Bernie had stayed back at Treptow. He had another important duty to perform when the time was right.

The senior officer at Bernau was not too happy about having secret police crawling all over his barracks, but once he had seen the letter from Mielke, he reluctantly permitted the search. He did, however, excuse himself, no doubt to make some frantic phone calls.

Once in the armoury, it took them fifteen minutes to find the relevant crates.

'These look like the numbers,' Neumann said, trying to clear the mud from the outside of the crate.

'Read them out,' Hans asked, taking out the manifest Kampmann had left on his desk in his haste to leave the office.

'Where did you get that from?' Neumann asked suspiciously.

Hans smiled genially. 'Never you mind. What's important is that it confirms these are the missing guns. The question is why they've been removed from a Volksarmee barracks and brought here without my knowledge? And who took them?'

'Is there a problem here?' The uniformed man who stood in front of them was used to being listened to. Hans thought he had the air of some old Prussian generals he'd come across in the last war. This man was much younger, barely thirty years old, but his uniform was that of the Felix Dzerzhinsky regiment. He was one of the regime's chosen ones. Hans couldn't help taking a dislike to the man and he could tell he wasn't the only one by the way Neumann was visibly bristling next to him.

'These items are the source of our investigation. They have been stolen from the Volksarmee barracks at Treptow. I would like to see the delivery notes for them,' Neumann said.

The man eyed Hans and Neumann with contempt. 'This barracks is off limits. You should not have been allowed access here. Please leave immediately, otherwise there'll be serious repercussions.'

'You don't understand…' Georg said, waiting for the name.

'Lieutenant Rainer Hellweg.'

'Lieutenant Hellweg, we have the highest authority to be here.' Neumann pulled out the paper from his pocket and handed it over. Hellweg took it like he didn't really have time to read it. However, the more he read, the more his face coloured, until in the end he looked like he was ready to blow a gasket.

'This is preposterous. Someone's head will roll for this.'

'Quite probably,' Neumann said. 'Now, do you have the delivery notes for these crates?'

'There must be some misunderstanding here.' Hellweg's tone was starting to change and his arrogance was waning by the second. Hans was really enjoying himself. He hadn't had to say a word so far and everything was falling into place. There was only one thing left that needed to happen, and Kampmann's appearance at the door of the warehouse couldn't have been better timed. Bernie had done his job back at Treptow.

'What is the meaning of this, Neumann?' Kampmann shouted.

'We've found the missing items, and Lieutenant Hellweg here was just explaining how they got here.' Neumann said, unperturbed.

Hellweg's focus had turned towards Kampmann. It was clear he was raging mad by this stage; it was just a question of who would feel the full force of that anger.

'Kampmann, a word,' Hellweg said sternly.

Evidently the two knew each other, which didn't come as a particular surprise to Hans. Their conversation was over twenty metres from him, but it didn't take a rocket scientist to see the exchange was heated. In fact, after a while, Kampmann said very little and appeared to be visibly shrinking by the second. Whatever the case, somebody was going to pay for the set-up which had clearly gone wrong. Fortunately, on this occasion, it wasn't going to be Hans.

After a short time, Kampmann shuffled over in their direction, apparently shamefaced. He addressed Georg Neumann in a different tone to when he had arrived.

'Georg, look, I'm sure we can sort things out here. It seems there's been a misunderstanding,' he said.

By now, Neumann had lit another cigarette and was slowly inhaling on his apparent lifeblood. He gave Kampmann a look of pure contempt.

'Inspector Kampmann, I will give my full report to your superior on what I have seen today.' Neumann shrugged. 'Then it's up to them what they do with you. Honestly, if it means I never see you again, then it will make me a very happy man.'

Hans couldn't have said it any better himself. He didn't need to add anything.

'Any chance of a lift back to Berlin, Georg?' he asked, with a wide smile on his face.

CHAPTER 19

FRIDAY, 11th AUGUST 1961,
WEST BERLIN

Klaus had left a message at Pullach for Markus Schram to contact him. It took exactly two hours for him to do so. Klaus wasn't the slightest bit surprised that Markus was in Berlin; if something was to happen, then the West German Security Services needed to be on the spot. Markus was an old comrade. He and Klaus had fought side by side in Russia and were taken prisoner by the Russians in Stalingrad. They had survived the camps of Kolyma together and that was only half of the story.

That Friday afternoon the Kurfürstendamm was bustling in the August sun. Klaus had his own experience of the *Wirtschafstwunder*, the German economic miracle after the war, but this place epitomised it. Women swinging shopping bags thronged the pavements and the roads were dotted with flashy sports cars in amongst the majority of beige Volkswagen Beetles. The place smelled of success and wealth. It was a far cry from the streets in East Berlin. The numbers of people brought anonymity, and Klaus knew that was the reason Markus Schram had suggested they meet there.

Klaus waited by the tobacco stall opposite the Pan-Am ticket agency within the shadow of the ruins of the Kaiser Wilhelm Memorial Church. As Klaus watched an unruly queue of camera-toting tourists forming vaguely around the beige double-decker bus in front of him, Markus suddenly materialised from their midst.

He was dressed in a modern suit, which fit well with the affluent surroundings. Klaus took him in a bear hug, genuinely pleased to see him again. 'You still look like a young man, Markus.'

'But not in body or mind, Klaus. How are you doing? I can see the country air is doing you good.'

'I have no complaints, Markus. I consider myself one of the fortunate ones.'

Markus nodded, pausing for a moment, no doubt to reflect on those who were no longer with them; that's certainly what Klaus was doing.

'Let's walk,' Markus said, eventually.

'So what brings Klaus Schultz back to Berlin?'

'Do you have to ask? You saw the papers.'

'I did.'

'But nothing has been done about it.'

'What makes you say that, Klaus?'

'Look at this place. Berlin's about to go up and everyone is content splurging cash on overpriced luxuries. The Amis are doing absolutely nothing; they are not prepared for what's to come.'

Markus didn't argue. 'We lost the war. We don't run things, Klaus. You should know that better than anyone.'

They stood at the side of the road waiting for a gap in the traffic, people all around them. As the crowd moved off the kerbside en-masse, Klaus was forced to manoeuvre around a strolling middle-aged man walking hand in hand with his giggling wife, who was sporting a fine, pale yellow summer dress, her designer sunglasses perched in her pushed-up hair.

Back at his side, Markus said, 'We gave them everything, including your papers and much more intelligence beside that.'

'So what are you saying? The Amis know exactly what Ulbricht is planning? They know he's going to close the door? And?'

'You're asking me what they will do?' Markus shrugged. 'Nothing. I believe they will do nothing. Nothing of consequence, at least.'

Klaus had difficulty believing it. 'How can they just let them build a bloody wall? It breaks the Four Powers Agreement, for starters. They have to do something.'

'Like what? Break it down with tanks? They won't risk a war. They believe a wall is better than a war...'

'And in the meantime, we have to suffer the consequences,' Klaus said, bitterly.

Markus raised his eyebrows in admission. 'Something like that. Anyway, you didn't come here to ask me what will happen?'

'That's true,' Klaus managed a laugh. 'But what you've told me doesn't exactly make me feel any better.'

'You know it's coming, at least. That's more than those poor sods over in the eastern sector.'

Klaus stopped walking and Markus turned, sensing something.

'They've arrested her, Markus. They have Eva.'

'What? *Now?*'

Klaus didn't want to say the rest. He couldn't get past the hopelessness he was feeling.

'It's not only that. Dobrovsky...' Klaus managed.

Markus sighed, 'I am so sorry, Klaus.'

Markus was one of the few who knew that that meant. He was one of those who were in Stalingrad when the prisoners had been shot. Dobrovsky's brother had been gunned down escaping whilst he was being snatched by Klaus and his men.

'He won't let her go, Markus.' Klaus was looking for some reassuring words, some hope. He wanted to hear they could get her out, just like the two of them had helped Ulrich to escape back at the time of the Workers Uprising.

'You want our help?' Markus said.

'I am not asking you to mobilise the forces of the BND, Markus, but anything you can do to help. I wouldn't normally ask, but I don't know what else to do.'

They were facing each other as the shoppers passed either side of them, oblivious to the tension.

'Did you tell Ulrich?'

'I haven't had a chance,' Klaus said.

'I don't think it would be a good idea right now,' Markus said.

'This is his sister we are talking about, Markus. Can't you stop playing God for a moment?'

Ulrich's choice of profession had always been a bone of contention between the two of them, or at least with Klaus.

Recognising they weren't exactly being inconspicuous, standing in the middle of a busy pavement, Markus took Klaus by the elbow and they started to walk again. Klaus didn't particularly care.

'I'll do what I can, Klaus, but…'

'I know. You can't do much.'

'We can't do much, but you know somebody who can, Klaus. And if he believes Dobrovsky is involved, I am sure he will help you.'

'I wouldn't ask that man for anything more.'

'I don't see that you have much choice, Klaus. Dobrovsky will not let Eva go. He will see it as the ultimate revenge after all these years.'

Klaus had a frustrated look. 'We didn't kill his brother.'

'I know that and you know that. But he holds us responsible, and you did kill Wiebke.'

CHAPTER 20

SATURDAY, 12th AUGUST 1961,
EAST BERLIN

Errors of judgement can impact you in certain ways. Some are small mistakes, and some are big ones, when you have the overriding feeling that the impact of the mistake will be felt for months, or even years, to come. I was sure it was one of the latter errors of judgement I'd just made. Trying to strangle Weber wasn't exactly the smartest of moves, but I just couldn't help myself. The bastard deserved it.

I had been in my cell for six hours now and it was getting on for Saturday morning. I knew this because I still had my watch, unlike last time. I also still had the film. Both of these things worried me; it told me Weber didn't care whether I knew what time it was or, more importantly, whether he got hold of the photos.

After having tried to squeeze the life out of Weber, he was well within his rights to keep me here. It was not his problem my decision-making proved to be eminently flawed. I could be here for days. Wondering how long you'd be sitting in a prison cell was the worst part of it; when you only had yourself to blame, it was a damned site worse. The victims of my folly were lined up in my mind.

Eva, Tanja, Gerd, even Klaus; I'd let them all down.

***

The room was strong with the overwhelming smell of disinfectant. It seemed it was one of the few items in profligacy in East Berlin. It wasn't the smell that was making Hans Erdmann feel sick, as he planned to brief his NCOs that Saturday morning. Looking at the map, his eyes followed the line of the proposed border that was about to cut Berlin in two. It was their job to restore order should things get out of hand, like they did in '53. He knew what it meant. He wondered if he could order his men to fire on his fellow countrymen. He didn't like it, but it was his job. As a soldier, he would do his duty; how long he would be in position was another question.

He turned to face his men. There were eighteen of them including Bernie. They were mainly fresh faced and bright-eyed, full of enthusiasm for the task ahead. Hans knew it would test their loyalty.

He rapped on the briefing board with his knuckles to ensure he had their attention.

'Right, let's get started,' he shouted.

Hans allowed the room to settle and waited for the obligatory nervous coughs to finish before ploughing on. 'Our role is to form the support for a large scale border operation commencing at 0100 hours tomorrow, Sunday thirteenth August.' He looked around the room, waiting before delivering the last line. 'The border is to be closed.'

Hans watched the men's reaction carefully. He saw some sideways glances to their comrades, some shuffling of feet, but there were no words. They knew better than that. One of the lights flickered annoyingly, as if sensing Hans' disquiet. He knew every man in the room would be thinking about his family and friends.

'Needless to say, you are trusted with this information and it must not leave this room. I don't need to warn any of you of the consequences if it does.'

Hans didn't enjoy saying it, but he felt duty bound to administer the warning. Aside from Bernie, these were younger men who had grown up with the Party and their ideas. They knew why the border was being closed. No doubt many of them agreed with the measures. That said, they all knew people, family who crossed the border in either direction, for work or play. They all did it in one form or another, whether to buy cigarettes or catch a movie. Whatever the case, in the future, it would all stop.

Hans tapped the map with his pointer; the big news done, it was time for the detail. 'Our area of responsibility covers the southern part of the Mitte, starting at the Brandenburg Gate, through Potsdamer Platz, around the railway yards, on to Friedrichstrasse, through Kreuzberg and along the river to the Oberbaumbrücke.' Hans followed the line of the sector border slowly along the map. Somehow he felt like he had a knife in his hand, slicing it through the heart of the city.

'It continues down past the back of Treptower Park, past the canal and the Plänterwald.'

'It's a wide area, Colonel. Is it our job to be present the full length of that border?' one of the younger NCOs asked.

'It's a good question, Riedle. The tanks and armoured cars will be stationed on Marx-Engels Platz, well back from the border. Like I said, we are to support the operation; we won't actually go to the border unless there are any problems at the outset. It's likely once the border is sealed, we will perform guard duties.'

'What does "any problems" mean?' Riedle asked.

'Civilian incursions from the west, or even from enemy forces,' Hans said.

Riedle looked straight at him and Hans felt he could read his mind. Hans felt it was better said. 'It also means we have to deal with any potential disorder from our side of the border.'

This brought chatter around the room. Hans didn't react. He had expected it. He would have been more worried if it hadn't happened.

'All right, settle down!' Bernie Schwarzer said from the back of the room.

Riedle wasn't giving up. 'Exactly how are we authorised to deal with any disorder, sir?'

'Initially, we'll use water cannons…'

'And if that doesn't work?'

Hans wondered just how loyal this group were to Ulbricht and the like. He knew what allegiance he once had, had waned, mainly due to Marks and the vendetta against him. He was sure he would find out about his men over the next few days.

'All units will be supplied with live rounds.'

Again, there was chatter in the room. Even the normally forthright Riedle looked concerned.

Hans raised his hand for silence. 'Gentlemen, we have to expect some form of reaction to these measures. Under no circumstances will anybody fire unless given the order.'

He slowly turned his head around the room, looking each man in the eye. 'Is that understood?' he said, eventually.

There were slow, awkward nods. Hans thought he saw fear in some of their eyes. He did wonder what they were getting themselves into. He hoped they remained well back from the border and all went without a hitch, without the need to use force of any kind. Somehow he doubted that would be the case.

'Dismissed.' Hans brought an end to the meeting.

The men filed inexorably out of the room, the enormity of what Hans had just imparted to them sinking in.

With the room empty, Bernie finally broke the silence. 'I can't say I like the sound of this one, Chief.'

'Not only the operation, Bernie.'

'Any comeback from Kampmann?'

Hans shook his head. 'Not yet, but I can't see Marks giving up that easily. We have to assume they'll try another way.'

Bernie threw a nervous glance over his shoulder. 'Don't you ever feel like getting out? You know…'

Hans studied him for a moment, considering his reply very carefully. 'I think it's a bit late for that, Bernie.'

Bernie raised his eyebrows. 'Yeah, I suppose as we're about to fence ourselves in, you might be right about that one, Chief.'

Hans glanced at Bernie and cracked into a laugh, thankful, at least, for their ability to joke at their situation.

CHAPTER 21

SATURDAY, 12th AUGUST 1961,
EAST BERLIN

As I sat in front of Major Weber of the Staatssicherheitsdienst, two angry red marks encircling his flabby neck, I really had to pinch myself, rather than his throat. He seemed a little reticent, even a bit standoffish, but I couldn't really blame the man. After all, I'd done my best to kill him a few hours earlier. Weber had taken the precaution of having three guards in the room this time. It wasn't really necessary, as I was still in shock that I was there in the first place, and positively delirious at the offer he'd just made.

'The deal to release Eva Schultz is still on the table.'

I managed a mumbled, 'What?'

'In exchange for the film. Of course, we have to establish the film's contents are genuine and worth the price I will pay.' Weber felt his neck gingerly as he looked at me. I think he was more wary than angry, but I wasn't paying him much attention. He was sitting here offering me the opportunity for Eva to be freed. The only thing that came into my mind, in fact screamed through it like a firework, was, why? Why would he offer me that after what I'd done? If it had been me on the other side of the table, I would have let me suffer. What could he possibly gain from this? After all, it was Saturday morning and the border was to be closed tonight. Leaking the photographs now would have no effect simply because it would be too late.

I didn't care why. I managed a weak nod. 'How long do you need?'

'It'll take a few hours to develop the film then we have to check its authenticity. Probably until tomorrow morning,' Weber said.

My mind had started to work at last. I didn't trust him. 'Yes, but then the border will be closed. How can we be sure you'll let us both cross into West Berlin?'

This was where he stopped. Weber seemingly returned, in my mind at least, to that hateful character box in which he'd been placed in my brain from the very first moment I had met him. 'You have my word.'

I raised my eyebrows. The word of a Stasi officer wasn't worth much in my eyes.

'I also have some questions.'

'Go on,' I said rather tiredly.

'I need some information about your informant.'

So this was why they still wanted to offer a deal. It was contrary to all my instincts. Sources were sacrosanct. It was only when I got down off my soapbox that I realised there wasn't anything I could actually say about my informant. It had been an anonymous call to the pub. It was a male voice with a Russian accent.

'That goes against everything I believe in, Major Weber.'

Weber shrugged. 'We could keep Eva here.'

I tensed suddenly and I saw Weber recoil slightly in response, like my hands had touched the reflex of his knee. It seemed the guards hadn't noticed it, but the two of us certainly had. Yet again I was in a position where I could've happily strangled Major Weber. This time, I managed to restrain myself.

Before I replied, I gave a look as dark as the Spree. 'Seeing as you put it like that, I can't honestly tell you much. He called me at the Leydicke pub on Mansteinstrasse most evenings. Sometimes I wasn't even there.'

'Anything else?'

'Only that he had a slight Russian accent.'

Weber's ears pricked up considerably, so much so that my heart sank. I was worried I'd dropped somebody right in the proverbial. It didn't last long, however. No sooner had I said that, than he held out his chunky hand for me to shake and I was handing over the film.

It was one of the strangest episodes in my life. Everything appeared to be back on track, if Weber was to be trusted, of course.

***

Hans was forced to raise an eyebrow at the feast on offer. Caviar on thick buttered bread, cold meats aplenty, and hundreds of bottles of chilled champagne from the Crimea were all laid out the length of the great hall. No normal person in East Berlin would have seen this kind of feast for years, if ever. But this wasn't a normal gathering. This was the last sendoff for all the NVA (People's Army) commanders and Grenzpolizei (border police) before the big operation started. Hans had expected something, so when the invitation summoning him to NVA headquarters at Strausberg arrived that Saturday evening, he wasn't in the least bit surprised.

The briefing had been going on a while. There was never an opportunity missed when it came to political indoctrination. They even showed a propaganda film, unabashed in its bias. Hans had switched off long before, not only because he wasn't interested, but because he felt anxious. He was fully up to speed with the logistics of the operation and his men had been fully briefed, but that wasn't the issue.

His mind was preoccupied with the skulduggery of his boss and his acolytes. Hans knew he had kept them at bay for now, with the help of his contacts, but it couldn't last for long. As General Karl-Heinz Hoffman got up to say a few words, his impressive array of medals making the jacket of his uniform sag, Hans was thinking about Bernie's

143

question of earlier. He really had thought about getting out, more than once. It was only because of the deep sense of duty he felt towards people like Bernie and his men that he had stayed put. He had even gone as far as to wonder how to make his flight west. He had some ideas, but they would now have to be changed due to the measures. With a sealed border, it clearly wouldn't be as simple as walking over the sector border anymore. He had to think about Bernie. This wasn't a decision he would be able to, or want to, make alone.

Hans tried to shake all thoughts from his mind. He had to focus on what was to be done in the early hours of tomorrow; the rest would have to wait. He slid towards the back of the main hall as the general was raising his hands in acceptance of the sycophantic applause. Hans didn't only want to get away from the drivel, he also wanted to call back to the barracks to check on preparations.

As he reached for the large brass-handled door, a hand took a firm grip on his forearm.

'Not staying for the rest of the speeches, Erdmann?'

Xavier Marks had been lurking at the back of the audience. In his preoccupation, Hans had failed to spot him. Hans continued out of the door with Marks in his wake.

'What could be more important than the morale boosting words before the big operation?' Marks was grinning, immaculately attired, as ever.

Hans felt compelled to answer, mainly because he'd been caught off guard. 'I wanted to check if all was going well back at the barracks.'

'Yes, that's very important, Erdmann. Nothing should be amiss at this late stage, should it?'

Hans looked at Marks, wondering what he meant, before answering. 'Quite right. In fact, if most of the men in the hall were with their men, there may be fewer mistakes on the day.'

Marks pondered for a moment, stroking his finely cut suit, his party badge gleaming on the lapel. He broke into a smile. 'You know what,

Erdmann, you might just be right.' Then he added, patronisingly, 'Why don't you run along and give Treptow a call right now?'

He widened his eyes, almost with a sense of glee. It made Hans feel ill at ease. He couldn't help taking Marks' advice, however; the quicker he was away from his presence, the better, as far as Hans was concerned.

Hans was directed to a line of phones just off the main entrance. He had the pick of any of them, as the speeches were still ongoing. He was connected to the barracks quickly.

'Put me through to Sergeant Schwarzer.'

As he waited to be connected, he couldn't help feeling Marks had been a bit too happy, given the failure of his latest attempt to discredit Hans. He did wonder if he might be slightly more hesitant, but then dismissed it as the way of Xavier Marks.

'Colonel?'

Hans didn't immediately recognise the voice on the line. 'I asked for Sergeant Schwarzer. Who is this?'

'It's Riedle, Colonel.'

'Ah, yes, Riedle. Get Schwarzer on the phone. It's urgent.'

'Yes, Colonel, that's the point. We can't find him.'

'Well, he won't have gone far, not with the operation and everything. Tell him to call me…'

'That's what I was trying to say, Colonel. Nobody has seen him in the barracks since dinner.'

Hans considered it strange. Bernie was normally around the barracks somewhere.

'At what time was he last seen?'

'Around six, Colonel. Nobody has seen him since.'

Hans let the phone hang limp in his hand and closed his eyes as the realisation struck him.

'Colonel?'

'Ok, Riedle. I'll be back as soon as I can.'

145

CHAPTER 22

SUNDAY, 13th AUGUST 1961,
EAST BERLIN

It was one a.m. The barracks forecourt was teeming with life. The troop carrier engines were being revved continuously, causing the air to become choked with clouds of grey exhaust fumes. The last of the men were scrambling onto the truck tailgates, their rifles and submachine guns slung over their shoulders. Hans looked down from his office window. He knew it was time to move, but it was something he couldn't bring himself to do. He didn't particularly agree with the mission, but it wasn't about that. It was because his right-hand man and comrade of the last twenty years, Bernie Schwarzer, wasn't with him, and Hans had more than an inkling why Bernie wasn't there.

When he'd arrived back at the barracks, Bernie still hadn't been seen. He'd ordered a search of the barracks, which was no mean feat considering the amount of equipment and manpower in the barracks. Hans had even gone to check on Bernie's small apartment, leaving the last minute preparation to the young Riedle, but the place was deserted. He knew Bernie wasn't a man to shirk his duty. Far from it—if there was a job to be done, Bernie had always been the first to volunteer. Hans did have some momentary doubts Bernie may have gone west, like so many others, but those thoughts were quickly dismissed. He wouldn't have done that without informing Hans first. The two of them had done everything together since those days in Russia; there was no reason that would change now, especially not now, with Marks breathing down Hans' neck. That left only one possibility in his mind. It was one that was reinforced by the bullish behaviour of Xavier Marks the previous evening.

With a heavy heart, Hans pulled himself up and into the cab of the first troop carrier.

'Ok, Riedle, let's move out!'

In a cacophony of roaring engines, the multitude of troop carriers bristling with armed men and equipment swept out of the barracks gate. Passing Treptow Park, Hans glanced to his left at the sea of tents erected to house the additional military personnel shipped into Berlin over the weekend. There was no doubt the regime was taking a big risk with this operation. They were hoping that a quiet weekend in the city would see its residents, and the Amis, either napping, enjoying the lakes around Berlin, or simply away on annual vacations. Hans knew his mind had to be on the job, but it was very difficult when his best friend of the last twenty years had gone missing. He'd not reported the fact to his superiors yet. He couldn't bring it upon himself to do it. He would have to do it eventually; he couldn't hide the fact Bernie wasn't there.

Hans stared at the light dipped onto the road by the shuttered headlights. He kept returning in his mind to Xavier Marks' behaviour the previous evening. He was almost encouraging Hans to call the barracks. The more he thought about it, the more he knew they'd taken Bernie. They'd taken him at the worst possible time, just before the operation. Riedle was coping admirably, but it still wasn't the same without the reassuring presence of an old hand quietly steadying the ship in the background. Hans shuddered involuntarily at what Bernie would be going through. There would be no charges and courts, and Hans didn't want to think about the consequences of that.

As the lead truck, they were the first to swing onto the wide open expanse of Marx-Engels Platz. The old bomb-damaged Berliner

Stadtschloss had long being blown up by Ulbricht to make a place for the constant parades of the regime. Now it provided a sensible and sizable marshalling area for Hans' men. This is where his men would wait for a call from the border, should they be required, should they be called into action.

During the short journey from the barracks, Hans decided on an action of his own. If he was to save his friend, he had to move fast. He would do anything for Bernie. That time had come. It would mean another favour he owed to his Russian contact, but Hans knew he had no choice. He had to do it.

***

The next morning, I was decidedly nervous. The squeaking of chairs and shoes on the waiting room's linoleum floor didn't exactly ease my anxiety. When Eva was brought up, her condition was infinitely improved. She seemed to have been allowed to sleep whilst all the drama had been going on, and some of the bruises on her face had lost the angry look they'd had in the dim light of the cell.

After a long, deep hug, she looked up into my eyes and said, 'What took you so long?' I had the feeling the old Eva was back.

All I could manage was a shrug. It wasn't really a question I could answer without revealing the fact she was condemning herself to a life sentence with an imbecile. Whilst we both took a seat behind the desk, I got hold of Eva's hand and squeezed. 'It'll soon be over. Trust me,' I managed through gritted teeth.

My words were uttered with such alarming ease, I had to wonder if it was somebody else saying them. In fact, I was trying to calm my own nerves. I was worried this whole thing was going to blow up in my face. And I couldn't shift that feeling from my bones when Weber came into the room and sat down opposite us.

'The photographs are as you described, Herr Kaymer. I must congratulate you on your skills as a journalist.'

I nodded. Compliments weren't something I'd expected nor sought. Eva even turned to me and smiled. Did I see pride in her eyes? If only she knew the full story. It was then, I decided, on the grounds of pure self-interest, that she had no need to know exactly what had happened.

'The information you have provided proved very useful,' Weber said with a smug smile.

'Oh? I can't imagine it was from anything I said.' I felt quite certain.

Weber smiled and I immediately winced. Maybe he was just saying it to make me feel awkward. Eva didn't look at me this time, but I could imagine what she was thinking. I managed to brush it off, however. I remembered how I'd felt on the other side of pride, sitting down there in the cells; being up here doing deals with the devil felt like a better place to be.

With that everything seemed to be done. 'So Mr Kaymer, I'm sure we'll have no need to meet again.'

'No offence, but I hope not.'

The smile on Weber's face as we he left the room was strange. It was hard to place, like he was happy, but a little bit awkward. I might even say it was as if he had been coerced to do the deal. It did nothing to assuage my feelings of unease.

***

It was early Sunday afternoon before Weber managed to organise a car to take us to the border. By this time, I was like a caged tiger, growling periodically at the impassive guards. We had no idea what was going on at the border, and that, along with the confidence I was forced to place in Major Weber, made me anxious.

Sitting next to Eva in the back of the Wartburg, I felt sick. I wasn't sure if the smell of sweat was coming from me or the two young pups Weber had gifted us as chaperones. They looked like they still should have been at school. Their pair of jutted chins had never seen a razor and their cheeks looked as rosy and soft as baby Tanja's.

By the direction we'd taken, down Karl Liebknecht Strasse and on towards the Unter den Linden, it seemed the handover was to take place at the Brandenburg Gate. The nearer we got to the Gate, the more the military presence grew. In fact, passing Marx-Engels Platz, Eva nudged me. Looking across the vast square, there was an array of tanks and personnel carriers covering every available inch of space. It was clear the authorities weren't taking any chances.

Eva had a ponderous look in her eyes, which was not really surprising after the last two days she had endured. She turned to me. 'Tanja is one today, Jack.'

In all the commotion of the last few days, I'd completely forgotten about Tanja's first birthday. 'Well, you know what? When we get home, we will do whatever you want together. It's going to be fine, Eva.'

The last words were for me, not for her. The fact it was Tanja's birthday had just turned my anxiety ratchet one notch higher, as if it wasn't tight enough already. Eva squeezed my hand, probably sensing my disquiet. She was one hell of a woman after all she'd been through.

As we crawled inexorably down the Unter den Linden, there were small crowds of people gathered on each corner looking towards the Gate. I noticed Weber's men glance uneasily at each other. From the looks on their faces, this operation wasn't in the school textbook. I felt they were ready to bolt at the first sign of trouble.

And it was trouble I was starting to feel brewing somewhere deep down in my stomach. On Parisier Platz, immediately at the rear of the Gate, a Vopo flagged down the car and leaned into the open window.

'You'll have to turn back,' he said. 'There's nothing coming through here. All hell's kicking off on the other side.' He flicked his head westwards.

The driver showed his identification card and said, 'We have to deliver these two over the border, orders of the Major Weber.'

The Vopo was unimpressed. 'Try telling that to my colonel. You've got no chance here. I suggest you go to one of the other crossing points.' With that he went to stop another vehicle pulling up behind us. I was starting to get panicky. Eva was squirming in her seat. She understood the full implication of what was happening. The two youngsters in the front were lost for words and ideas, and I couldn't help offering a useful suggestion.

'We should make the rest of our way on foot. I'm sure your authority could see to getting us over the border. After all, those were your orders,' I said, more in suggested hope than in latent expectation. The two men eventually nodded their reluctant agreement and I jumped out of the car. Grabbing hold of Eva's hand, I could feel the tension in her. Her face was taut, her teeth no doubt grinding like my insides.

We heard screams. We could see a crowd gathered on the western side of Hindenburg Platz. There appeared to be a protest going on. Three water cannons were spread in front of the western side of the Doric columns (though still in the eastern sector) facing the crowd. Most of the militiamen were armed with submachine guns. Right on the border line, two rows of barbed wire and numerous metal obstacles were kept company by hundreds of brown uniformed Grepos.

On the western side chaos started to reign. People were hanging over the barbed wire, shouting insults at the guards. There were harassed looking Schupos, the West Berlin border police, not sure exactly what to make of the situation. Taking in the scene, our two minders had not shaken their decidedly nervous appearance.

Suddenly there was a great deal of screaming and shouting from the western side and missiles started to rain down in between the columns of the Gate. A half brick landed by our feet, breaking into pieces with a thud. Our two Stasi guards made a bolt for the car. I chased after them, but they were in the car and it was moving before I could stop them, despite my banging on the roof. Before I knew it, I was chewing on blue exhaust fumes as the car screeched off back down the Unter den Linden, leaving Eva and me to fend for ourselves. We were now fully exposed to the riot ensuing in front of us.

I instinctively pushed Eva behind one of the Gate's pillars to avoid exposure to the onslaught. I thought I'd been in pressure situations before. Korea had always taught me things couldn't get any worse. This was different. It was difficult to know which side was which and who we could trust.

The crowd suddenly broke through the barbed wire. The Grepos immediately retreated 20 metres to just in front of the Gate itself, within touching distance of us. Some protestors were now over the border line. It was then the huge water cannon kicked into life. The progress of the protestors was halted rapidly as the water swept them off their feet. The ones caught in the full force of the jets were tossed around like rag dolls and back over the border line. Eva and I, meanwhile, were in the midst of a mass of East German uniforms; Grenzpolizei, NVA, we could take our pick. We were as vulnerable as two sitting ducks on a fair shooting range.

I felt a rough hand on my shoulder. I was being dragged back, eastwards from the Gate on to Parisier Platz. All the while I was frantically looking around for Eva. Some thirty-seconds later I found her, but now we were under the gaze of a submachine gun and two long in the tooth Kampfgruppen. I say long in the tooth, but one actually had no teeth; the other had a few, but they were as yellow and stained as the sink in the Stasi cell. I had the feeling this wasn't going to be the most intellectual of exchanges.

'Kennenkarten,' one of the men demanded.

They wanted our identity cards. It was time to do some fast-talking. With my passport in hand, 'Look, I'm an American citizen, and this,' pointing to Eva, 'is my wife. We just need to be placed back over the border.'

The man with no teeth grimaced and turned to Eva. 'Kennenkarte!'

Now, we were in trouble. Sure, Eva had been returned her identity card, but, of course, it was only for East Berlin. Slowly she took it out. This time the guard took one look and started to separate us with a few sharp, insistent prods of his gun.

I was back by Eva's side in a flash. 'No, no, you don't understand.' Eva was looking disconsolate by now. 'Major Weber of State Security brought us here. We are to be put on the western side of the border. I wouldn't like to be in your shoes, my friend, if you don't do what he wants.' I made a sign of a finger across my neck and nodded knowingly. It was dramatic, I know, but in the circumstances, it was the best I could think of.

Fortunately, it seemed the words had their effect. The soldier with the stumps for teeth said, 'I'll stay here and watch them. Fetch the colonel.'

I breathed a short-lived sigh of relief. I did consider making a run for it, but looking at the gun, it was well oiled and maintained, and looking at the man holding it, it didn't appear he would think twice about using it. On this occasion, I thought caution was the better part of valour. I knew I was right when I received a friendly tickle on the ribs from his gun when I made the mistake of looking around the area over his shoulder. Apparently, we were staying put and waiting for the colonel.

This was like the wait for the walk to the gallows or out on to the plank over a choppy Baltic in February. Our fate was in the hands of the colonel, whoever he was. It was then, out of the corner of my eye, I was aware of a tall, striking figure in a Volksarmee uniform, striding purposefully towards us.

***

The morning had gone to plan. Hans and his men had been able to have breakfast without any particular alarm. However, by late morning, Berliners had grasped the significance of what was happening and the atmosphere started to be change. Groups of youths had gathered on the eastern side of the border on the Unter den Linden, well back from the Gate, but it was the western side where the real trouble was brewing.

At noon Hans had been called to the Brandenburg Gate crossing to assess the increasingly unruly protest gathering pace there. He was met with a crowd of at least a few thousand people on the western side of the barbed wire coils, which temporarily marked the border. For a while, he monitored the crowd, and whilst they were only shouting and hurling abuse at the militia men and some of Hans' NVA units, he took no action. Within an hour, the crowd had started to throw missiles. Soon after, the border was breached as the crowd surged over the wire, throwing coats on top of it so they could trample over it. Reluctantly, he gave the order for his men to pull back and to use the water cannons.

In the midst of this chaos, Hans was approached by one of the rough looking Kampfgruppen.

'Colonel, you must come at once to deal with some people who want to cross the border!'

Hans glared at him. 'Are you mad, Corporal? Deal with the situation yourself. You can see I am busy here.'

'Sir, I must insist. There is an American citizen with them. I cannot decide what to do.'

Hans shook his head. The water cannon had pushed the crowd back for now, but who knew what they would try next. He didn't really have time for interruptions of this nature. However, he couldn't deny being slightly intrigued by the militia man's story and, more to the point, he didn't need an incident with a US citizen at a border point for which he was responsible.

Hans strode across Parisier Platz, directly behind the Gate. He shook his head on seeing another militia man holding a man and woman at the point of a machine gun.

'What the hell is going on here?' Hans said to the militia man.

Before he could answer, the man held at gunpoint was talking. 'Like I explained to these two goons, I am an American citizen. Me and my wife,' he waved his hand towards the woman at his side, 'are to be safely placed over the border by order of Major Weber of State Security.'

The militiaman said to Hans, 'The lady has only an East Berlin identity card, Colonel. No permit.'

Hans turned to view the couple. The pair of them looked stressed. The man was waving his arms in exasperation. The woman looked exhausted and was clearly sporting recent injuries by the cuts and scratches on her face.

'Please can I see your passport?' Hans asked the American.

Reluctantly, the man handed it over, eyeing Hans with suspicion.

'Kaymer?' Hans had heard the name somewhere before. 'I know that name.'

The American smiled, gaining a slightly smug look. 'I am a journalist.'

'Ah, yes.' Hans recalled some of the man's articles. 'I am not surprised you want to leave, Herr Kaymer. Your articles have not exactly been complimentary to the DDR in the past.'

Kaymer lost his easy manner, quickly regaining the hassled appearance. 'Look, Colonel, we have orders to be put over the border. I wouldn't want to be you…'

'Yes, Herr Kaymer, I get the picture,' Hans interrupted, annoyed at the implied threat. He turned to the woman. There were large black rings under her eyes, that didn't seem to be present only through excessive tiredness. The small scratches and cuts had been summarily repaired, but were still visible. In spite of that, and the tousled hair, there was no doubt the woman was beautiful. Looking at her condition, and the American's insistence on naming the Stasi major, Hans could piece together where the woman had been.

'Your identification, please, madam?'

Hans took the pass. 'Eva Schultz?'

'That's what it says.' She was surly and defiant in the face of authority. That would be no surprise if Hans' deductions about her had been correct. Hans handed her the identification card back. They all turned towards the Gate, their attention grabbed by a particularly blood-curdling scream. Hans needed to be rid of this issue.

'Your identification is only for East Berlin. My orders are not to allow anybody to cross this border without permission,' Hans said.

Kaymer started to wave his arms in protest, so Hans raised his hands to quiet him. 'I haven't finished yet.'

Hans was still intrigued by the woman and her story, in spite of his need to get back to the Gate.

'Were you arrested by the State Security, Madam?'

Kaymer was chirping away again, 'I don't see what that's got to do with it...'

'I asked the lady a question. Please keep quiet, Herr Kaymer.'

She nodded, forcing her hair to fall in front of her eyes.

'May I ask why?'

'This is ludicrous...' The militiaman stepped forward and forced the muzzle of his machine gun under Kaymer's ribs.

'That's enough, Corporal,' Hans chided.

'It's a long story,' she sighed.

'Humour me.'

'Jack is the father of my child. He wanted to write a story about all this.' Eva pushed her chin defiantly towards the continuing chaos at the

Gate. 'The closing of the border and whatever else you people are doing.'

'And?'

'They arrested me to blackmail Jack.'

Hans took a breath and held the back of his neck for a moment. He knew this kind of thing went on. Their story had a ring of truth about it.

'So where are your guards with the papers to legitimise this…' Hans searched for the word.

'Deal,' the American said.

'Yes, deal,' Hans said, eyeing Kaymer warily.

'They ran off ten minutes ago when the bricks started to fly,' she said, with scorn.

Hans smiled. He liked her spirit. He couldn't help thinking about Bernie, hoping he was bearing up under likely the same treatment the woman had received.

Hans took one last look at the American. His eyes were pleading now, all the pretence of bravado long gone. He cut a desperate figure. Hans felt sorry for them, especially the woman. He had difficulty understanding just what the regime was hoping to achieve with all these measures and, more to the point, he had no more time to waste on the matter.

With a deep sigh, Hans turned to the corporal. 'Take them further down towards the back of the Reichstag and put them over the border there.'

The militiaman looked doubtful. 'Colonel?'

'Do as I say, Corporal! And if it's not done, you will end up on a charge. Do I make myself clear?'

'Yes, Colonel.'

Hans turned to walk away, but Kaymer stopped him. His eyes were full of gratitude. Hans even noticed a tear pricking at the corner of Kaymer's eye.

'I want to thank you, Colonel. It's good to see people can still think for themselves in East Berlin...' His words started to trail off, like he had said too much.

Hans smiled. The man couldn't help himself. He was starting to understand how he had managed to get himself in so much trouble with the East German authorities. 'If I were you, Herr Kaymer, I would leave quickly.'

For once, Kaymer didn't say anything. The woman grabbed his arm and they turned to the Kampfgruppen corporal who was to lead them to the border.

Hans had to get back to work. He had not taken two steps back to the Gate when a black sedan screeched to a halt beside him. The driver was out and around to the passenger door. There was no need; it was already open. A short man in the uniform of a KGB general jumped out of the car and was staring intently across at Kaymer and the woman.

He turned to Hans. 'Colonel! A word!'

***

I couldn't begin to express my gratitude to this man. As he walked away, I realised I didn't even know his name. I only knew his decision would allow Eva and me to be a family again, to be father and mother to our daughter. He was a colonel in the People's Army of East Germany. I couldn't understand why he had decided to allow Eva to leave; as he said, it was against his orders, but he had judged the situation for himself and made a choice. It was one kind act in amongst all the political chaos. In the midst of two posturing superpowers and a delinquent nation trying to save itself from extinction before it was out of diapers, there was, after all, some humanity.

I was oblivious to the screeching tyres of the large black limousine. I only half heard the involuntary moan from Eva, 'No! It cannot be him.'

Before I was really back from my woolly world of intense happiness, I vaguely noticed the colonel talking to a squat man in a Russian uniform. I felt my stomach start to move as if in a fast descending elevator. I recognised the man as the one who had interviewed me with Weber. I couldn't recall his name.

'Dobrovsky,' Eva mumbled.

'You know him?'

Eva turned to me with a burning fear in her eyes. 'Jack, he won't let me go. I have to get out of here,' she hissed.

I held on to her, preventing her from bolting there and then. 'Are you mad? We just need to talk to the guy. He knows Weber. It'll be fine...'

'Jack, you don't understand. Dobrovsky knows my father.' She was still pulling away like the proverbial bull at the gate.

Eva's eyes were wide, the fear turning to panic. My mind was racing now. I knew there was something that Klaus had been holding back on me. I recalled the feeling I had at my apartment. I was coming to the conclusion this whole thing was bigger than just my story. This went way back. What was the connection between Dobrovsky and Eva's father?

I could see the colonel and Dobrovsky were by now in the middle of a heated exchange. Involuntarily, I let go of Eva. I moved closer so I could hear what they were saying above the din of the protestors.

'He has an American passport. You can't keep him here,' the colonel shouted.

'You would do well to recall who you are talking to, Colonel.' The Russian's German was nearly perfect.

'They are to be released over the border on the orders of a Major Weber. This is what I know.'

'Those orders are countermanded by me. They are not leaving.' Dobrovsky was adamant.

The realisation hit me. Eva was right. There was no way this man would let us leave East Berlin. Either Weber had stitched us up or Dobrovsky himself had set the whole thing up. Either way, we were in the shit.

The colonel took off his hat and mopped his brow. The sun had appeared momentarily, even if the heat was caused more by the situation than the weather.

'General, you can see I am rather busy at the moment.' The colonel motioned towards the Gate.

'Yes, Colonel, you should get back to your duties. I'll deal with things here,' Dobrovsky said, turning to face me. As he did, the colonel grabbed his forearm. 'My duties include recognising and upholding the law and the regulations currently in place in this city. That man,' he pointed at me, 'is an American citizen and is thus free to cross the border.'

'This is not your business, Colonel Erdmann,' snapped Dobrovsky.

The colonel was put off his guard for a moment. 'So you know who I am?'

'You'd be surprised what I know about you.'

Their eyes were locked on each other. Dobrovsky looked like he would blow a gasket and it seemed the colonel was not backing down. I could feel my whole world crashing down to earth like the bricks from the protestors.

I turned to check on Eva, but she wasn't there. Only the two militiamen stood, staring, transfixed, like me, on the confrontation between a general in the KGB and a colonel in the NVA. I looked around frantically but there was no sign of her. I went to shout her name, but the words didn't come out. Something stopped me. It wasn't intelligence because I had been slow on the uptake for the last few days. It was something else. Gut instinct, probably.

Nobody else had noticed she'd disappeared. There was no way we were getting out of here together. The only place Eva was heading was back to Höhenschonhausen, or worse. I didn't care about me. As much as I couldn't bear to see her go without doing something, as much it made my heart ache, I knew I had to let her go. The quicker she got away from here and the seething Dobrovsky, the better.

Instinctively, I walked towards the two men. The longer this went on, the more time Eva had to run. It was about survival, once again.

'The colonel is right, General.'

Dobrovsky's face whipped around like he'd been slapped.

'You have no say in this matter. This is about the security of the East Berlin border.' Spittle was hanging from his lip.

The anger was rising in me. This little man had led me on a merry dance over the last few days. Together with his monkey, Weber, I had a made a deal with the devil which the little Lucifer with the cardboard shoulders had no intention of keeping.

'I suppose you and Weber cooked this one up? Actually, no, he's not clever enough for that. This one has to be all yours, Dobrovsky.' I was in front of him now, or I should say, leaning over him. He stepped backwards, no doubt looking for a soapbox to hitch up on, but only bumped his backside on the body of the car. His driver was round quickly to protect his boss.

Dobrovsky was brushing himself down, despite the fact I had not actually touched him. Dobrovsky shouted, 'Take this man and do what you want with him, Colonel. I don't need him.'

'No, you don't need me now you have kept your dirty little operation hidden from the world.' I pushed towards him again, but the driver held me back.

The colonel snapped an order to the militiamen. 'Take this man and put him back over the border. Quickly!'

As they dragged me away, I winked at the colonel. He didn't acknowledge it. He only shook his head slightly. He had bigger problems to worry about.

'Where is the girl? Where the fuck has she gone?' It was Dobrovsky. It might actually have been a Katyusha rocket battery, as there was little difference in the screeching noise.

As I was being dragged away, I could hear Dobrovsky shouting insults, then threats, mainly in the colonel's direction. I even heard the car being kicked. Eventually, in the distance, there were some intelligible orders.

I knew he would organise a thorough, painstaking search. A search I imagined he would personally orchestrate. I just hoped Eva had moved fast.

CHAPTER 23

Eva Schultz knew. She just knew. The attention of the two militia men was focused on Dobrovsky and the colonel. Jack was also transfixed, letting go of her and moving closer to the confrontation. Eva glanced nervously to her left. There was a small crowd looking towards the chaos at the Brandenburg Gate. She hated to leave Jack, but this was her chance. This was her only chance. She moved off slowly, careful not to attract anybody's attention. It took all her effort not to break into a run. She was dreading a shout at any moment. She made it through the crowd of East Berliners and turned to see Jack arguing with Dobrovsky. She wondered if Jack could see her. Dobrovsky had his back to Eva and the car was between her and them.

This was no time to wait around. She started to walk quickly back down the Unter den Linden, from where Weber's men had brought them what seemed like only minutes before. Her mind was racing. She needed to clear her mind and think. She passed the Soviet Embassy, all brass plates and gold fittings. It helped focus her mind. *Get off the main streets*, she told herself. Instinctively, she turned to her right. When she took the time to look, she could see other ordinary Berliners milling around in a state of confusion and fear. She passed a young couple in a shop doorway arguing about his work in West Berlin, just like Eva. His ability to earn now cut off, just like the official at the town hall had warned it would be.

She turned onto Französische Strasse, now heading in the opposite direction to the military traffic. Each time a truck passed she expected it to stop and take her away. She was at pains not to draw attention to herself. She tried to maintain a strong but even pace. She crossed the bridge, lifting her head left momentarily to catch a glimpse of the shattered dome of Berlin's main cathedral. She didn't dare look behind her. It was only about putting distance between herself and the Gate, herself and Dobrovsky. She wasn't going back to a Stasi cell for anybody. There would be no free passes now. It was all down to Eva.

She crossed the Spree, brown and swirling in the wake of a laden barge. She kept on past the Rotes Rathaus, Berlin's distinctive red-bricked town hall. Where was she heading? She needed a quiet place to think, to gather her thoughts, plan her next move. She kept moving. Flight first, think later. All the time, she was pushing down the feelings of fear and distress. She couldn't think about Tanja; she couldn't think about Jack. Focus, Eva, focus.

She walked until she started to tire and feel a slight chill. She was only wearing the clothes in which she'd been released, a t-shirt, a thin jacket, and slacks. She didn't know how long she'd been walking, but by now she was at Friedrichshain Park. She dared to turn around and look behind her. There were no military uniforms, no Dobrovsky. There were only families out strolling together in the park. Surely they knew what was happening on the border. Everybody must be aware by now. Eva passed through the small gates of the Marchenbrünnen, the fountain of the fairytales. What had happened to her over the last few days was more nightmare than fairytale.

Eva allowed herself to breathe properly. She felt the hunger for the first time. Tiredness was seeping into her muscles as the urgency of flight subsided. She walked through the statues more slowly. Some of them remained headless, the place overgrown. Ulrich had brought her here when she was younger. He would tell her about her father and how they came to the park before the war.

Eva thought about her father. She wondered how he'd become embroiled with Dobrovsky. The war with Soviet Russia had cast a shadow over all of them. They had all paid for it: the people of Russia, the Berliners, her father, her mother, Ulrich, and now her. But her family had survived. Her father had survived Stalingrad and the Gulag. Her mother had survived the invasion and all it brought with it. Ulrich had escaped from the Stasi back in 1953. Eva would do the same. She would find a way out of this mess. She would find a way out of East Berlin and back to her daughter, back to Jack.

She started to think about what she needed to do. She needed help, some money, food, and clothes in the short term. She had nothing but the clothes she stood in. She couldn't return to the apartment. They would be watching, waiting for her to make that mistake. Dobrovsky would search for her. Helmi was out of the question. It was too obvious and she'd already done enough for Eva. Helmi didn't deserve to be dragged into this anymore than she already had.

Eva needed somebody she could trust, someone the authorities would not suspect. Then she needed to get out of the eastern sectors under her own steam. She knew Berlin like the back of her hand. There was no way they could close all the borders overnight, not tight anyway. She started to think of all the places she might escape. It wasn't long before she had some ideas. She would need to check them out, of course, but it was the start of her plan, the start of her fight back.

Whilst the possible places of escape flicked through in her mind, Eva had already decided on the person she would approach for assistance. It was a risk, she knew it, but she felt it might just work.

She smiled to herself, feeling better that she had the formation of a plan in her mind. It was time for Eva Schultz to act.

CHAPTER 24

SUNDAY, 13th AUGUST 1961,
WEST BERLIN

Away from the protest in front of the Brandenburg Gate, the last coil of barbed wire was lifted aside, and I was manhandled through the gap by the helpful Kampfgruppen corporal. I was being ejected from the DDR, forever an undesirable to them. I walked back down to Platz des 18 März oblivious to the tumult around me, and hailed a taxi. I hoped to God Eva could stay out of the grip of the Stasi long enough for us to get some help to her. The journey back to Schöneberg allowed me time to reflect. It was hard to do. Not only had I failed to get Eva back home, I'd been using a sixteen-year-old boy to run my errands and look after my daughter without a word to his family. I felt down on myself in the way I imagined only an alcoholic felt right before he reached for the bottle one last time.

I knew when I reached the apartment I'd have some explaining to do. However, in spite of all that had happened, in spite of my pathetic failings, what had just happened to Eva had an air of inevitability about it. As if whatever I had done, even if I'd hit a homerun, Eva would still have been in East Berlin. As I turned the key in my apartment door, I wasn't the only one with questions to answer.

Gerd jumped up when I walked in. I shook my head. Fortunately for me, Eva's lack of presence told its own story. I didn't need to speak.

'What happened?' Gerd said.

Klaus hadn't moved. He had Tanja in his arms. I glanced at the table and noticed a birthday cake and some unopened presents. The presents gripped my heart and left a lump like a rock in my throat. I needed a drink. I poured myself a generous measure of bourbon and sank it in one. It didn't touch the sides, so I helped myself to another.

'Don't you think it's a bit earlier for that, Jack?' Gerd said.

'Very probably, but the one I just downed is for last night, and this one,' I held up the tumbler, 'is for what I'm about to get off my chest.'

I stared at Klaus. My eyes must have been trained on him like a pair of battleship guns, because he stood, and turned away from my gaze, putting Tanja over his shoulder and patting her back.

Gerd seemingly felt the atmosphere and tried to help. 'Why don't you sit down and tell us what happened?'

I didn't sit down. 'I couldn't get her out, Gerd. They wouldn't let me take her over the border, in spite of the film. It was a setup.'

'Setup?'

'A man called…Dobrovsky…'

Klaus flinched as I said the name, like a bullet had whizzed by his ear. The next one wouldn't miss. With Tanja placed back in the cot, Klaus sat down and finally faced me.

'They were never going to let her go, were they, Klaus? You knew that all along.'

'The last time I saw you, I didn't know Dobrovsky was involved, but yes, it did worry me they wouldn't release Eva regardless.'

'And you didn't think to let us in on your little secret?' My arms were wide now, voice lifting in intensity.

'I didn't want to worry you…'

'You didn't want to worry me?' I screeched. 'Well, right now, Klaus, I am pretty fucking worried. I can tell you.'

My antics had caused Tanja to cry out. Gerd went to her, looking confused at the turn of events.

'Has he got her?' Klaus asked.

'I don't know, Klaus. The last time I knew she was on the run.'

'She's free?' Klaus said, standing up, some hope returning.

'Free? Free? How can she be free, stuck in that mousetrap?'

Klaus appeared lost for words for a moment. 'I meant Dobrovsky didn't have her,' he managed, quietly.

'And how long will that last, Klaus? Dobrovsky will search high and low for her. He won't give up. And you know why?' I pointed at him, just in case he was in any doubt where my anger was focused.

Klaus started to move to the door, seemingly searching for his jacket. 'We have to help her. We can't just sit here.'

'Sit down!'

'We must look for her,' Klaus pleaded.

I don't know why I did it, but I launched the tumbler. I half aimed it in Klaus' direction, but not exactly at him. It crashed against the frame of the door, showering the floor with glass, and its contents.

I said, 'Sit down. You're not going anywhere until I know what the hell is going on.'

I thought for a moment Klaus would ignore me, or even fight back, but eventually he threw his jacket on the back of the chair. Crunching gingerly over the glass, he came back and sat down.

By now, Tanja was screaming. Gerd said, 'Was there any need for that? Can't you see she's upset?'

I took a deep breath and a few seconds to compose myself. I motioned for Gerd to pass me Tanja. He looked at me, slightly unsure.

'Come on. Give her here. I am okay now.'

I took her rabbit from the cot and soothed her. Before long, she was sucking on her thumb and flicking furiously on the rabbit's ear. I took a seat opposite Klaus. Gerd sat down as well. We were all ready to listen to Klaus.

'I am sorry about the glass,' I said.

Klaus shrugged, 'I can't say I blame you for being mad.'

'So, just who is Dobrovsky, apart from a full-fledged general in the KGB, that is?'

Klaus let out a deep sigh. I had a feeling we were reaching into places he'd rather not go, but if it took the odd tumbler or two for it to come out, I was all for it.

'I will say this all as quickly as I can. Time is of the essence; after I've told you, we all have to work together to get Eva out. Are we agreed?'

'I thought we were all already working together to get Eva out, Klaus?' I couldn't resist.

Gerd nodded his head in agreement.

'I suppose I deserved that one,' Klaus said with a wry smile.

Something told me I was slowly breaking this deep and complex character down, but we weren't done yet, not by a long shot.

'So? Dobrovsky?' I said.

Another sigh. Pulling teeth with a piece of string and a door handle would have been easier.

'It goes right back to Stalingrad. In the late summer of '42, we were ordered to snatch a couple of "tongues" from the front line?'

'Tongues?'

'Prisoners, for intelligence.'

I could see Gerd's eyes popping out of his head. Not many made it back from Stalingrad. In Germany, it was stuff of legends.

'Anyway, we grabbed the two prisoners from the front lines. When we were bringing them back to our lines all hell broke loose, mortars, machine guns. We were pinned down in no man's land. The prisoners took their chance and ran, despite the fact they were blindfolded and bound. One of our lot gunned them down.' Klaus shrugged, 'As we sit here now, it sounds a harsh thing to do, but in the middle of the battle for Stalingrad, it was commonplace.'

'So why was it so different?' I asked, keen to keep him talking now that the floodgates were open.

'We didn't believe it was at the time. A few months later, we were taken prisoner by Ivan, which was no picnic.'

'I can imagine.'

'Some of us survived. It was hard, but we got through to the end of the war. Late in '45 we thought we were going home, but we didn't count on Dobrovsky. As we were lined up to get on the train back, we were arrested.'

'So what happened then?'

'There were only four of the original group from Stalingrad arrested. The rest had already perished in the camps. They took us to the Lubjanka.'

'In Moscow? Jesus!' I'd heard horror stories about the place.

'It was Dobrovsky's doing. He'd been in Stalingrad at the time we took the prisoners. One of them turned out to be his brother.'

Gerd let out a low whistle.

'We were sent to a Gulag in Siberia. The sentence was 20 years, but in effect we were to die out there. The worse thing was none of the four of us actually pulled the trigger.'

'You didn't kill Dobrovsky's brother?' I asked.

'No, I was in charge of the troop, but neither me nor my remaining comrades shot the man.'

'So how did you get back?' Gerd asked.

'There was an amnesty when Stalin died in 1953.'

'And Dobrovsky let you go?'

'Not exactly. I had help.'

'And what then?'

'He followed me to Berlin and well…you know now why he won't let Eva go. The man is hellbent on revenge.'

The room was quiet whilst we digested what Klaus had said. The man had lived one hell of a life. It was a miracle he was sitting in front of us. I had so many questions. In fact, I wanted to take out a pen and write it all down. I couldn't shake that professional instinct.

For Klaus, the talking was done. 'Now we have to make a plan to get Eva out...and quickly.'

Sounding a note of caution, I said, 'That's not going to be easy, Klaus. We've got to find her first. If she's hiding from Dobrovsky, and doing it well, she'll take some finding. Then we have to get her out.'

Gerd was confident as ever. 'There are plenty of places we can get through. They can't just shut the place up overnight.'

'Do you have a good map?' Klaus said.

'Sure.'

Before I went to get it, Klaus said, 'Ok, Gerd should work on the places we can get her out. You'll need to do some scouting up and down the border, what measures are in place, guards and the like.'

'Don't worry, I will sort it out. We won't exactly be bringing her through the Brandenburg Gate,' Gerd joked.

I winced at that one.

'You're missing the big point, Klaus. How the hell do we find her?'

Klaus was quiet, pondering something. I'd had the same feeling previously when I felt he was holding something back.

'Come on, Klaus, out with it. No secrets this time,' I said.

He looked at me, weighing me up. I don't think I'd ever met a more closed person. Given his past experiences, it wasn't the biggest surprise.

After what seemed like an age, he said, 'I told you I'd had help to get out of Russia when we were released.'

I nodded. It was on my list of questions.

'I think we're going to need that help again,' Klaus said, almost reluctantly.

CHAPTER 25

SUNDAY, 13th AUGUST 1961,
EAST BERLIN

It was early Sunday evening. Eva had left a note earlier in the afternoon. It was simple and to the point. She had asked for some money, but mainly clothes and some camping equipment. She knew she was taking a big chance. Not only on her choice of assistance, but asking to meet like this. She knew it could be the Stasi waiting for her. Eva had to go with her instinct; if it went wrong, she'd be in a cell again in a couple of hours. If it went well, it might just have been an inspired choice.

Seemingly, Sophie Reinhardt had everything going for her. She was in her final year of medical school, studying to be a doctor, just like Eva. Sophie was training in East Berlin and the Charité Hospital. Unlike Eva, her political credentials were squeaky clean. Her father was a high ranking official in the East German government. She had been Eva's best friend all through her school years. They'd not seen as much of each other recently, mainly due to Eva having to go to West Berlin to work, and the time she spent looking after Tanja. Eva trusted Sophie. She knew Sophie would do anything to help her, just like Eva had helped Sophie in the past. Eva also knew, with Sophie's background, she wouldn't be under suspicion. As Eva sat waiting near the café, at the edge of the Plänterwald, she hoped she'd judged it correctly.

On seeing Sophie, Eva couldn't hold back the tears. All the emotion of the last few days flooded out. Sophie put down the rucksack and took Eva in a tight hold. Sophie was tall, a champion swimmer at school. She was a big character in many ways. At that moment, Eva only felt relief.

Sophie let her go. 'What did I tell you about getting involved with an American?'

They both laughed. It was typical of Sophie to make a joke. She didn't even know Eva's story yet, but all that was important was that she was there to help.

Eva was about to start explaining, but Sophie stopped her. 'Not here.'

They looked around. Some of the tables at the café were occupied. It was best not to talk in the open like this, and Eva had to be careful not to draw attention to herself.

'Let's get you some food first. We can talk after,' Sophie said.

Sophie didn't say much as Eva wolfed down some cold meats, cheese, and bread. This wasn't the time for niceties. Eva noticed the rucksack, stuffed to the top. There were some small pots and a cooking burner attached. It looked like Sophie had thought of everything. Eva did think there looked to an awful lot of stuff in the rucksack; she didn't intend to be staying in East Berlin long.

Sophie paid and heaved the rucksack onto her shoulder. Once they were well clear of other people, Sophie said, with a wry smile, 'Eva Schultz, my mother always said you were trouble!'

'I was never politically reliable enough for your mum.'

'Yeah, well, the old bat was never much of a judge.' Sophie had never got on with her mother. Sophie hated the politics. At work it was bad enough, but her mother insisted on the indoctrination continuing at home.

Eva raised her eyes, 'Given my situation, she is actually very perceptive.'

173

Sophie laughed. 'Yes, I have to say when I read your note, I wasn't surprised. I still had to come, though.'

'And I am truly grateful, Sophie.'

'I know you are. You've helped me out before. Anyway, I'm not only here for you.'

'What do you mean?'

'Never mind that now. What exactly have you got yourself into?' Sophie said.

Eva told Sophie about her arrest, about Jack and the story, and about the fact she was on the run.

'I have to get out, Soph. And I think this is the best place to do it…'

'As good a place as any, I suppose.' Sophie said, letting out a deep sigh. 'I can't believe they've actually gone and closed the border. We knew they'd do something, but this sounds permanent.'

'I have no doubt it's permanent,' Eva said.

'We've been on double shifts at the hospital for the last month, to cover all my colleagues who have left.'

'You can't blame them, Sophie.'

'I don't blame them one bit. I am only annoyed I didn't get out before they closed the border.'

Eva looked quizzically at her.

Sophie pointed to the rucksack, 'Well, you don't think all this bloody stuff is only for you, do you?'

It started to dawn on her what Sophie was talking about.

'I'm coming with you, Eva.'

CHAPTER 26

MONDAY, 14th AUGUST 1961,
EAST BERLIN

The last 48 hours had been tough for Hans Erdmann. He felt like he was trying to do his job with both hands tied behind his back. On one side, he had Marks and his men chipping away at him, doing their best to make him fail and to bring him down. On the other, Bernie Schwarzer had now been taken out of the game. They had managed during the operation the previous day. The initial operation had been judged an overall success. However, for Hans, without Bernie it could never be the same. He badly needed some rest, but he knew he couldn't sleep until he did something to help his comrade.

He would have preferred to let sleeping dogs lie. It had been eight years since he'd agreed to get involved. He knew he wouldn't have got involved if his wife had still been alive. It had been just after the Workers' Uprising and he'd thought about his decision every day since. He didn't want anything like the Uprising to happen again. Indeed, that's why he agreed to help, to stop those actions, to prevent the extreme measures. In the end, it hadn't been successful; the sealing of the border had been another of those draconian reactions. He couldn't have done anything more to prevent that. Now, Hans wanted something in return for all the information he had given.

175

He'd made the emergency call to arrange a meeting with his controller. Hans waited, as agreed, close to the memorial for Soviet soldiers in Treptower Park. He had his back against one of the stones of the granite memorial. It was a time he preferred not to think too much about, but the sheer size and scale of the memorial, dominating the park, made it difficult to forget. The war had brought only disastrous consequences for all it touched. It was not only his comrades and himself, but Hans couldn't help thinking about them, thinking about the times in the camps as prisoners of the Russians, where he and Bernie fought to survive. Many didn't survive. At least, he was grateful to be alive, even if his body was crying out for rest right now.

'Are you with us, Hans?'

He was shocked from his reverie. His controller, Alexei, was at his side. Hans hadn't even noticed him approaching.

'You look a little stressed,' Alexei said, sweeping the park with those sharp, cold eyes Hans remembered. Alexei looked older, grey hairs poking out at his temple under the fedora he always seemed to wear.

'Let's walk,' Hans suggested.

'I thought you would have been busy with the operation,' Alexei said as they left the memorial behind them.

'I was, still am,' Hans said. 'I need some help, Alexei.'

'Slowly. Let's start from the beginning. We've not heard anything from you since the incident with the missing weapons. What happened in the end?'

Hans filled Alexei in on the last few days. 'Your help was much appreciated, but it's gone past that now.'

'You need to remain calm, Hans.'

Alexei started to cough, his eyes watering in the process. Hans was grateful for the interruption. He didn't want to reveal what he wanted too early in the piece. He knew what Alexei's reaction would be.

'What the hell has been going on, Alexei? I joined to prevent these sort of measures, "a more progressive socialism", you said.'

Alexei shrugged his shoulders. 'Khrushchev didn't listen to my boss. I don't know exactly. I tend not to ask too many questions. It's not healthy.' Alexei laughed, which only brought on another bout of coughing.

'Sealing off a city to stop people from leaving is not what I call progressive,' Hans said, bitterly.

'I take your point. I am sure it won't end well, if it means anything.'

It was Hans' turn to show indifference. 'I'm done caring about what happens in this country, or trying to affect it, for that matter. It's time to look after myself and those closest to me.'

'Yes, you said you needed help?'

'Bernie Schwarzer has gone missing.'

'Fled west?'

'Not Bernie. He wouldn't just leave like that without saying anything and certainly not before a big operation. I am convinced Marks has arranged his arrest.'

'What makes you so sure?'

Hans told Alexei about the incident with Marks at the NVA headquarters. 'Put together with everything else, it's the only explanation.'

'Let's say you're right, Hans. What is it you're asking?'

'I need you to get him out, Alexei.'

Alexei was shaking his head, 'We're not even sure he's been arrested and even if we find him, we can't just go taking prisoners from their cells.'

Hans held on to Alexei's forearm, enough to make them stop walking. 'You're the bloody GRU. You do what you want.'

Alexei glanced down towards his arm for a moment. 'You know we're not one big happy organisation, and not to mention the reaction of our German cousins. They can be quite stubborn, you know?'

Hans smiled.

They started to walk again, the birds chirping in the trees. It was the dawn of a lovely summer's day. It was hard to imagine what was happening so close to this scene of relative tranquillity.

Hans changed the subject, 'What do you know about a general called Dobrovsky?'

Alexei stopped in his tracks and said gravely, 'Where did you hear that name?'

'Our paths crossed yesterday. I may have… upset him.'

'Christ, Hans, you don't do things by half measures. That man has serious power.'

'In that case, you might have to arrange my release from Hohenschönhausen as well,' Hans said, smiling.

Alexei was still serious. 'You should try to keep your head down once in a while, Hans. It helps you to survive in our kind of world.'

'It's too late for all that, Alexei.'

'That sounds very terminal.'

'I want out, Alexei.'

Alexei became animated. 'What do you mean "out"? You don't resign from the GRU. It doesn't work like that.'

'Don't treat me like a naïve idiot. I mean out of East Berlin. Once you've found Bernie, I want you to get the two of us over the border.'

Alexei started to cough again, like an old dog barking.

'You should get that looked at,' Hans said.

'I am going back to Moscow next week.'

'I hope for your sake you're only going back to see the doctor.'

Alexei smiled and held up his hand, seemingly not wanting to laugh in case it brought on another bout of coughing.

Hans turned to Alexei, noticing the water in his eyes. 'I am serious, Alexei.'

Alexei looked nervously to either side. Fortunately, as it was so early, they were alone in the park. 'Hans, do you know what you're asking? I wouldn't even take these things to my boss. In fact, I didn't even hear it. If you want to defect, do it under your own steam.'

Hans felt himself getting angry; the lack of sleep didn't help. Suddenly, he grabbed Alexei's lapels. 'After eight years of risking my life for you people, I expected more. It's payback time, Alexei. Go and tell your boss what I want, and do it now!' Hans shoved him away.

Alexei brushed himself down, looking flustered. 'I would think very carefully about this, Hans. If I go to my boss, it's out of my hands. You know what that could mean?'

Hans sighed and rubbed the grit from his eyes. 'I don't care about the consequences. Just do as I ask.'

Alexei paused for a moment, seemingly gathering his thoughts. He then held out his hand. After a moment, Hans shook it.

Alexei looked into his eyes. 'Be it on your head, Hans Erdmann.'

CHAPTER 27

MONDAY, 14th AUGUST 1961,
WEST BERLIN

It was Monday before Klaus could arrange the meeting. Back at Jack's apartment, they hadn't wasted any time, but Sunday still seemed to drag on. They alternated taking care of Tanja whilst the others reconnoitred the border. Klaus knew he should have asked Maria to come to Berlin to help, but he didn't want to worry her about Eva's plight. What Klaus had seen on the border had lifted his spirits. Not in the central sectors, where the barbed wire had already been replaced by concrete posted wire fence. From Potsdamer Platz along Ebert Strasse to the Brandenburg Gate, the fence was reinforced by strong patrols. That clearly wouldn't be the place to attempt to cross. Away from the Mitte district, however, there were weaknesses in the border. The waterways, the parkland areas, were difficult to guard. These were the places on which to focus. They were racing against time, however. The East German authorities would ensure the measures increased in their efficiency in all places. They also had to find Eva before they could help her, and most importantly, they had to get to her before Dobrovsky did.

Klaus had to call the meeting. He didn't want to owe Burzin anything, but he felt he had little choice. Pride had long gone out the window where his family was concerned; he'd learned that harsh lesson when he came back from the camps. Klaus sat by the window in a small *Kneipe* on Bernauer Strasse. He'd been here before, years ago when he was searching for Ulrich. His girlfriend Ursula had lived there with her family. Not anymore; they had gone to West Germany in 1953. Klaus hadn't really thought why Burzin would want to meet him here, of all places. There wasn't time to think about things too deeply.

'In all the time we have known each other, it's the first time you've requested a meeting.' Burzin was standing in front of him, with a cigarette in his hand. Klaus had been so preoccupied, he hadn't seen him enter the small bar.

'I wouldn't have thought this was your type of place,' Klaus said, purposely not getting up to greet Burzin.

'There's a reason we're here, but we'll get to that later.' Burzin took off his coat and folded it neatly over the back of a chair. He waved to the proprietor, 'Schnapps,' he said, pointing at their table.

Klaus turned to look around the bar. They were the only customers except an older man, deeply engrossed in his newspaper. The headline screamed, "Barbed-wire Sunday!" Klaus preferred the view out of the window. On the street he could see a crowd gathered at the junction of Wolliner Strasse. Barbed wire was stretched across the road marking the boundary into East Berlin, and armed guards manned the crossing. The apartments directly opposite Klaus were actually in East Berlin, the pavement in front of it, the start of the French sector of West Berlin.

With a bottle of schnapps and two glasses placed on the table, Klaus turned to face Burzin. He had to do it sometime, even if it nearly killed him. With the cigarette in his mouth, Burzin filled up both glasses, his eyes smarting as the cigarette smoke caught them. He lifted one of the glasses in a toast and motioned for Klaus to do the same. Klaus didn't move.

'To…families,' Burzin said.

The bastard never missed a trick, Klaus thought. Burzin knew exactly why they were there and was, as usual, toying with him. Klaus took the glass and tossed back the contents, feeling the hot liquid grip his throat.

'How many years have we known each other, Klaus?'

Klaus shrugged. He barely managed to hold back the reply, too many. It remained unsaid. After all, he needed the man's help.

'It must be fifteen years. That lovely summer's day in Kolyma,' Burzin chuckled.

Even Klaus couldn't help a smile. 'If it was a summer's day, it was the only one in the seven years I was there.'

Burzin nodded, 'Yes, it was a tough place.'

Klaus had been Burzin's prisoner. Burzin had been his reluctant Camp Commandant, during the years Dobrovsky had consigned Klaus and his comrades to mine gold in the gulag. Klaus saw Kolyma as the arsehole of the world in no uncertain terms. Burzin himself had been there under sufferance, exiled for political reasons. Klaus and his comrades learned to survive the extreme weather and working conditions; Burzin only cared for his own skin, but was pragmatic enough to know that well fed prisoners were productive. At least, Klaus did his best to make Burzin keep his promises.

'Here we are again, with the fences going up and people stuck behind the wire,' Burzin said.

'And the Russians are at the back of it all again,' Klaus added.

Burzin poured two more glasses, unperturbed by the slight.

'You'd be surprised, Klaus. Ulbricht is a persistent so and so.'

'You're telling me Khrushchev doesn't have the power to stop him? Come on, Burzin, nobody would believe that.'

'Oh, he had the power to stop him, but he needed a solution to the problem in Berlin, and Ulbricht gave him one.' Burzin eyed Klaus now, looking for a reaction. 'In fact, not only the Russians needed a solution; the Americans did as well.'

Klaus looked puzzled.

'Think about it.' Burzin took his glass, tapped Klaus' glass, and launched the fiery liquid down the same way the first one went. 'It couldn't go on. All these people leaving their posts, something had to be done.'

'And this? Is this the right solution?' Klaus asked, reaching for his glass.

'Right solution for who? The people of Berlin? No, of course not. I told you before, I honestly believe socialism can work, but these measures, just like tanks on the street in '53, won't work. Not in the long run. That's why we're back here eight years later.'

'So who is happy with the outcome?'

'Ulbricht, Khrushchev…Kennedy.'

'How are the Americans happy? You don't know how they will respond yet.'

Burzin laughed, smoke blowing from his mouth and nostrils simultaneously. 'What have they done so far?' Burzin clicked his fingers. 'Absolutely nothing. And believe me, they will continue to do nothing, because this, the sealing off of the border, is better than the worst outcome for them.'

Klaus didn't look convinced as he threw back the contents of his glass. The second felt better than the first.

'Nobody wants another war, Klaus. And what Ulbricht is doing is better than a war.'

Klaus looked down the street, his eye caught by a man in his fifties wearing a flat cap, tattoos on his bare forearms. He stood on the pavement looking up and down the street directly in front of a window of an apartment on the eastern side.

'You seem to know a lot about this. If you don't like it, why didn't you do more to prevent it?'

Burzin shrugged. 'I tried, if you remember? Gehlen's mob didn't believe me and somehow, the Stasi stopped your American friend from publishing his article. If I could have done more, I would have. This won't work. You cannot keep people against their will.'

It's the first time Klaus had felt honesty from the man. At least it boded well for what he had to ask; humanity existed beneath the cloak Burzin had always seemed to operate behind.

Once again, Klaus' attention was drawn to the man on the street. After a last check up and down, the man turned and threw a small stone against the window just above his head. Suddenly the window was open. A man's arm passed down a large box. The man on the pavement placed it beside him on the floor, before taking another.

'So you need my help again?' Burzin asked.

The word "again" cut through Klaus. He hated the thought of asking the man who had imprisoned his comrades for more help. Klaus hadn't worked out just who Burzin did work for, apart from himself. The KGB, for sure, but that was such a large organisation and there always seemed to be competition, even in-fighting going on. Yet Burzin had helped Klaus to release Ulrich from Hohenschönhausen in 1953. He had saved Klaus' life by keeping him out of Dobrovsky's clutches. There was no doubt the man had delivered on his past promises. Klaus believed he still despised the man for his motives and the world he operated in, rather than his actions.

'Before, your son, and now, I assume, your daughter,' Burzin said.

Klaus sighed.

Back on the street, a pair of white stilettoed feet appeared out of the window. The man on the pavement reached up and helped a woman to the ground. She immediately picked up one of the boxes and ran across the street into the French sector and West Berlin. Two more men dropped out of the window, down on to the pavement. One of them reached up to take a small suitcase from the man still in the apartment. These people were escaping from East Berlin whilst they could. It made Klaus feel there was still a possibility they could get Eva out.

184

Burzin turned around and looked over his shoulder out of the window. 'They're still getting out, I see.' He was smiling.

Klaus focused on Burzin. Now he knew why Burzin had brought him here.

Burzin leant forward, the next cigarette already lit, his hands either side of the Schnapps bottle. 'You see how easy it can be, Klaus. It can all be organised.'

Klaus felt uneasy this close to Burzin, this close to the chance to get his daughter out. He grabbed for the bottle and poured himself another glass. He picked up the glass and sent another one down the hatch.

'So what is it you want this time? You want me to kill somebody again, is that it?'

Burzin sat back, more relaxed. 'No, I won't ask that. There was good reason last time. Dobrovsky and Wiebke had to be stopped. What they were doing was wrong.'

'They incited the Uprising, for sure, but it was too late when I went to Wiebke's place. The damage was already done.'

It was Burzin's turn to reach for the bottle. After pouring the schnapps, he held the glass in his hand, seemingly deep in thought. 'Of course I will help you, Klaus.'

'Why? What's in it for you? There's always something in it for you.'

Burzin shrugged. 'In the past, yes. Dobrovsky and I go way back. You weren't the only person he sent to Kolyma. In that sense, I am the same as you.'

Klaus was shaking his head. 'No, Burzin, me and you will never be the same. I just wanted my family to be reunited and then for them to be free.'

'Ah, but that's not quite true, is it? You killed Wiebke, but you didn't only do it to get Ulrich out, did you, Klaus?'

Burzin had hit a weak spot and Klaus felt the blow. It was like the carpet of the moral high ground Klaus always thought belonged to him had been swept from under his feet.

Burzin topped up the glasses. Klaus sensed it was a peace offering, his point made. Perhaps Burzin had made Klaus see that things weren't quite as straightforward as he thought it had been back in '53. For the first time in his life, he felt Burzin was genuine in his motive.

'I will do what I can for you, Klaus. I will do that because I believe that you deserve some peace after all you've been through. Even I deserve some peace.'

Klaus laughed. 'Don't tell me you're going soft on me, Burzin?'

'Maybe I'm getting too long in the tooth for all these games.'

'You're planning to retire?' Klaus asked, incredulous.

'Perhaps, but not just yet. I have one last thing to do… one last score to settle.' Burzin smiled wickedly.

Not wanting to miss the opportunity, Klaus said, 'So where do we start?'

'Well, Klaus, we need to get to your dear daughter before Dobrovsky, don't we?'

CHAPTER 28

MONDAY, 14th AUGUST 1961,
EAST BERLIN

Their night had been as comfortable as it could have been in the circumstances. Sophie had arrived well prepared. The small camouflaged tent fit the two of them snugly. The other equipment she had brought was all they needed for a few nights whilst they figured out exactly how they would make their escape. The relatively dense woodland of the Plänterwald was a perfect place for them to hide overnight. The sector border was only a short walk from this point.

As much as Eva tried to push the events of the last few days out of her mind, it still kept popping up. No matter how much she wanted to be with Tanja and Jack, she knew she had to stay focused. This might be the only chance she'd have to escape. Anyway, Sophie being there was like a crutch to Eva. Her strength was something Eva badly needed at that moment. In some ways, Eva was still shocked at Sophie's revelation from the previous evening.

As they sat amongst the morning birdsong drinking coffee brewed with Sophie's small stove, it was difficult to believe what was happening in the wider city.

'It's hard to imagine you managed to pack everything so quickly, Soph. I mean, I am really grateful, but it almost seems like you were prepared for this eventuality,' Eva said, still trying to understand Sophie's decision.

'I just guessed something was brewing by my father's behaviour. He's been constantly in meetings for the last few months, and then he insisted we cancel our holiday. Put that together with what's been going on at the border for months, it was clear something was coming to a head. There's no way I'm getting stuck here.'

'But you of all people, Soph. You have everything you need compared to the rest of us.'

Eva recalled the time Sophie had brought her some bananas. It was the first time Eva had ever tasted one. Sophie was kind like that. The way Sophie gave things away, Eva felt she had never really seemed comfortable with her position of privilege.

Sophie shrugged. 'Sometimes, that's part of the problem. Their politics are supposedly based on equality, but it's nonsense. There's as much disparity in East Berlin as in West. Anyway, I hate being told what to do.'

Eva laughed, 'Yeah, that's the biggest issue here.'

'Well, that's part of it,' Sophie agreed, 'but all the people I respect are leaving. My lecturer at Humboldt, Doctor Folt, maybe you've heard of him?'

Eva had heard the name. He was one of the chief medical staff at Charité Hospital.

'Well, he took me under his wing.'

Eva looked at her with a knowing smile.

Sophie tapped her arm playfully. 'There was nothing like that in it; I just admired him. For a year, I watched all of his operations, noted everything he did. I had total respect for the man.' She was staring out into the trees now, deep in thought. Her hair looked rough and tousled and her skin slightly dirty after a night out in the damp atmosphere. Her eyes shone in defiance. 'He left, Eva, two days ago, before the border was sealed. I had no idea he felt like he did. I heard him talking on

RIAS. He was scathing about the government, the shortages of medical supplies, political interference and corruption. You know, the stuff that doesn't happen, according to Ulbricht. It made me look at my situation, my parents, why I had what I had.'

'I take it your parents don't know you're here?'

Sophie quickly shook her head. 'God, no, my mum would have kittens, or report me. Probably both.'

'You're not even going to tell her, say goodbye?'

'No.' Sophie was adamant.

Eva only raised her eyebrows in response.

'I know what you're thinking. I'm a spoilt little rich girl who doesn't know she's born, but it's not like that. I just want to live a free life. I don't know, maybe I'm escaping my parents as much as the political oppression.'

'You have to tell her at least,' Eva said.

After a long pause, Sophie eventually muttered, 'Maybe.' She quickly changed the subject to Eva. 'Anyway, you make me out to be some kind of rebel. What about you, Eva Schultz?'

'Yeah, well, sometimes I wish I could keep my mouth shut. I might not be in so much trouble.'

'Well, you were always like that, Eva, let's face it.'

The two of them laughed together, forgetting their troubles for a moment. As the laughter subsided, Sophie turned to Eva. 'So now we know we are both going. We just have to decide how.'

'Finish your coffee. We've got some scouting to do.'

'No need. I know how I am getting out,' Sophie said with certainty.

'You sound very sure of yourself. You've not even checked it out.'

'I've got a very good idea, though.'

'How?'

Sophie started to rummage down into her rucksack, which Eva noticed was complete with a plastic internal liner, and pulled out a swimsuit.

'The Teltow Canal. They can't put barbed wire or a fence across that. It'll be a cinch. So are you coming with me, or what?'

As she watched Sophie holding up the swimsuit, Eva Schultz felt the panic rising in her throat.

CHAPTER 29

MONDAY, 14th AUGUST 1961,
WEST BERLIN

Through the remainder of the Sunday afternoon and evening, we'd been up and down the border. I used the Karmann-Ghia to get around; Klaus, old fashioned shoe-leather; and Gerd, on a bike. I didn't ask where he'd got it from; there were bigger priorities. By midnight, between the three of us, we'd checked the border from Nordbahnstrasse in the north of the city right around the Teltow Canal in the south. We had a good idea what measures were in place. By the end of the day, we were all done in. Only the thought of Eva all alone in East Berlin drove me on; I know it was the same for Klaus. In spite of his problem with talking to people, there was no doubt the man had grit. Gerd continued to be resourceful, even brilliant. He had no reason to be here. There was nothing in it for him; it said a lot about him that he still was.

When I came round, my head throbbing slightly from the one too many whiskeys, Gerd was already at the table poring over the map.

'Tanja seems content,' I said. Her blue eyes followed me across the room, not missing a beat.

'What?' Gerd was miles away. 'Oh, yes, I've already changed and fed her.'

'Where's Klaus?' I said, looking around, noticing his absence for the first time.

'He went to meet the Russian.' Gerd pointed at the map. 'Here. That's where we should get her out.'

'That's water, Gerd. We told you she can't stand water.'

'I heard. No, here, further up.'

I peered over, the words and symbols still slightly blurred.

'We used to play down there when we were kids.'

I raised my eyebrows. Seemingly, I'd witnessed a boy turn into a man overnight. Gerd didn't notice.

'Treptower Park,' I said.

'Well, the area is called Plänterwald. There are lots of trees, small streams and becks, and some allotments. It will be difficult to patrol and a great place to hide. That's exactly where I would get Eva out,' he said with the certainty only Gerd could.

The kid didn't lack confidence. Judging by the way he'd spirited us in and out of that meat factory, I didn't lack confidence in his knowledge of Berlin.

He was staring at the map intently. 'We've been up and down here, the Mitte. This area is no good. Too many guards, fences already in place. People shouting from the western side. Not a chance.'

'I can't fault your reasoning, kid.'

Gerd frowned at me. Sometimes, I was slow at understanding that people of Gerd's age liked the universe to believe they were older than they actually were.

Gerd went on, 'She doesn't swim, so that removes the Spree and the canals.'

'Looks like you've got it all worked out,' I said with a sigh.

'Don't sound too pleased about it,' he said, slightly aggrieved.

It had been eating away at me all through the night. We'd bust a gut up and down that border, checking, watching, and counting guards. We'd looked for any weaknesses we could find. But none of it made the slightest difference. It was about then I got the whiskey bottle out.

That's what had kept me awake, walking up and down, watching over Tanja sleeping.

'Working out where to escape is irrelevant until we've found Eva.'

Gerd was about to say something, when I clarified my assertion. 'More to the point, finding her before Dobrovsky does.'

Gerd was shaking his head. 'I've thought about that as well.'

'Why am I not surprised by that?' I said, laughing.

Gerd ignored me and carried on. 'If I've worked out the best place to escape, so would Eva. She's smart.'

I shook my head. 'It's a big city, Gerd. How can you possibly predict what Eva will do, where she would go?'

Gerd pulled a face. 'Well, it's just a hunch, but I bet I'm right.'

My negativity was blighting my thoughts, or was it my blinding headache? The last few days had knocked me. I could only admire the kid's energy. He reminded me of me before I went to Korea, where I had turned into a bit of a cynic. A horrible thought ran through my mind. I felt Gerd's eyes on me. He was looking at me strangely, almost pityingly. I did start to wonder if I was getting like Klaus. Was I really that cynical and suspicious? Had it got that bad? I took a very a deep breath.

'Ok, let's just run with this,' I said.

Gerd smiled and nodded eagerly, like he'd seen the cent drop in my spacious head.

'Let's say this place is a good place to start. This Planter...'

'Plänterwald.'

'Yeah, so we need to search this place. How the hell can we do that?'

'I know that you're thinking,' Gerd said. 'You can't go east, they'll be watching for you. You wouldn't know what to do anyway.'

I ignored the slight.

'Klaus can't go back there. Dobrovsky wants him more than he wants Eva.'

'No, Gerd,' I was shaking my head, seeing, at last, where he was heading. 'You've done enough already. Which reminds me, I need to get in touch with your parents.'

Gerd screwed up his face. 'I make my own calls. Anyway, I've got West German documents. They can't stop me coming and going through the border.'

'You don't know that. They could have changed it at any time.'

'No, I have checked already.'

'When?'

'Yesterday.'

I stopped. 'What?'

'I used the checkpoint at Schlesische Strasse. No problem,' he said, like it wasn't worth mentioning before.

'You're crazy,' I said.

He winked at me, then flicked the fringe out his eyes. 'Stick with me and we'll get Eva out,' he said.

***

I let the boy go back into East Berlin. Again, I'd done something I wouldn't have dreamt of doing only a few days ago. The urgency of the situation, coupled with the fact of my emotional disorientation, maybe even the alcohol, was playing havoc with my decision making. As I sat waiting at the apartment with Tanja on my knee, I fully expected a thunderbolt from Klaus when he returned. Gerd and I had gone on without him, making our plans and acting accordingly. There I was again exploiting a teenager, but then again, Klaus Schultz was full of surprises in his own right.

As soon as he walked in, he looked lighter than before, more positive in his manner.

'How did it go?' I asked, trying to hide Gerd's lack of presence for a while, by getting Klaus talking.

'He's going to help us,' Klaus said with meaning, his eyes focused, if slightly watery.

'Have you been drinking?' I asked.

'A couple of glasses of schnapps with Burzin.'

I was a bit surprised and evidently it showed on my face.

'I know, I know,' Klaus said, defensively, 'but the man seemed almost humble for once in his life.'

'Can we trust him, Klaus?'

He sighed, seemingly coming back down to earth. I had that ability, grounding people, or dragging them down, I wasn't sure which.

'Believe me, I have asked myself that question a few times, Jack. I don't like the man, or, at least, I didn't...'

'You don't sound too sure now?' I teased.

'All I can say is, in difficult times, you form unusual alliances. I have relied on him twice, once in Kolyma, when he saved my life, and once in Berlin, when he saved my son's. What would you Americans say? He's got a pretty good strike rate.'

'It sounds like you've been hard on the man.'

'Maybe. He was still camp commandant when some of my comrades were killed at the mine in Siberia. And he's still KGB, whichever way you look at it.'

'So what exactly brought you together?'

'And keeps bringing us together,' Klaus said. 'Circumstances, I suppose. That, and one man. Dobrovsky.'

He was staring at the map now, his mind seemingly ticking over.

'Where's Gerd?' he asked, looking around the apartment.

'Ah yes, I meant to mention that.'

His eyes narrowed and I waited for the explosion.

'He's gone to look for Eva,' I said, rather meekly.

He glanced up from the table and looked straight through me. His eyes moved slowly back to map. 'Where, exactly?'

I stood up and joined him at the table, thinking this was going better than I expected. 'By his thinking, and all the reconnaissance we did yesterday, he thought here in the Plänterwald area.'

Klaus nodded briefly. 'And why?'

I shrugged. 'It's the best area to escape, in his eyes. Away from the centre, away from the guards and crowds. He thought Eva would have figured that out and headed there. I know it's a long shot...'

'He's smart.'

My mouth hung open, expecting him to be angry he'd not been included in the decision making. He turned at looked at me. 'Well, the boy is showing initiative and besides, we can't help her until we find her.'

I must have looked slightly flabbergasted because he went on, 'Who else is going to look, Jack? You? Me? We're slightly more sought after than Eva on the list of undesirables.'

He was changing the subject now, keen to dig. I was still too shocked to move on. 'Tell me, apart from Helmi, who were Eva's friends? I didn't really know anybody.'

'She had friends at the hospital, but she didn't have much time to socialise, what with her work and looking after Tanja.'

'No, I mean in East Berlin,' Klaus persisted.

'Oh, I see. She didn't really mention many people, aside from Helmi. She did mention someone she used to go to school with. I believe she was training to be a doctor too, at the Charité.' I racked my brains for a moment. 'Sophie Reinhardt. They were friends from way back, but I never actually met her. Have you asked Maria?'

He looked sheepish now.

'She doesn't know Eva is stuck in East Berlin?'

'I will tell her. I just thought we might get her out before I rang her. I didn't want to worry her.'

I had to raise my eyebrows at that one. It was a bit late for that.

'Anyway, why do you want to know about Eva's friends?'

'It's a matter of knowing where to start the search. Gerd's idea is a good one and he is free to move around there, whereas we are marked men, as I said. Burzin can only really help once we've found her,' Klaus explained.

'And her friends?'

'Well, yes, Burzin can also use his contacts to check out her friends, maybe follow them discreetly. They might lead us to Eva. I'm afraid finding Eva is pretty much up to us.'

I swallowed hard. I felt a wave of anxiety wash over me again. I don't know if it was Klaus telling us we were on our own, or relying on Gerd, or simply the alcohol wearing off.

'When did Gerd say he would be back?'

I shrugged, still lost in my momentary depression. 'When he finds her, I suppose, even if it is a long shot.'

'I'll give Burzin a call with this name. It's something, at least. Until then, we'll just have to wait and see what Gerd can turn up.'

I was taken aback by his almost nonchalant nature, relative to previous encounters with the man. It wasn't the Klaus Schultz of the last few days. 'What? We can't do anything else?' I asked.

'Not unless you know anybody in East Berlin who can help us. Someone who knows the place very well, knows Eva and also, and this is most important, you would trust with your life.'

This didn't feel like enough for me. I needed more. I wasn't really in a place to be as accepting as Klaus. It was like his mood of the last few days had transferred to me.

'What about another check of the border?' I said, grasping at straws.

Klaus had started to warm up some milk for Tanja. 'We already know where we can get her out. There are a number of places.'

'You seem pretty relaxed all of sudden,' I said, snapping.

'I'm not relaxed about anything, Jack. I am just focused on what we can do, what we can control. And at the moment, we are doing all we can. I have every faith in the boy and...'

'The Russian?'

Klaus shrugged.

I was finding him a difficult character to fathom. Maybe I was finding my own emotions difficult to deal with, too. Either way, I couldn't sit in the apartment any longer. I needed to do something. Exactly what I was going to do, I wasn't sure, but I couldn't just sit tight and wait. I grabbed my jacket and headed for the door.

'Where are you going?' Klaus asked, milk bottle in one hand, baby in the other.

'Out. I need some fresh air,' I said, moodily.

***

Matt Collins stared back at me, wide-eyed. 'No way, Jack. You're crazy.'

He didn't like my request, but that wouldn't be the first time.

'They'll have no idea it came from you, if I get caught. Just some papers, that's all I need, Matt.'

I'd come to another decision whilst stomping around the streets of Schöneberg like a man possessed. Probably another bad decision, but I wasn't about to sit around and wait. I couldn't. Matt wasn't exactly in agreement with my current line of thinking. His high-pitched response gave me a hint. 'That's *all* you need?'

It was time to plead. 'Look, Matt, I'm in a difficult place. I've got to find her. It's driving me crazy sitting here and doing nothing. I've got to do something.'

'Ok. Let's just say I go along with this madcap plan, and by the way, this does not mean I am agreeing, far from it. I just want to know how far ahead you've planned on this one. Come on, if I give you the papers, what are you going to do when you get over there?'

It was at that moment I realised I was hopelessly out of my depth. I was a journalist, so I knew how to get information. The problem is, without a network of informants I could tap, I was lost. Alone in a hostile city, finding Eva was already like looking for the proverbial needle in a haystack. Without help, I was as lost as the next man. Even with the papers, I knew I at least needed Gerd to guide me through. But somehow I was under an obsessive need to do something, so all these logical reasons not to go and find her became mere operational details. On top of that, I wasn't about to let Matt Collins know how desperate I was really feeling.

'Don't worry about me. It's all taken care of. I have contacts over there, people who know their way around every corner. I just need to get back over.' I was lying through my teeth. I knew it and I didn't like it. Well, I suppose lying, per se, was a part of my daily life as a journalist, but to my best friend, it was hard.

Matt wasn't giving in though. 'Not good enough, Jack. I want to know details.'

I sighed. This was putting me on the spot. 'We have intelligence, people who have seen Eva. She's going to try and escape and I've got to be there to make sure she does, Matt. Come on, for me. I wouldn't ask you for anything.'

'I've helped you many times, Jack. You should be taking care of Tanja, rather than thinking up harebrained schemes like this. The list of favours has to stop somewhere.' He paused and stared at me for a moment.

I gave him my best wounded look.

Matt said, 'What you are asking is highly irregular. I will get fired if I'm found out. These IDs are for our operatives, not for some lovesick friend who has gone over the edge. Now, if I was to go along with this in a professional manner, I would want to hear the plan, and challenge it, to ensure it has been considered properly.' He looked at me again. I was feeling nervous now, even a bit desperate. I was hoping he couldn't sense it.

'My intelligence tells me she's headed for the Treptower Park area with supplies. The area is on the border with Neukölln and the Teltow Canal.'

'So how will you locate her, considering she'll be hiding?'

'I have informants helping me.'

'You trust them, Jack? East Berlin has many informants, not all what they seem to be.'

'Sure, I trust him...'

'Him? You said informants before. So it's one person?'

My mouth opened and closed without anything coming out.

'What else are you not saying, Jack? What are you not telling me?'

I hung my head. I was ashamed of myself. Here I was bullshitting a man who had saved my life on more than one occasion and I, his, if the truth be known. It was time to come clean and give him the full story.

So I did. I told him about Gerd, what he had deduced about where Eva would go. I knew it was tenuous at best. I told him about Klaus and Dobrovsky. It was out in the open and even if I felt better, I knew my chances of getting Matt to help me were dwindling.

I looked up and could see the pity in his eyes. I could see whatever he wanted to say was difficult for him. 'They know you, Jack, by sight. They'll be looking out for you, not only the Stasi, but after the scene at the Brandenburg Gate, many of the soldiers and militia, too. I can do some things to help you, to try and locate her without you having to go over there...'

'No, Matt. I have to do this myself.'

There was a pause. I knew I had said something which summed up the situation and my predicament. I also knew what was coming, and honestly, I didn't want to push him anymore. I couldn't find it in me.

'You're right. You do have to do this yourself. I'm sorry, Jack, but I can't help you this time.'

***

My solitude was complete. No Matt and, most of all, no Eva. Sure, I had Tanja and, thankfully, Matt's rejection of help over the papers didn't stretch to his wife helping with Tanja. Gerd was hopefully in the eastern sectors searching for Eva, but it wasn't enough for me. My anxiety was pushing me to act. I was banking on myself, which, knowing my past record on reliability, frankly made me scared; not only for me, but for Eva, too.

For some reason, I had driven back towards the border and was wandering aimlessly around the Tiergarten. That Monday evening was warm, so it wasn't a bad place to be physically, even if, mentally, I was somewhere altogether more hostile. I was desperate to get on with things, even if I knew the rush to do so was at the expense of any rational, workable plan. It was then an opportunity presented itself.

There was a crowd of what the East German newspapers would call "rowdies" on the western side of the fence on Lennestrasse. I estimated there were a couple hundred of them gathered over the road from the edge of the Tiergarten. This area was between the Brandenburg Gate and Potsdamer Platz and by now, around six hours since I'd last parked in the area, the fence posts had been well and truly hammered into the asphalt and a simple wire mesh fence connected the posts.

As I moved closer to the group, I could see there was also a crowd, albeit a smaller one, gathered on the eastern side. There were only two rather worried looking guards between the two groups and the fence. The atmosphere was spicy, to say the least. Many of the West Berliners were hurling insults at the guards. The people on the eastern side were taking a growing interest in the situation.

The thing that surprised me, given the central area, was the lack of guards. It wasn't what we'd witnessed the day before. Maybe it was the relatively late hour or maybe the East German authorities thought they had the situation under control, but to have only two guards in the area proved to be a mistake on their part. It was only when a handful of the group on the western side started to vehemently shake the fence that I really started to take notice. Suddenly the group on the eastern side were alive and looked ready to rush to the fence at any time, even if the guards were doing their level best to hold them back.

Then it happened. The fence gave way. The crowd on the western side held back the open fence. They started to beckon those on the eastern side towards them. Some of them made an immediate bolt, taking their chance of freedom with both hands. Others looked decidedly more reticent, like they were agonising over the decision to leave friends and family. Eventually people started to move westwards through the gap. People of all ages made their bid for freedom. It was difficult to tell who had been on the western or eastern side before the fence had been breached. The scene was one of utter tumult.

To make matters worse, one of the guards had disappeared to summon help. It tended to heighten the panic; everyone knew this opportunity wouldn't last much longer as the fence would be resealed soon. I estimated up to fifty people had escaped to the western side before it dawned on me what a chance this represented for me. I only had my American passport. I knew I was a marked man. But here was the chance to get into East Berlin without having to take the risk of being discovered at a border checkpoint. Here was my chance to get to Eva.

I felt the elation rush through me. Maybe it was adrenalin, I don't know. I didn't think too much about it, or what I would do when I got to the other side. I just did it. The fence was held back, people were flowing in all directions, and I just slipped through like a ghost, unnoticed. I didn't look back. Whatever was going on behind me wasn't my concern. I did have a fleeting thought that the episode would have made a great story, but it didn't last long. Before I knew it, I was away from the border and back on the streets of East Berlin.

CHAPTER 30

MONDAY, 14th AUGUST 1961,
EAST BERLIN

Hans Erdmann slept fitfully that day. He found it difficult to relax let alone sleep. His meeting with Alexei hadn't exactly filled him with hope. He was under no illusion how his wish to leave the DDR would be perceived. Hans worked with a particular faction within the GRU, and nobody in the East German hierarchy knew of this work. Hans had believed Alexei and his colleagues could influence things in East Germany for the better, to keep the Stalinist hardliners like Ulbricht in check. It clearly hadn't worked. To Hans, the recent measures on the border were like 1953 all over again. Personally, he felt he had done all he could. He had nothing here. In fact, he'd had nothing since Monika died.

In contrast, his work back at Treptow barracks seemed meaningless. Sitting at his desk, Hans forced himself to keep up the pretence. He took a gulp of coffee and picked up the day's report from his overladen desk. From the reports he read, the border operation continued to hold. There was more work to be done, however. Along most of the border section for which he was responsible, a simple fence had been erected. All along Ebertstrasse from the Gate, across Potsdamer Platz and along Zimmer Strasse, the fence and a high number of guards had proved effective so far. The trains travelling to

West Berlin had been stopped and the train stations closest to West Berlin closed. Entrance steps to the stations, such as on Potsdamer Platz had already been bricked up and the station platforms were heavily guarded.

There were more difficult areas to police, such as the waterways, the Spree, and the canals. The border followed the Teltow Canal for three kilometres in some places. These areas remained the weakness in Ulbricht's whole plan. While people were still able to escape in numbers—the Marienfelde refugee camp arrivals were still very high, according to secret reports—the project would fail. It gave Hans hope on the one hand, for him and for Bernie, but Hans knew the regime. They wouldn't stand for the current position. They would continue the push to plug the gaps.

Hans arrived at a signed order close to the bottom of his pile. His instinct had been right, and he was glad it wasn't yet failing him. The order was about working harder to prevent escapes. He focused in on the important words, that they should use "all possible measures" to prevent the continuing "border transgressions." He shook his head, knowing what the euphemism meant. They were already implementing forced rehousing of inhabitants living in apartments directly on the border line. It wouldn't be long before they were being urged to ever greater measures against escapees. Closing the border was never going to be the end. Hans made a mental note to check the time of the order. He had little intention of passing on these orders to his men. At the very worst, he could delay them.

His mind was only focused on what he perceived as his lifeline. He hoped Alexei had contacted his controller to pass on his demands. He was well aware of what it could mean. He knew he could disappear into the night, just like Bernie. Hans felt he had little choice. It had happened to Bernie and he'd only been doing his job, so he weighed up his options and selected one. Not the safest option, but it was all or nothing.

His thoughts were interrupted by the young Lieutenant Riedle entering his office.

'Permission to give my report, Colonel.'

He wasn't used to such formality with Bernie. The boy looked worried.

'Go ahead, Riedle.'

'No major incidents in the Mitte, sir, except for one small breakthrough on Lennestrasse a couple of hours ago. The fence was quickly repaired and the situation is under control.'

'Good. I will go and inspect the area myself.' Deep down Hans could feel his hopes surge at the news. He was elated to hear the population weren't just standing for the measures. There was some fight in them, after all.

'Anything else, Riedle?'

Riedle started to look a little uncomfortable, shifting on his feet, his lips pursed like there was something bothering him.

'What is it, Riedle?'

Hans looked into his eyes and could see what he had seen in so many people over the last few years. Fear.

'Come on, man, out with it. We don't have time to waste,' Hans barked.

'I received a call earlier this morning, just after you left. It was from the deputy minister himself.'

Hans felt his stomach lurch. 'Go on.'

'He was very hard, Colonel. I didn't know what to do. He threatened me with arrest if I didn't comply...'

'Just stay calm, Riedle. What did he want?'

'He wanted me to pass on the order...'

Hans picked up the piece of paper from his desk. 'You mean this order...'

Riedle didn't even look, 'Yes, the one about escapes. He told me I must pass the order on to all sectors in person.'

Hans took a deep breath. In front of him was a scared young man, his lip quivering. He wondered what would come of his city.

'You should have tried to contact me, Riedle.'

'I sent a car to your apartment after you left. I am sorry, Colonel...I had no choice.'

Hans knew he must have been watched. As soon as he left the barracks, the order was sent and the call was made.

'So Deputy Minister Marks asked you to say what, *exactly*?'

'That I must tell the men to protect the border using all possible measures...'

'Yes, I can read that, Riedle. But that wasn't the end of it, was it?'

Riedle looked very uncomfortable now. Hans feared what was coming. It was typical that the orders should be given in person, so nothing was committed to paper.

'He told me I should inform all sectors that all possible measures should be used to prevent escapes, including the use of force.'

Hans shook his head, not wanting to believe what he was hearing, or to consider the consequences.

'He told you that all escapees are to be shot, didn't he, Riedle?'

Riedle closed his eyes and nodded.

'...And to only pass the order on verbally?'

'Yes, Colonel.'

***

Eva and Sophie did not know what to expect when they left the tent that morning. They were taking no chances. They had little idea what they would encounter in the border areas, so they dressed as if they were simply out walking for the day. They were keen to blend into their surroundings and not attract any unwanted attention, given people would be looking for Eva. They need not have worried, however. As they got closer to the border they could see people hanging around,

207

waiting and watching. They were in groups, young and old alike. Eva saw young children on bikes, housewives with shopping bags, and people around her own age. Many appeared simply curious. They watched what was happening on the border for the spectacle it was.

Along Kiefholzstrasse the fence posts were already in place. People on the western side were standing right up to the fence, some even leaning on top of it with their forearms, talking to people on the other side. On the eastern side, Eva could see smaller groups standing as close as a metre from the fence. The fence itself contained no barbed wire. Eva noticed it wouldn't be much different to that of a garden in some of the nicer districts of Berlin. They were watched by guards, albeit in a very relaxed manner. They were in groups of two or three, talking and smoking, but present nonetheless. Eva counted twelve NVA guards on the street, all armed with rifles or machine guns.

From there, they moved on. There were so many people milling around on the eastern side, it made Eva feel more comfortable, and allowed them to move around without fear. Many of the people were carrying bags and even suitcases. These people didn't care if the authorities knew they were trying to escape. There was desperation now in the people. It had been 36 hours since the borders had been closed. The gloves were off. It was clear to most, if not all, that these measures were permanent. There was no going back from here.

As if to prove this point, in the Heidekampgraben area, a ditch ran through the wood, although the beck tended to be dry in the summer. Even in this semi-rural area, the guards worked shirtless in the warm sun, knocking in the fence posts under the watchful gaze of the armed guards. Behind them was a long coil of barbed wire to prevent impromptu escapes whilst the more permanent fence was completed. Slowly but surely, the authorities were plugging the gaps in the border. It made Eva feel anxious to get out now. On more than one occasion, Sophie reminded her they were only there to check the border. When they attempted escape, it would be under the cloak of darkness.

Eventually, they reached the area where the border followed the Teltow Canal. Through the trees, where Eva and Sophie stood watching with a group of other people, guards patrolled periodically up and down the edge of the canal. Here there were no physical barriers in place, only the guards, and, of course, the water providing its own natural hurdle. The canal itself was no more than ten metres wide in places. On the opposite bank lay Neukölln and the American sector of West Berlin.

After a long day checking along the border, Eva and Sophie finally made it back to the tent. As they cooked a final meal before nightfall, Sophie's view remained unaltered. 'The canal is the easiest place. They only had guard patrols, and in darkness, there's no way they can stop people crossing over.'

Eva remained silent. She couldn't argue with Sophie's logic. Of all the places they'd seen, there was no doubt it was the weakest section. The canal was also long enough to select a quiet place to cross. It made it very difficult to guard. However, logic was all well and good, but it didn't stop Eva hating the thought of getting into the water. Ever since that day on Mügelsee when she'd nearly drowned, except for a hot bath, she'd not been in water of any description. If it hadn't been for Ulrich hauling her out, she wouldn't be here today.

'Eva?' Sophie was chewing on some bread with her usual tenacity. 'Are you with me?'

Eva screwed up her face.

'Oh, come on! It's not even deep. Don't tell me you're still petrified of water!'

'You know I can't stand it, Soph.'

'Where's the rebel now? Here's the woman who survived a Stasi interrogation, but she's scared of the water,' she teased.

Eva just scoffed and turned away from her.

'Look, we can walk across. It won't even reach your chin. I'll be with you all the way.'

Eva wasn't convinced. She knew the fear was irrational, but it didn't matter.

'Eva, look at me!' Sophie's voice was stern. Eva reluctantly lifted up her head. 'We are getting out of here and the canal is the easiest and safest way. We will get out together. I promise you. There won't be any problems.'

Eva found it impossible to counter what Sophie was saying. She didn't have a reasonable argument. In all the other places on the border, fences were in place and the guards more numerous. There was no rational defence, only that she was more scared of the water than the guards.

Sophie wasn't giving up. 'It's like this: We have to go into the water to get out, for you to see Tanja again, to see Jack again, to start our lives over again. We have no choice. For you, it's that or a Stasi cell, because, if you don't get out, you know they will find you eventually.'

Eva put the down the piece of cheese she'd been trying to eat for the last five minutes. There was no way she could eat, giving the way she felt. She knew Sophie was right. She'd put things in stark perspective. She had to be strong. Eva took a deep breath, 'Ok. Soph, you win. The canal it is.'

'Good girl.' Sophie tapped Eva's shoulder. 'Now, get some food down you. I reckon we've got two hours before it gets dark. Then we are out of this place, for good.'

***

Hans headed back to his apartment in Friedrichshain, his jacket slung over his shoulder. The walk in the warm, slightly humid air could only do him good. The climate didn't relax him, however, and his pace only mirrored his frantic thoughts. He had been toying with ideas to limit the impact of the order Riedle had passed on to the men from

Marks. Hans cursed Marks' duplicity, in going directly to his chain of command, bypassing him, and more to the point, giving the order as soon as Hans had left the Command Centre for the first time in 36 hours. It was all well planned, another way to undermine him and push him off course. He'd told Alexei he didn't care anymore, but he couldn't help worrying about his men, nor for the innocent people who would be caught up in the effects of such an order. If Hans Erdmann would have been concentrating on what was going on around him, rather than focusing on his troubles, he may well have noticed the innocuous looking beige delivery van over his right shoulder. Such was his inner turmoil, he didn't.

He first noticed the man on his right, as tall as Hans, but much stockier. 'Got a light?' The voice was gruff, the manner curt.

Hans turned to answer, catching a scent of sweat as he did. This allowed the man on his left to link under his arm. Another strong man, he had the grip of a vice. The van was now level with them and Hans tried to struggle free. The last thing he saw of the outside world was a man walking his dog. The man turned away, petrified, pulling his small, white terrier after him.

Now at the back of the van, doors open in preparation, Hans felt a large paw on the top of his head, forcing him downwards. He tried to prevent the inevitable, by locking his legs and digging his heels into the cobbles. His knees were fast against the back bumper of the van. A forceful thump in the back took the wind out of Hans and put paid to his brief resistance. He fell, hands first, onto the splintered wood of the van floor. Both of his legs were then lifted, one man each side, and he was deposited in the back of the van. He couldn't see through to the front. He heard the doors slam shut and Hans rolled over to get a view of his silent assailants. Immediately his head was covered with a dark bag. Hans went to kick out, taking a swipe at mid-air with his right foot. That was the last thing he remembered.

211

***

He felt the throbbing at the back of his head. Instinctively, Hans went to check the damage with his hand, but found he couldn't. He was sitting, his hands and feet bound to a chair, the bag still in place. He was relying on his senses. It was a quiet place, but he could hear voices talking in the distance. It sounded like Russian. Every small sound echoed. He was in a large, empty building. He smelled tobacco smoke, smooth and silky, more American than Russian.

'Heh!' Hans croaked.

The talking stopped and footsteps moved in his direction. Hans steeled himself, expecting a blow at any moment. He felt a presence close to him now. They were watching over him; the smell of tobacco smoke was stronger.

The hood was whipped off, which shocked Hans. He flinched, expecting more punishment. He heard laughter. There were two heavyset men to his right, leaning, arms crossed, against a black saloon car, no doubt his abductors. In front of Hans was a well-dressed man in his fifties. His suit was smart, rather than expensive, his shoes well-polished. His manner was calm, even a touch languid. A cigarette was held leisurely in his hand, close to completion. He was in control.

Hans had expected Marks, or at least Germans, if this is how his disappearance was to happen. The Russians had brought him to a large, bomb-damaged, unused warehouse. They could leave him here and nobody would find him. Not until it was too late.

The man deliberately took another cigarette from a pack, Lucky Strikes, and lit it with the dying embers of the previous one. He pulled on the new cigarette and expelled a large cloud of smoke above his head.

'Alexei sends his greetings,' the man finally said. There was little warmth in the sentiment, but at least Hans knew who they were now.

He could breathe a bit easier. The meeting wasn't exactly as he'd envisaged it.

Hans remained silent, unsure just how to begin. His own manner was far from relaxed. He was on the defensive, scared. Hans knew that was the purpose of his dramatic abduction from the street. He was well aware just how precarious his position was.

The man moved slowly towards him. 'I got Alexei's message.' He was in front of Hans now, who could only look up at him, smoke floating from his nostrils. As he bent down, Hans smelled a very faint whiff of cologne. 'I want you to know, you are not in a place to make demands, Herr Erdmann.'

Hans found his voice from somewhere. 'I asked for help. After everything I've done for you people, I feel I am in a position to do that.'

Hans felt a foot on the chair between his legs and he was pushed backwards. He knew he was toppling over but there was nothing he could do to prevent it. The back of the chair hit the ground with a thud, but without injuring Hans. He rolled onto his side, his cheek landing in a small pool of rusty water.

The man crouched down in front of his face. He moved the burning cigarette close to Hans' left eye, enough for him to feel the heat. 'You work for me. Don't you forget it.' Hans was waiting for the cigarette to be applied to his eyelid, but the man immediately stood up and barked instructions at the other two.

They ran to Hans and quickly brought him upright. They untied his hands and feet and walked back towards the car. He rubbed the cold water from his face and neck. Better water than blood, Hans thought.

'Now,' the man was talking again, before Hans could react, 'your comrade has disappeared, one Bernhard Schwarzer?'

Hans nodded, 'I believe he has been taken...'

'I know who has him and I know exactly where he is being kept.'

'You know? Is he okay?'

'He's alive...for now.'

'We need to get him out quickly…'

The man raised his hand. 'Slowly, Erdmann. One step at a time. We'll get to Schwarzer.' He flicked some ash from his sleeve. 'You mentioned a KGB general to Alexei?'

Hans was surprised at the sudden change of subject. 'Yes, Dobrovsky. What about it?'

'Tell me how you met him.'

Hans sighed, a little impatient at the diversion. He knew he had no choice in the matter, so he told him about the incident on Parisier Platz with Dobrovsky, Kaymer, and the missing woman, Schultz. Hans noted a small smile of satisfaction on the man's lips when he got to the part about the woman's escape.

'Good. That is useful information, Erdmann.' The man was pensive now. So much so, he didn't have a cigarette in his hand. Hans noted the two butts by his right foot, the last still burning.

'I need you to get Bernie out,' Hans said, firmly.

'I know what you want.' The man seemed relaxed now, as if what Hans had asked might not be out of the question. He didn't want to miss an opportunity, especially as he felt the Dobrovsky story had been something more than just slightly useful to the Russian. 'And when you release my friend, I want you to get both of us out of East Berlin.'

The last comment brought the cigarette pack out again. The man started to tap an unlit nail on the packet. He shrugged. 'That's not totally impossible.'

Hans breathed a huge sigh of relief. He wasn't sure if it was elation or shock.

'You will be useful to us in the West,' he said, before expertly flicking his lighter and taking another gulp of his apparent lifeblood.

It certainly wasn't what Hans had in mind, but he was ready to agree to anything, for now. 'That's possible,' Hans said.

The man smiled quickly. 'Oh, I know it is.' He was still thinking, computing the possibilities; then, he looked like he had made the decision. 'So, here's what you'll do. You go back to work. Carry on with your job as normal and I will be in touch.'

Hans was incredulous, wondering how he could continue as normal after everything that had happened. 'That's it?'

The man shrugged. 'Well, I am finished, unless you have any other *demands.*'

Hans was still in shock, but managed, 'Your name, perhaps?'

'I am sorry?'

'You told me I am working for you now. Who are you?'

The man flicked his spent cigarette into a puddle, causing it to sizzle as it was abruptly extinguished.

'Burzin,' he said.

CHAPTER 31

MONDAY, 14th AUGUST 1961,
EAST BERLIN

I wasn't thinking clearly. If I had been, I wouldn't have been walking the streets of East Berlin as a wanted man, without either Klaus or Gerd knowing where I was. It was getting late and with the sun fast disappearing, I was only heading for where I thought Eva to be. It wasn't as if I was going to walk into a hotel and bed down for the night. To go to a hotel meant I had to be registered. To be registered, I needed an identity, and I only had my passport with me. That identity was compromised. To an uninvolved onlooker, analysing my situation, I was an idiot. To me, my emotions were ruling my head. To Treptower Park, and the Plänterwald area, I headed.

On the way, some military vehicles passed on the roads, heading to and from the sector border. Each time I saw one, my heart sunk. I averted my gaze to the pavement and kept moving, much like the few ordinary Berliners I encountered. Even I worked out this wasn't the time to be asking for directions. Any request to see my documentation could have been the end of my foray into the eastern sectors.

It took me over an hour to reach the park. On the park, there were a few long military tents. Presumably they didn't have required barracks space for the influx of military personnel required for the operation. In my haste to get to Eva, I wasn't prepared, nor had I even considered how I might react to any Vopos I might come across. At the edge of the park I saw two guards no more than twenty yards in the distance. They had stopped a man on a bike. I felt a momentary shame that I was glad it wasn't me; even at that distance I could tell they weren't making a polite enquiry about his health. The way the man fumbled nervously in his pocket, presumably for his ID card, was testament to that.

In hindsight it wasn't the brightest move, but I figured the guards were more preoccupied with the poor soul they were harassing than noticing me suddenly change direction and take the sidewalk on the other side of the road. What I didn't bargain for was anybody behind me who might have seen my eagerness to avoid the hazard up ahead. Unfortunately, the shout from behind me belatedly alerted me to that threat.

I didn't stop. I reached the side of the road with my mouth fast becoming as dry as a desert. I had an innate urge to glance over my shoulder. I didn't though, I just quickened my pace.

'You, halt!' the shout came again. This time it was harsher, more insistent.

There's something about the German language and how it can appear barked and dangerous at certain times. The familiar "Du" term undoubtedly had a menacing tone to it. As familiar as it was, if I did stop, I knew I wasn't about to be invited to a garden party.

I didn't look back, I just kept moving. It was a ridiculous thought, but I was still grasping on to the hope that they were making their overtures to someone else. My fast walk broke into an anxious trot. If I was hoping not to draw attention to myself, I knew I'd now broken all the rules in the book. I could see Matt Collins shaking his head at me.

There were more shouts behind me now. It was difficult to judge how far away they were. With the adrenalin now well and truly pumping, every noise was magnified tenfold. What made matters worse, the shouts had attracted the attention of the original guards, now away to my right. They had suddenly lost interest in the man on the bike, who was peddling gleefully away into the distance. The threat to me had consequently doubled in its intensity.

Up ahead the street hit a crossroads. My only choice was to take a left away from the immediate danger. All the pretence of a trot had now been dispensed with and I was moving at top speed. That was, of course, my top speed, which, after all those long days and nights in Leydicke, didn't amount to any sort of rate at all. Fortunately for me, my pursuers were weighed down with heavy boots and uniforms. To this point, I'd not seen any weapons, but the mere thought made me move a little quicker.

Behind me I could hear more angry shouts, seemingly closer, but it could well have been the fact we were now on a street with buildings on either side. I was starting to get desperate. My mind was working fast. I glanced quickly at the opportunities on either side; there were alleyways and courtyards. However, with the men on the same street as me, and clearly able to see which direction I would take, I figured that wasn't a good plan. Actually, maybe I should have thought through a plan earlier, then I wouldn't have been in this mess.

I was up to my neck in it and escape looked all but impossible. After all, I wasn't in any state fit enough to maintain my mediocre speed over a distance. The guards chasing me were probably conscripts and undoubtedly fitter than me. I was about to give up and take a gamble on one of the off street options I'd already rejected, when I saw the last passenger getting on a tram about twenty yards in the distance.

I didn't even think about it. Much like my instinctive decision to walk through the open fence on Lennestrasse, I knew my target. Unfortunately, with me still ten yards or so short of it, my target started to move off. I knew they were closing in on me because I could clearly hear the boots stomping behind me, like they were flattening the road. I felt like a condemned man, in all but name.

The rest became a blur. My mind flashed between Tanja and Eva and the power in my legs took on an extra dimension I thought I'd left behind in Korea. My lungs were fit to burst, but the back of the tram was now no more than two or three yards in front of me. It wasn't quite close enough to stretch out and grab the rail, mainly because I feared losing my balance.

Then, and to this day I don't know how, the handrail of the steps of the tram was in my hand. The second hand joined the first and I hauled myself up on to the back step in the nick of time. I didn't have the energy to look behind me straightaway as my eyes were losing focus behind the stars, and the ringing in my ears meant I couldn't do anything useful.

When I did look back, I could see at least six of them. They had all given up the chase, doubled over at their exertions. For now at least, I was still a free man.

***

Eva didn't know if she was more scared at the thought of getting caught in the act of escape or of slipping into the cold, murky waters of the Teltow Canal. However, she felt, they had agreed to the plan, and there was no going back. They dressed in the darkest clothes they had between them; Sophie a dark pullover and trousers, Eva a T-shirt and navy slacks. It was a warm, humid night, so they weren't going to suffer from cold. If all went to plan, they'd be across the canal and in the western sectors minutes after entering the water. If it did not, well, those thoughts were for the weak, according to the ever ebullient Sophie.

Sophie led the way when they left the tent just after eleven. Eva's nagging doubts about their method of escape slowed her pace. On more than one occasion, Sophie turned and hissed at her to keep up. There were other people around in the dark wooded area, no doubt finalising their own escape plans. Back from the border, there were no guards; they probably had enough to do guarding the expanse of the border area itself.

They first crossed a wooden footbridge over a tributary of the Spree River. After the river, the area of the Plänterwald was wooded, interspersed with open grassed areas. They came upon a small road. As they crouched behind some bushes, they heard voices ahead of them. They saw a young man pushing a scooter over the road and into the trees on the other side.

Sophie whispered, 'We should let them go on. We don't want to get too close.'

Eva wasn't in a rush to get to the canal and was quite content to watch others make their escape. There was no other reason to be in that area at the dead of night. Although how they planned to carry a scooter across the water was anybody's guess.

'Are you okay?' Sophie asked.

Eva nodded. She wasn't, but this wasn't the time or the place for another lengthy pep talk.

The road ahead clear, Sophie motioned to her and they quickly crossed over and on into the trees. There was little noise except the swish of the shoes in the longer grass. An evening dew had formed, leaving the bottoms of Eva's trousers damp. She'd soon have more than just wet trousers, Eva thought. The canal was no more than 200 metres from this point. They had to be totally silent now. Guards had been patrolling the track by the canal during the day; it was possible there were others hidden in the trees. Eva could feel the tension rising in her body, the closer they moved towards their target.

They reached a small clearing in the trees. They could now see the last bushes before the canal, perhaps ten metres ahead of them. Sophie gestured to her right. Eva could just make out two figures carrying a large board between them. Sophie flicked her head left. It was best to stay clear of other escapees.

They covered the final distance to the canal crouched down. They were at the last line of trees. Immediately in front of them was a track of around two metres in width, then the banking fell away to the water's edge. Eva could hear the lapping of the water. Here, they would wait, as already planned back at the tent. They were to check the frequency of the guard patrol before going anywhere near the water. Sophie appeared to be in control and focused. Eva could only feel the tension across her forehead. She felt the ringing in her ears, every sound amplified. She was sure this was about the last few days she'd endured, as well as her fear of the water, now that they were so close.

They were both lying on their front, peering out across the canal. The far bank signified freedom to them; on a normal map it would mark the start of the district of Neukölln. That was their target. Sophie smiled at Eva. She looked faintly ridiculous; Sophie had insisted on smearing their faces in black boot polish for that last bit of camouflage.

'Look over there,' Sophie whispered, her eyes now wide with excitement.

Eva strained her eyes looking across the water to the far bank, but seeing nothing. Sophie pointed animatedly this time. About twenty metres to their right, Eva could now see what looked like young men carrying a small raft down to the water's edge. Immediately behind them, another man pushed a scooter over the track and down the bank. Eva couldn't quite believe what she was seeing. Were these people really trying to escape to the west with their scooter? Sophie shook her head in awe. Eva really hoped they would make it to the other side.

They watched transfixed, willing the group to get over before any of the patrols appeared. Two of them were in the water with the raft, holding it against the bank. One of the others pushed the scooter onto the raft and over onto its side. They were now four of them in total, all in the water, one each at a corner of the raft. Eva was amazed the raft floated. She felt a pang of anxiety as she saw the water lapping around the men's shoulders. She couldn't tell if they were actually swimming or touching the canal bottom, but they were moving.

Eva gripped Sophie's hand. She didn't know if it was fear or the excitement of witnessing this daring escape. She was willing the men over to the other side, as if it were she and Sophie making their escape. They were halfway across now, their progress painfully slow. The noise of splashing arms and feet could be heard from their position. Eva thought she heard voices away to her left. She strained her eyes in that direction, but it was impossible to make anything out due to the lack of any artificial light.

Finally the group made it to the far bank. Two of the young men were already out of the water. Lying down, they dragged the scooter from the raft onto the bank. Immediately, the other two pushed the raft away and clambered onto the grass. Just as they made it out of the water, Eva spotted the guard patrol on the track. They were around ten metres to Eva's left. The young men pushed the scooter up the bank and dashed into the trees. They had made it and Eva felt truly elated.

'You can let go of my hand now,' Sophie hissed.

Eva smiled. They turned their attention to the guards who were now heading towards them on the track. They pushed their faces down into the wet grass to wait for them to pass. Eva dare not breathe. She could hear them talking. They sounded so young, only interested in what would be for supper. They were oblivious to the escape that had just taken place, a few minutes before. As they passed, Eva popped up her head to see their backs disappearing down the track, rifles slung over their shoulders. Eva shivered at the thought of men so young having guns in their hands. Who knows how they could react in a pressured situation.

After a minute or so, Sophie rose, proceeding carefully out of their hiding place and onto the track. She checked the path in either direction then made her way back to Eva. 'Ok, let's go!' she whispered.

Eva felt her mouth go dry. It had been fine to watch other people trying to escape. Now, it was time for her to do it, to get into the water, but she found it difficult to move her legs. Sophie sensed her reticence and held out her hand, glancing nervously up and down the path as she did.

'Come on, Eva. I can't stand here all night.'

From somewhere, Eva found the power in her legs to leave her comfortable, sheltered position and move out into the open. Eva focused her eyes on the far bank. It seemed such a long way away at this moment in time.

They scrambled on hands and knees across the path, the soil slightly damp and gritty on Eva's hands. Now they were at the top of the bank. From here, the distance down to the water was much more than she had imagined. Sophie slid down expertly into the water. As she stood at the very edge of the canal, the water still reached just below her chest. Eva wished they could have used the raft like the men before, but with her as the passenger instead of an old scooter. She didn't want to go any closer to the water, but she knew she was a sitting duck at the top of the bank. To be caught would mean arrest for certain, perhaps even worse. She knew she had to move.

She could see Sophie's eyes wide, imploring her to get a move on. Eva felt sick at the thought of getting into the water. She could feel it around her nose and mouth, struggling for air, even though she wasn't yet actually in the canal. Then, Tanja came into her mind. It was a focus, a way to overcome her demons. She felt herself starting to slide down the wet grass and reeds towards the water's edge.

Suddenly the bank ended and the cold water rushed up her legs to her stomach. Her left foot touched the bottom, her right went deeper, the depth increasing quickly. She wanted to cry out, but Sophie held her with one hand, the other was clamped over her mouth, for both their sakes.

'You're okay, you're just fine,' she whispered, reassuring her.

Sophie started to move her away from the bank. Eva felt her eyes widen in panic, but Sophie was stronger than her. Before she could do anything about it, they were out of reach of the bank. Sophie spun her around, so Eva was facing backwards, and thrust a strong arm under, and across, her chest. Eva's feet still scrambled along the bottom, but the water was getting higher, up to her chest, lapping under her chin. Eva couldn't see how far they had to go, but the eastern bank was getting further away.

It was then Eva felt her right foot catch on something. Sophie continued to pull her body, but as much as she struggled to move her foot, she couldn't.

'Soph, my foot is stuck,' Eva managed.

'Eva, this is not the time.'

Eva tried to kick herself free, but it was stuck fast and whatever was holding her, was starting to hurt her ankle.

'I am telling you my foot is stuck and I cannot move it!'

Sophie moved back towards her. Eva was still struggling to get free, but she just couldn't lift her leg.

'It's not moving, Soph.' Eva was starting to panic.

Sophie said quickly, 'Ok. Don't move, I am going to take a look.' She took a deep breath and disappeared under the surface. Eva felt alone. She couldn't believe it was happening all over again. The water seemed to be rising closer to her mouth. She closed her eyes, trying to keep her emotions in check. She couldn't believe she'd even made it back into the water. She had to stay strong.

She felt Sophie pulling on her leg below the surface. Seconds later, she reappeared. After a second to regain her breath she said quickly, 'It's stuck between some railings.' She took another gulp of air. 'It's too heavy to move. We should try and take off your shoe to see if we can make your ankle smaller.'

Eva turned and looked over her shoulder. She could see they weren't even halfway across the canal. She seemed to be stuck fast, vulnerable and easy to spot from the bank. She felt the idea to escape across the canal had been doomed from the beginning. In fact, that went for both her attempts to make it to West Berlin.

It was then Eva heard voices away to the left. She immediately started to move her leg, but the more she did, the more pain she felt.

The voices were coming closer, even if the people were not yet in view. The fact they were talking openly suggested it was the guards, returning sooner than they'd anticipated.

'Sophie, you have to go.'

'You must be joking. I'm not leaving you here.'

'You have no choice.'

Eva looked to her left again and could see the two figures approaching. They had not been spotted yet, but it was only a matter of time. Eva turned back to her friend. Even she was looking anxious. Time was running out.

'If you don't go now, you'll never make it, Sophie!'

'Halt!'

Eva's heart sank.

In a flash, Sophie was off, not towards the western bank, but along the canal towards the approaching guards. Eva wondered what she was doing. She was already ten metres away from Eva, but no closer to the western bank, when she started to splash and shout. 'Over here!'

The guards started to flash lights further down the river close to where Sophie had been.

'Stop or we'll shoot!'

The attention of the guards was well away from Eva. Their flashlights were focused much further down the canal close to the western bank. Eva could see one of the guards was pointing his rifle at the water. Sophie was nowhere to be seen. Her attention distracted by the action, Eva didn't see the figure slip into the water directly opposite her on the eastern side.

Then she spotted Sophie scrambling up the bank on the western side. Sophie had made it across. The light followed her into the trees and the guard lowered his gun. It wouldn't be long before they spotted Eva marooned in the water.

Suddenly, Eva felt her foot lifting slightly. She turned her ankle and then she was free. A face broke the surface, covered in grime, dirt and hair over his face. He quickly grabbed Eva and pulled her back to the eastern bank, three metres away. It was too far to the other bank. Eva felt her head pushed down and into the grass close to the surface of the water. She turned to look at his face. She couldn't see him properly, only that he put his finger to his lips.

Torchlight flashed to and fro along the canal, moving towards them. The guards chatted excitedly to each other. Eva only pressed herself against the bank, making herself as small as possible. There was no time to think about anything else. The guards seemed to be on top of them now. Eva could hear them saying the person must have been alone. After what seemed like an age to Eva, they passed by and continued on down the canal.

Eva felt herself starting to breathe. She also felt the pain in her ankle for the first time. She allowed herself to turn to one side, to see who had helped free her. There was nobody there. Then an arm reached down in front of her face.

'We need to get away from here before they come back with reinforcements,' he said.

The arm pulled her onto the grassy bank. She looked ruefully to the far bank, grateful at least that Sophie had escaped. As much as she wanted to, Eva didn't have the energy to reach the far side of the canal. There wouldn't be time. He dragged her up and onto the top of the bank. She scrambled after him, limping back into the trees.

She fell on to the damp grass on her side, grateful to be out of the water. She pushed herself up on her elbow and tried to catch her breath. He was smiling at her, pushing his wet fringe out of his face. Eva was looking at the boy who worked for Jack, the one who had given her the film on the street.

CHAPTER 32

MONDAY, 14th AUGUST 1961,
EAST BERLIN

It was dark when I slipped back into the park area proper. It was a warm, sultry evening. There was a real stillness in the air, which magnified every sound. I'd just about physically recovered from my earlier close escape. Mentally there were question marks, but I had to admit a strange calmness had fallen over me as I went about the task of finding Eva. I was doing something, and that's exactly what my mind needed at that moment. If it was something useful, something sensible, well, that was another matter altogether.

I had a map of the area in my mind; God knows we'd studied it enough over the last couple of days. I knew the Spree was at my back, running alongside Treptower Park. Under normal circumstances, this would have been a nice place to relax in the sun. As it was, with sweat dripping down my back and my senses on high alert, I was far from a sun lounger. With its many trees and shrubs, at least the park provided good cover. I skirted around a lake, where the squawking geese made me feel uneasy, and crossed over a small beck using a wooden footbridge. To that point, I hadn't seen another soul. I did wonder where I was heading, and what my overall plan was, but being there wasn't about that. It made me feel closer to Eva, even if it was a harebrained scheme. For all I knew, she could have already escaped, or she could have been in another area of East Berlin altogether. As long as she wasn't in a Stasi cell, I would keep on searching.

I eventually came to a small road. Taking care to cross, I knew now that I was in the Plänterwald. With my jacket in one hand, I wiped the sweat from my brow with the other. Once over the road, I heard the sound of breaking branches in the trees to my right. It was difficult to see anybody, but then I heard voices. In a mild panic, I crouched down and scrambled across the twigs and damp grass to the base of a large tree. I heard cursing. I started to think. I was still quite a distance from the actual border area. I could have possibly mustered a legitimate reason to be here, if challenged, but I was jumpy after earlier. With my clothes and accent, even if my German was pretty good, I was out of place, just like Gerd had so kindly pointed out.

I waited a couple of minutes then got up to move. Within seconds I was back on the floor. I heard laughter. It was louder, closer. Then I heard a slight whimper. Allowing myself to peer around the tree, I could see two guards crossing a small opening. Straining at a tautly held, thick, leather leash was a large Alsatian. I tensed, wondering if the dog would pick up my scent. It wouldn't be difficult given how profusely I was sweating. They were opposite me now and I dared not let out a breath. I couldn't tell if they were patrolling the area, or just making their way back from the border. I looked again, my cheek pressed against the rough bark. They seemed in a hurry to get somewhere.

They were past me now, heading back in the direction of Treptower Park. I recalled the military tents on the entrance to the park, and supposed that's where they were heading. As long as they were away from me, I didn't care.

I waited what seemed like an age until they were out of earshot. I cautiously left the sanctuary of the tree line and made a quick jog across the clearing. I pushed quickly through some bushes on the other side, scratching the skin on my forearms in the process. My jacket got caught. It took me a few seconds to release it. I pulled on it, cursing to myself. Finally I freed it, and whipped round, nearly bumping into a man as I did. I saw another man with him. It all happened so quickly I didn't react. The man in front of me was in his early twenties, small and wiry. He eyed me suspiciously, then went on his way. His larger companion had a small bag over his shoulder. Both dressed in dark clothes, I figured that they were only heading for one place, and for one thing. I was just grateful they weren't guards. I was in the process of reminding myself to be more careful, when I had a brainwave.

Even I wasn't naïve enough to believe I could ask the men if they'd seen somebody of Eva's description in the area, I knew if I followed the pair, albeit from a safe distance, they might lead me to a place where other escapers were gathered. I was grasping at straws again, but the thinking that had led me here was built on conjecture and opinions, and it definitely beat fighting around in sharp bushes as a plan.

I guessed by the direction they'd taken, they were heading for the border. Recalling the map, the sector border ran along Kiefholzstrasse, through the Heidkampgraben area, then on to the long stretch of Teltow Canal. I wasn't keen to venture too close, as I knew there would be an increased guard presence there, but I also knew, unless I took some risks, I wouldn't have a chance of finding Eva.

I waited a minute or so, then set out in the same direction the two of them had taken. Before long, I reached some houses. The trees went right up to the small picket fences of the properties' back gardens. I couldn't see the two men in front of me, but I didn't want to be in a residential area. I skirted the fences and arrived on a small street. I popped my head around the side of a house and looked down pavement. There at the end of the road, I could see a number of troops in front of the fence. If my sense of direction was working, this was Kiefholzstrasse. I headed back into the woods, away from the border for a short time, before turning south again.

It didn't take long to reach the sector boundary again. Running through the wood was a stream, known as the Heidekampgraben. Gerd told me the stream ran from the lake I'd seen in Treptower Park, and the southern part was close to the border area. From my spot behind a fallen tree, I could see a number of guards and the type of fencing and posts I had first seen in the meat factory warehouse. Coils of barbed wire were laid out in front of the fence as a first obstacle. The fence itself was on the far upward bank of the stream. I could see an armed guard patrolling the area between the coils and the fence. I moved down the trunk to get a different view. It was then I spotted a man crouched in the tree line, not three metres from the coil. I assumed it was one of the men I had followed, but couldn't be sure.

I was gripped now, wondering if the men were going to make a dash for the fence. Immediately to my left, I saw smoke drifting up from the ground. I strained my eyes, not sure if they were fooling me. It was then I saw a head pop up briefly. There were guards in a foxhole. I wondered if the men trying to escape had seen them. I held my breath wondering if these men were going to risk everything.

I didn't have long to find out. A dark figure scrambled on his elbows and knees, commando style, to the first coil. He was out in the open and the guards in the foxhole only had to turn their heads to see him. The man was on his front, passing the coil over his head like an expert at work, however, just as he was nearly through, his clothing snagged on the coil. I felt sure he would be seen, as he waved and pulled his arm in desperation. I didn't want to look. Then he was free and crawling towards the stream. He disappeared from view as he reached the ditch.

I strained my eyes hard, waiting for him to reappear at the fence on the far bank. The man wasn't wasting any time. He was up the bank and at the fence already, on his back, clipping at the fence with some cutters, arms over his head. He snipped once, twice, three times. Then he was through the gap he'd created. He jumped onto his feet and sprinted on into the trees on the other side. It had taken less than two minutes. My heart was thumping, as if I had played some part in it all. No sooner had he reached safety, when a second figure darted from the trees to the coil. I felt sure now this was the two men I'd seen, as he pulled a bag behind him.

The second man was less nimble than the first. He struggled under the first coil, taking much longer. It wasn't long before he'd given up on the bag, leaving it tangled in the coil, and continued his fight with the barbed wire. It was hard to watch and I felt sure he would be spotted, given the time he was taking. Finally, he freed himself on the far side.

Then I heard a shout. 'Halt!'

The figure froze for a second, then he made a dive for the ditch. The guards started shouting to each other, trying to locate the figure in the darkness. The abandoned bag was illuminated in the torchlight. The man was only halfway through the border. He still had to make it up the other side of the ditch and through the gap in the fence.

One of the guards leapt out of the foxhole, his rifle raised, walking slowly towards the coil. Another guard, between the coil and the ditch, was closing on the man's position, even if he didn't know it. The escapee didn't have long to make his move.

The figure scrambled up the ditch towards the gap in the fence his friend had made. With guards descending from all sides, I did wonder if it was time to make myself scarce, but I couldn't move. I was hooked, hypnotised by the drama of the scene unfolding in front of me.

The sound of gunfire ripped through the wood. I ducked instinctively. The man was still moving and halfway through the fence. It was either a warning shot, or it missed its intended target. Either way, the man made a desperate last attempt to wriggle through the gap. A second shot rang out and this time the man cried out. The man at the fence was motionless. The guards stopped for a moment, not daring to move any closer. I was transfixed, fearing the worst. The whole scene was macabre in the torchlight.

Then, the man lunged his body through the fence, kicking his feet like a maniac to free himself of the fencing. He was through the fence, but immediately fell as he tried to stand, clearly injured. He scrambled along the floor, clawing at the grass, desperately trying to reach the safety of the trees. Suddenly, his comrade jumped out and started to drag him the last few metres to safety. Two guards watched on, standing at the gap in the fence.

My mouth was dry. I was in shock at what I had witnessed. I had a feeling of exhilaration at the men's successful, daring escape. On the other hand, I was appalled they'd been shot at, like rabbits in the wild. By now there were more guards close to where the fence had been breached. They were pointing and talking animatedly. I knew it was time to move on. It was amazing how gunfire had the ability to make you move quicker. I covered the ground quickly whilst still gathering my thoughts, amazed at what I had just witnessed.

It took me some time to regain my composure. I was away from the sector boundary, but was still keen to check out the canal area. I had nothing to lose now. Shooting of escapers meant I had to find Eva now. In a few days, escape would become increasingly risky. I rubbed my face, tasting the salt on my lips. I wasn't sure if I was sweating due to the humidity, fear, or excitement. With the adrenalin still pumping, I pressed on.

Whilst I wanted to head for the canal, my first instinct had been to put distance between myself and the scene of the escape. As I turned south once again, I put my jacket back on, feeling a chill as the sweat dried on my skin. I crossed over another waterway close to the S-Bahn line. I'd not stopped to think how I felt now; the action was keeping the emotion at bay. I was content that way. The thought drove me on.

I checked my watch. It was now after one a.m. A short distance further on, the trees thinned out and I reached a road. I knew I had to cross it in order to reach the canal. Suddenly, I heard an engine approaching. I ducked back into the thicker foliage. The engine was deep and throaty. I envisaged a truck of some sort. It was getting closer to my position in the trees. I stayed low and watched as first the headlights lit up the road and then a military truck trundled by at slow speed.

I waited until the engine died away into the distance. After another few minutes, and as there was no further traffic, I took a deep breath and edged forward towards the road. I peered out from the leaves, checking to the left, where I saw nothing. I turned my head to the right and instantly dropped down to the floor. The truck that had passed had stopped twenty metres further on. Worse still, guards were fanned out across the width of the road, walking slowly in my direction. I scurried back to tree line, straining my ears for any sound.

I held my breath for a moment and then raised my head. I could see them now, no more than ten metres away. There wasn't a word between the men. They looked concentrated on their task, as if they expected to find someone. I pushed my head back down into the grass, my heart thumping once again. I dared to lift my head to check on their progress. As I did, something caught my eye opposite, in the trees on the other side of the road. A teenager pushed through the leaves, turning to help another, seemingly struggling to walk behind. The boy turned to face me. My stomach lurched. It was Gerd. There was a woman with her arm around him, limping. I could see it was Eva. I turned to the right, the guards were closing in.

I wanted to jump out and shout to warn them, but I knew this would have alerted to guards to all of us. My heart was somewhere at the top of my mouth. Gerd and Eva were about to walk right into the guards' arms. If Eva was caught, that would be the end for her.

There was only one thing I could think to do. I wanted to run out and embrace Eva and tell her everything would be fine, but that wasn't an option. I jumped up and out onto the road, without looking at Gerd and Eva, and ran towards the guards waving my arms like a madman.

'Hey!'

At first, the guards just stood in utter shock. Their attention was focused firmly on me, and that's exactly how I'd planned it. The apparent shock wore off and one of them eventually raised his rifle. I held up my hands. The guards closed in on me cautiously, as I was about to spring out of their encirclement. One of the guards stayed where he was and turned his head towards the trees. I started to make as if I would make a bolt for it. That soon grabbed his attention, especially after a barked order from the one seemingly in charge. They had their prize and weren't letting me go, seizing me on either side, with the others following. For once, I was happy to be the sacrificial lamb.

I didn't look back, making it as clear as I could to them that I was alone. I continued to struggle to retain their interest. Fortunately, they didn't seem interested to search further. When we reached the truck, the tailgate was dropped and I allowed myself to be slung into the back.

Two guards followed me in, and the back was snapped shut. I laid on the floor, praying none of the guards would return to the search.

Then I heard two cab doors slamming shut. The engine roared into life and we set off with a lurch. I closed my eyes, realising by being here in East Berlin, I had been able to do something useful after all.

***

Eva's ankle was swelling fast. The pain was excruciating. It didn't help that they were both soaked to the skin. Even with Gerd supporting her, it had been a struggle to get away from the canal. She knew she needed to get the weight off her ankle as quickly as possible, but they could only rest once they were back at the tent. Whilst they were still close to the border, and with the guards on high alert, they were not out of danger.

They made it back to the road she and Sophie had crossed only a few hours before. Gerd placed Eva down carefully.

'Let's have a break,' Gerd said, slightly out of breath.

Eva still hadn't worked out why the boy was here helping her. She wasn't complaining. There was no doubt he had saved her from arrest, and probably a whole lot worse, if Dobrovsky had his way. She watched him peering out through the leaves, checking the road.

'Can I ask a question?' Eva whispered.

The boy glanced back, seemingly preoccupied. 'I'm not sure it's a good time for questions.' He flashed a brilliant smile back at her.

'Why are you here? Helping me, I mean?'

He shrugged like a shy teenager.

'You saved my life back there.'

Eva could see he was blushing now. Then they heard an engine. Gerd dipped down, suddenly wary. He carefully popped his head out in the direction of the noise.

'Troop truck,' he said.

He jumped back from the road and grabbed Eva under her arms and pulled her behind a tree. He sat down next to her. They could hear the truck getting closer.

'Do you think they're looking for us?'

He shrugged, 'Maybe. They're probably just twitchy at the number of people trying to escape.'

Eva nodded, recalling the young men with the scooter. They went quiet then. Eva held her breath as the engine passed them, the headlights momentarily illuminating the leaves around them. The truck continued on down the road.

They listened as the engine tailed off into the night.

'Do you think we could have made it over the canal?' Eva said.

Gerd shook his head. 'No chance. We didn't have time.'

It was what Eva wanted to hear. She knew he was right. She'd been so close to being free. Now she had to do it all over again with a busted ankle as an impediment. She wondered if she would ever see Tanja again. Right now, the safety of Jack's apartment seemed a long way off.

She wanted to ask Gerd more questions, but the priority had to be to get clear of the canal and the border.

They'd waited at least five minutes and whilst she was glad of the rest, Eva knew they couldn't stay there too much longer. As if her body was pushing her on, she felt a twinge of pain. 'We should get moving,' she said, 'while I can still can.'

Gerd nodded. He heaved her up under her shoulder and they started towards the road, breaking cover of the last bushes. Eva was looking down, concentrating on keeping moving.

She heard a shout from the other side of the road. Eva looked up in shock to see a man walking away from them down the road, shouting and waving wildly.

'It's Jack!'

Gerd quickly dragged her back into the trees.

'What the…?'

Gerd hissed, 'Guards!'

Eva felt her mind whirling, 'But Jack…'

Gerd grimaced. 'He's just stopped us getting caught, Eva.'

'You mean…?' She went to push herself up, but Gerd pulled her back down.

'He's done that for a reason, Eva. If we go out there, we'll get arrested, too.'

Eva thought about what Gerd was saying, amazed how he could grasp it all so quickly. Eva felt her heart sink, knowing they had Jack. She'd been so close to seeing him again. She could almost touch him.

Gerd sensed her unhappiness. 'We'll get you out. Your father is organising help.'

'Dad is here in Berlin? But what was Jack doing in East Berlin?'

They heard the engine gun and start to move away from them.

'Come on, we need to get moving,' Gerd said.

***

Once I knew we were clear of the area, I started to talk to the two guards who were in the back of the truck next to me. I had to think quickly. I couldn't end up back in Weber's hands, and more importantly, those of Dobrovsky. My mind was working overtime.

Unfortunately, the guards were just two young kids who didn't seem to care what I said.

'Look, I'm American. You can't keep me here. I was just out for a stroll in the park.'

I wasn't exactly convincing myself and I certainly wasn't getting anywhere. I took my passport out of my pocket and shoved it under their nose, to garner some kind of reaction. One of them, with a bad case of acne, took a curious interest, then handed it to the other guard. He said something derogatory about Americans that I didn't quite catch. The more confident of the two sniggered and threw the passport back in my direction.

It was then I noticed the uniform. I knew it was Volksarmee, but it wasn't only that; I'd seen it close up somewhere before.

'Erdmann,' I said aloud, almost surprising myself.

Both of them turned and looked at me.

'Colonel Erdmann.'

The name made them take notice. They looked at each other and I realised I had a way in.

'Take me to see Colonel Erdmann.' My voice was becoming stronger, insistent. 'I wouldn't want to be in your shoes if you don't take me to your see your commanding officer. I know him really well.'

The one with the spots was looking at the other one for guidance. The older guard was rubbing his face now, the sure look of before had evaporated into the night.

I focused on him. 'I need to speak to your commanding officer, Colonel Erdmann.'

That did the trick. He was up on his feet banging on the cab for them to stop. The truck eventually ground to a halt and a cab door slammed.

Within seconds the back flap was lifted up.

'What's the problem here?' a voice shouted.

'The prisoner knows Colonel Erdmann, Corporal. He requests to speak with him,' the older guard said. He stepped back now, his responsibility passed on to the next rung of the ladder.

'Does he indeed?'

The corporal clambered up onto the tailgate to get a better look at me, shining his torch in my eyes. 'Name?'

'Would you put that thing out?' I bawled. He moved the beam from my eyes and I thrust out my passport.

'I'm an American citizen. You've have no reason to arrest me.'

'You were in a restricted area, no doubt helping escapers,' the corporal said, waving my passport away.

'I was out walking. I got lost,' I said.

The corporal was more experienced that the others. He had a scar under his chin. He eyed me doubtfully, like he'd dealt with this kind of thing many times. 'You know the Colonel?'

'Yes, very well. He's a friend of mine,' I lied.

I could see he was getting edgy now. He looked at the other two, who avoided all eye contact. This was his call, and his call alone.

'Take me to see him, if you have any doubts. He will vouch for me.'

The corporal weighed things up for a moment and I tried to remain calm whilst retaining my feigned indignance. I knew I was getting somewhere. That's not to say Erdmann wouldn't throw me to the dogs when he saw me, but I would take my chance with a reasonable man like him. At the very worst, it would delay the inevitable.

The corporal shrugged. 'Ok. I'll take you to the colonel. He can decide what to do with you.'

As he jumped off the tailgate, and the back of the truck resumed near darkness, fortunately, the two young guards didn't see me heave a huge sigh of relief.

***

The birds had started their morning song by the time they made it back to the small tent. Eva slumped down, exhausted, but relieved they were clear of danger.

'You need to get out of those wet clothes. Do you have any more?' Gerd said.

'In the rucksack.' Eva nodded towards the bag Sophie had brought.

'Ok. You should get changed.' Gerd looked around at the utensils. 'I'll make us a warm drink.'

Eva didn't argue. She was happy to be led whilst her mind processed everything. Since she'd seen Jack, it felt like her bubble had been pricked. Her moment of hope had been snatched away from her. She was more scared for Jack than herself.

It had been a struggle, but she felt better now that she'd removed the wet clothes. Gerd handed her a cup of coffee and she sighed as it warmed her insides.

'You said my dad was in Berlin?'

Gerd nodded. 'At Jack's place. We were working on a plan to get you out. I came to find you first.'

Eva raised her eyebrows. 'Well, you did a great job. How did you know where to start looking?'

He smiled, full of pride. 'Just a hunch.'

Her ankle was griping at her. It was twice the size it should have been. Gerd wrapped it up tight in Sophie's swimming costume. 'Make sure you keep it rested, for now,' he said. He got up and started to check everything within reaching distance of her.

'You're not leaving me?' Eva said, feeling like a frightened child in need of protection.

'Don't worry. It won't be for long. Now I know where you are, I'll go back into West Berlin and tell your father. He has some help, from a Russian.'

Eva looked at him suspiciously. 'A Russian?'

Gerd shrugged. 'Don't ask me. It's somebody from that war that helped him before. He doesn't much like the other one?'

'Dobrovsky?'

Gerd just nodded. 'Right,' he said, fishing out some wet papers from his pocket. 'I hope these can get me back over the border,' he said, with a smile. 'Don't move from here. I'll be back with help.'

Eva suddenly felt very scared.

'What about Jack?'

It was the first time she'd seen the boy lost for words. 'I don't know, Eva. I'm sure he'll work something out. He's a smart bloke. Stay out of sight. I'll be back as soon as I can.'

Then he disappeared through the bushes, and Eva was alone.

CHAPTER 33

It was early in the morning. The sun was low and barely poking between the barrack blocks, but Hans Erdmann was at his desk. He'd not yet read the night's reports. He'd barely touched the coffee which had been prepared for him twenty minutes before. He looked at his phone, desperate for it to ring, willing Burzin to call and tell him everything was on; Bernie would be freed and they could both get out of East Berlin for good. It's why when the office door opened without the customary knock, he wasn't really prepared.

Even at that hour, Dobrovsky was in full uniform, his face grave and serious. He stood for a moment, while Hans got used to his unwelcomed presence. Eventually, he closed the door silently and strode to the desk as manfully as his short legs could muster, his pristine brown leather boots creaking on the way. He took a seat in front of Hans, uninvited, and placed his cap on the centre of the desk. He wasn't one to scare easily, but the blue of the KGB still made him nervous.

'People are still escaping from your sector, Erdmann. I'm surprised you are sitting at your desk drinking coffee.'

Hans raised his eyebrows. At least the attack was between his eyes; he could deal with that.

241

'Thank you for the reminder, General. I was about to make a tour of my sector. To what do I owe the pleasure?'

Dobrovsky ignored the question and reached for the coffee pot. He helped himself to a cup. He tasted it then pulled a face.

'Not quite up to the standard at Karlshorst, General?'

Dobrovsky placed the cup down. 'I've drunk the ersatz stuff in a bunker in Stalingrad, Erdmann. I don't need to remind you how that turned out.'

Hans didn't respond.

'I am here to give you a friendly warning.' Dobrovsky smiled. Hans thought he heard his face creak like his boots. His smile was as warm and unwelcoming as the coffee.

'You will send out extra search parties in all areas close to the border.'

'That sounds like an order, rather than a warning.'

Dobrovsky leant forward, and growled. 'You'll step up the searches to locate the Schultz woman and when you find her, you make sure your men bring her to me.'

'If we find her,' Hans added.

'You'll make sure you find her, Erdmann.' He stared at Hans now. One side of his mouth loped down manically, as he smiled again. His head reflected the rising sun that was now shimmering through the window. 'And you'll find her because it might just keep your comrade alive.'

Hans' mouth started to move, but he didn't find any words.

Dobrovsky nodded, a manic smile etched on his lips, as his eyes widened. 'Now you understand me. That's good.'

Dobrovsky stood and snatched his cap from the desk. 'I suggest you get to work, Colonel.'

Dobrovsky spun on his extended heel and squeaked out of the office, leaving Hans in a state of shock. At least he knew exactly who had Bernie now and it didn't make him feel at all comfortable. He was still gathering his thoughts when one of his corporals knocked on the door and popped his head in his office.

'Colonel?'

'Yes, what is it?' he snapped.

'There's a suspected escapee in the holding room, Colonel.'

Hans looked disinterested. 'So hand him over to State Security. You know the procedure. Why did you bring him here?'

'Normally, Colonel, I would have done, but he asked for you by name.'

'And?'

'He's an American, Colonel. Name of Kaymer.'

***

The last time I'd seen him, I had felt that he was almost on my side. This time it was clear by his expression, I was a problem to him. He appeared distracted, almost troubled. His grey-blue eyes were almost looking straight through me. His hair was dark, if peppered with individual strands of grey. There was no doubt he was a figure of authority. But as he stood there seemingly analysing his next move, I had the feeling I wasn't exactly his favourite person at that moment in time.

I thought I better start talking. 'Colonel Erdmann, thank you for agreeing to see me...' He held up his hand for me to stop.

'What are you doing back in the eastern sectors, Kaymer?' It was a simple enough question. The answer fell out before I had chance to think about it.

'I came to find Eva.'

It was a straight and honest answer. It could've landed me in a whole heap of trouble. It confirmed I was there illegally and, in attempting to help an East German national to escape, I was right in it.

They would throw the book at me. But deep down, I'd seen this man in action. I felt I could level with him.

He raised his eyebrows slightly in response, then took a seat at the battered table in front of me.

'And did you find her?' As soon as he said it, he held up his hand, 'Perhaps it's better if you don't answer that question.'

I shrugged. 'I wouldn't tell you if I had.'

That made the colonel smile. 'Why come back, Kaymer? You're a marked man. I don't need to tell you certain people will be looking out for you, especially after the incident at the Brandenburg Gate.'

I shifted uneasily in my chair and he saw it.

'People like Dobrovsky don't give up.'

I wondered what was coming next. I knew he should hand me over to Dobrovsky. I knew I was causing a problem for him.

'Colonel, I have a 12-month-old baby wondering where the hell her mother is. This country wrenched her mother away and I've come back here to find her. I am just…'

I stopped trying to think how my actions of the last couple of days could be put into words.

'I am just desperate. I want to get Eva back to our baby, all of us together so we can be a family. I don't think that's too much to ask.'

I had that feeling he was looking through me again, like he was in another time or place. Then he blinked and looked me up and down; maybe he gave me a look of pity, or maybe even sympathy.

'In another time or place, I would agree that it's not too much too much to ask, but humanity is thin on the ground right now.'

I thought back to the men escaping through the fence and remembered the way they had been shot at. I found it hard to believe a man like Erdmann would have anything to do with something like that, but they were his men on the border.

'That said, you're in East Berlin illegally. You've admitted you're here to help a citizen of the DDR flee the country. These are all serious offences.'

Now I was facing Erdmann the soldier, servant of the state. Maybe I'd misjudged the guy. Perhaps he would throw me to the dogs after all. I was almost past caring.

'If wanting to take a mother back to her child, and have her with her family where she belongs, is a crime, then I am as guilty as hell. Lock me up and throw away the key. In fact, you should call Dobrovsky now...'

'Do you think that's what I want to do?'

Erdmann seemed piqued now, offended that I should suggest such a thing. My big mouth had dug me into another hole and I wasn't sure of the way out of it. The last thing I wanted to do was to antagonise the man.

'I just thought you may not have too much choice in the matter, Colonel. Dobrovsky is a general in the KGB.'

He was studying me intently now. His eyes weren't vacant anymore; they were boring right into my forehead. I imagined my fate was being decided at this point. My mouth was dry.

'You're in the custody of the Volksarmee, Herr Kaymer. That means you are under my jurisdiction.'

I was quite relieved to hear it, at least I think I was.

'So what exactly will happen to me, Colonel? You know I am an American citizen.'

He snapped, 'You've tried that one before, Kaymer. It won't wash this time. If Dobrovsky got his hands on you, they'd hang you as a spy. That's if they bothered to grant you a trial.'

I gulped visibly. He wasn't pulling punches anymore. I sensed there was a lot going on behind those steely blue eyes that I couldn't read. I also believed that may be in my favour.

After the burst of anger, he seemed to be a little bit calmer now. 'I have not decided what I will do with you yet. That's something I will have to consider.' He stood up, the chair scraping on the linoleum floor.

'Until then, Kaymer, you will remain here. I advise you say nothing to the guards. Try to keep your mouth shut for a change. It might work out better in the long run.'

I was lost for words. It was a good thing because he'd already left the room. However, I was starting to believe I might yet get out of the mess I was in.

CHAPTER 34

When Gerd returned to the apartment with the news he'd found Eva, Klaus Schultz was ecstatic. When he learned she was injured, and also what had happened at the canal, his excitement soon evaporated. He was eternally grateful to the boy. He had done far more than could be asked. Klaus suspected he was underplaying his role in getting Eva out of the water and back to comparative safety. Klaus was baffled by Gerd's account of Kaymer's sudden appearance in East Berlin, but that explained his absence from the apartment, and his strange behaviour the previous day. He had no time to worry further about that now. He had found the courage to call Maria and ask her to come to Berlin to take care of Tanja. Klaus hadn't wanted to worry his wife about Eva; he felt he could get her out of the eastern sectors before he would burden her with it. But the situation was too grave for that now, and Gerd had done more than enough; it was time for him to get some rest. Klaus had already contacted Burzin to make plans for Eva's escape. They had arranged a meeting for later that morning.

As Klaus waited for Burzin on the periphery of the Tiergarten, he looked across the sector boundary. The fence had quickly become a way of life. There were no East Berliners close to it; they had been pushed back, kept at a distance by the seemingly endless supply of border police and Volksarmee troops. The wide open expanse of the old Potsdamer Platz was desolate. The only activity in the whole area was from militia men placing large crossed metal barriers. The Allies had still not reacted at all. Willy Brandt, West Berlin's mayor, had protested, but was powerless to actually do anything against the measures. Klaus, however, was ready for action. Whilst he'd been waiting for Gerd to find Eva, he'd been thinking and planning. Now that they knew where she was, it was time to move.

Klaus felt Burzin's presence next to him, the perennial cigarette stuck to his lips. Klaus nodded at the array of news reporters and cameramen filming at the border on the western side. 'It's like a bloody circus.'

'I am not sure there's too much to see anymore. They'll get bored in a few weeks when all this becomes normality.'

'Ever the optimist, Burzin.'

'Ever the realist, Klaus.' He grinned in that way that made Klaus believe the man always knew what was coming next.

'Come on, let's walk,' Klaus said. 'It's depressing watching it all.'

They turned into the Tiergarten proper, its trees green, if slightly parched in the late summer sun. Klaus was in shirt sleeves, his jacket carried over his shoulder. Burzin sported a linen jacket, zipped half way over a light coloured shirt.

'You must be delighted the boy found her,' Burzin said.

Klaus pursed his lips. 'Now for the hard bit: to get her out with a twisted ankle.'

'Yes, that makes things more difficult.' Burzin flicked his spent cigarette onto the pavement. People were sitting out on the grass enjoying the weather. The area was full of people riding bikes, walking dogs, and generally going about their daily business. It was surreal to Klaus that such normality could exist within a few hundred metres of life and death at the sector border, but that was Berlin.

'She'll have help, of course?' Burzin asked.

'Yes. Did you manage to get the papers?'

Burzin stopped walking and turned to look at Klaus. 'Are you sure about this, Klaus? It's one hell of risk you're taking.'

Klaus had thought about it, even if he hadn't talked about it with Maria. She would only worry more. Did he really want to go back into East Berlin with Dobrovsky on full alert? It would be just what Dobrovsky wanted: Klaus, and his daughter as a bonus. When he learned she was injured, that had been the final straw. He had to be the one to get his daughter out. After all, he couldn't rely on Kaymer.

'It's your neck,' Burzin said, taking out another cigarette. They started to walk again, strolling as if it was part of the morning constitutional.

'They will need an up-to-date photograph. I will give you the address to attend. Two o'clock this afternoon.'

'Thanks,' Klaus said quietly.

'I never thought I'd hear Klaus Schultz utter those words, not to me, at least.'

Klaus would have normally made a bitter remark, but it didn't feel appropriate. Burzin had done for him something that nobody else could do, and it wasn't the first time.

'How will we get out?'

'It's all in hand.' Burzin pulled hard on his cigarette, as they manoeuvred either side of a young mother fussing over her baby.

Klaus wanted to press for details, but thought better of it for the moment. He did wonder if he was actually starting to trust the man, but it didn't prevent Klaus' urgency. 'We need to do it quickly. She's sitting there in the Plänterwald alone. We need to move tonight. Is that possible?'

Burzin let out a huge plume of smoke, as if the effort of thought required an extra shot of nicotine.

'It can be organised.'

Klaus was starting to feel uncomfortable with Burzin's vaguely positive retorts. It seemed too easy, like the arrangements had already been made, like he had an ace up his sleeve.

'Why do I get the feeling there's something you're not telling me?'

Burzin laughed, his deep voice echoing against the trees on either side. 'I thought you were being too nice to me. That's more like the Klaus Schultz I know.'

'I am putting my neck on the block, as you said. And more to the point, I am putting my daughter's life in your hands. I need to know; I think it's fair.'

'You put your son's life in my hands some years ago, Klaus. I delivered that day and I will deliver now.'

They walked in silence for a while. Klaus did start to wonder if he was being paranoid due to all the stress and worry.

Then Burzin said, 'There is a reciprocal favour I need.'

Klaus felt his heart sink. The old Burzin was still there under the surface. He should have known. He turned to Burzin and administered a filthy look.

'What? You expected all this assistance for nothing?' Burzin's arms were wide, *that* smile on his face again.

Klaus shook his head. 'I should have bloody well known better.' He could feel the anger rising inside him. 'What is it this time? You want me to find Ulbricht and shoot him? Or simply Dobrovsky, this time?' Klaus was starting to shout.

Burzin looked around nervously. 'Keep your voice down, will you? Look, this is a genuine request...'

'Request? Who's the one being polite now? Last time you asked me to murder somebody. What is it now?'

Burzin shook his head. 'No, it's nothing like that.'

'Well, come on, what is it?'

'You won't be escaping on your own tonight,' Burzin said, eventually.

'I know that, me, Eva. The boy Gerd can come back through the border with his own papers once he's taken me to Eva.'

'No, I mean, there will be other people escaping with you.'

CHAPTER 35

TUESDAY, 15th AUGUST 1961,
EAST BERLIN

The call from Burzin finally arrived. It wasn't from him personally, but the code word was supplied so Hans Erdmann knew when and where the meeting would take place. It was for later that afternoon. That implied an urgency, which suited Hans just fine. He had been searching for ideas about how to handle the problem of the American. He did have some ideas, but one thing was certain, Hans had no intention of giving him up to Dobrovsky. Kaymer would not have been aware of the effect his appeal for having Eva Schultz back with her baby had on him. He couldn't have known Hans lost his wife whilst she was in labour all those years ago. His son didn't survive the ordeal either. Since then Hans hadn't really been living. Now was his chance to start his life again.

Hans had taken precautions to ensure he wasn't followed, with Burzin's reminder to follow his training still fresh in his mind. His convoluted route to Friedrichshain Park had taken in the S-Bahn, a taxi ride, and a long walk. The afternoon sun had made him feel better, giving him some perspective and preparing him for tests ahead. He just hoped Burzin would fulfill his side of the bargain.

He made it to the Grossbunkerburg in Friedrichshain Park. He stared at the large, grassy, manmade hill. Beneath it sat some of the bombed ruins of Berlin. It was a timely reminder of the effect the war had, and continued to have, on the city. To the kids it was a great place to sledge when the snows blew in; to the people who remembered how and why, it was a painful.

He caught sight of Burzin walking away from him, deeper into the park. Hans took his cue to follow on, catching up with him a couple of minutes later.

'You sure you don't have a tail?' Burzin asked gruffly.

Hans simply nodded.

Burzin kept up a brisk pace and Hans was struggling to keep up.

'Spending too much time behind a desk, Erdmann?'

He was beginning to sound like Dobrovsky, thought Hans. He didn't rise to the bait, though.

'Your man will be freed tonight.'

'Freed? He's been released?'

Burzin growled, 'Don't be bloody naïve. We're getting him out.'

'That's good…great. How is he?'

Burzin flashed him a look that told him he was being naïve again. 'I wouldn't count on him walking too far, but I am sure he'll manage.'

Further on, there were few people around, the park quiet on this mid-week afternoon. In between puffing on his cigarette, Burzin walked quickly and talked quictly.

'We'll bring him to you. You'll be informed of the details later when the plan is finalised, but you should prepare yourself.'

Hans was confused. 'It's all a bit vague. How can I prepare if I don't know where or how?'

'You'll work it out.'

Hans was growing tired of the games and half-answers. 'Our deal was that the two of us would be safely delivered into West Berlin. It sounds like you're leaving a lot to chance.'

'I am getting your man out. That was the deal.'

Hans stopped Burzin, grabbing hold of his forearm. 'Exactly what are you saying?'

Burzin angrily pulled his arm free. 'You're in charge of the border and the men guarding it; if you can't find a way out, who can?'

Hans thought the whole thing had been too good to be true.

Burzin added sarcastically, 'Do you think you can manage that?'

Before Hans could answer, Burzin continued, 'One more thing: You'll have some other people with you when you escape.'

'What? Now just a minute…'

'Erdmann, it's up to you. Either you help the others get out or I don't deliver Schwarzer. What's it to be?'

Hans was struggling to keep up with everything. Now he not only had to organise Bernie's and his own escape, he had to take other people with him.

'How many people? Who are they?'

'I can't tell you who, but there will be two others.'

Hans shook his head, not liking what he was hearing one bit.

Burzin added fuel to the fire. 'It has to be tonight.'

Hans' head was spinning. How would he have time to organise everything?

'I would suggest the Plänterwald area for the escape.'

'That's precise. Any particular reason?'

'Because that's where we'll deliver Schwarzer to you.'

'You sound like you have it all planned out, Burzin.'

'Not quite all. The rest is for you to sort out. I'll be back with final details later.'

Burzin turned to leave; for him the meeting was finished.

'Wait!'

Burzin looked annoyed, so much so he felt the need to pat his pockets in search of another cigarette.

'I have an American, named Kaymer, in my custody. Any ideas what I should do with him?'

254

For the first time, Burzin smiled. 'If I were you, Erdmann, I'd be looking for an insurance policy.'

Hans' mind was still in a whirl from all the other instructions. He had difficulty to catch his meaning.

'I believe Dobrovsky has been to see you…'

'You think I should hand him over?'

Burzin inhaled hard on the cigarette he'd finally located, then, he shrugged. 'The more contingencies you have in place, the better for you.' Burzin started to walk away, then turned back for a final time. 'Like I said, you'll work it out.'

***

The nightmares kept coming. She was always on the move, chased by something, someone. At one time she was in a pit of poisonous snakes, with no way out. Eva woke up sweating profusely. She checked on her watch. She'd barely slept, but whenever she closed her eyes, the worries were there. She felt like she was in the worst of all places. Trapped, but unable to even try and find a way out.

It was late afternoon. She'd heard people moving around close by, children playing, but she remained well hidden. Her only fear was to be discovered by a policeman or guard; the rest she could manage to talk her way through. She'd eaten the last of the stale bread, but she wasn't really hungry anyway. She was doing her best to stay positive. Gerd would have told her father where she was by now. They would be here soon to help her, to find her somewhere safer to stay until they planned the final escape or to make the escape itself.

Her worries about Jack wouldn't go away. What was he doing in the Plänterwald? Eva could imagine he was searching for her, but why send Gerd and then come himself. She could accept Gerd's explanation that Jack sacrificed himself to keep them out of the hands of the Stasi, but the rest of it didn't make much sense to her. Jack had always been prone to emotional outbursts from time to time. She put it down to his time in Korea. He was like her father: very quiet and calm, and then there were sudden bursts of emotion and anger when put under pressure.

She longed to be back with Tanja, to take care of her. She would do anything for the simple life now. She'd had enough shocks and excitement to last her a lifetime. She checked her watch for the tenth time that hour. Eva Schultz had a feeling there were more surprises to come before the day was out.

***

After Burzin left him, Hans Erdmann's mind was in turmoil. He hated the man for what he'd pushed upon him. He appeared no better than others he'd met in the KGB, even Dobrovsky. Hans had no time to feel bitter, however, and it wasn't his way. He had to organise the escape of Bernie, himself, and the others. He had little idea what Bernie's exact condition would be, but he could imagine what his time in captivity would have been like. And did Burzin really want him to give up Kaymer to Dobrovsky? Did he really want Hans to use him as a bargaining chip as Burzin seemed to suggest?

That wasn't Hans Erdmann's way. He had done tough things in his time. He'd killed with his bare hands when he had to, but giving up innocent people to the KGB, especially people with families relying on them, that wasn't his way. So when Burzin went off in a hurry, Hans continued walking through the park, right up to the Kleinerbunkerburg, past the lake, and around the memorial to the anti-fascist fighters. His mind was working so hard, he didn't notice any of the sights. However, one hour later, when he appeared at the Marchbrünnen (fountain of fairytales) at the entrance of the park, he had his plan worked out. He knew how and where they would escape, and how he would organise it.

He also knew exactly how he would deal with the problem of Jack Kaymer.

***

They'd given me blankets and some food, but I couldn't eat. It had taken me half an hour before I was pacing up and down the room they were keeping me in. My mind was racing. I had seen with my own eyes Gerd helping Eva to walk. She seemed to be injured somehow. How had it happened? Did she need urgent medical attention? We'd found her, at least. The boy Gerd was something else. I just hoped he could keep her safe and lead Klaus to her. We had to get her out quickly. Since I'd slipped through the fence on Lennenstrasse the previous evening, I had experienced so much. I had been able to see firsthand what the East Berliners were going through. It was difficult to imagine the risks that were being taken to cross the sector border from the safety of West Berlin. The rest of Europe, and definitely the people of the US, would be oblivious to the effect this was having on families. I had to get out of here and tell the world what was going on. Before I could do that, and more to the point, if I was ever going to be able to do it, my fate had to be decided by the seemingly pre-occupied Colonel Erdmann.

Erdmann left me kicking my heels until late afternoon before coming to see me. When he did, he looked much more relaxed than earlier. I would go so far as to say assured.

'Take a seat, Kaymer.'

I had been pacing around when he came in. I moved around the table and quickly sat down, anxious to hear my fate.

He sat, crossed one leg over the other, and gently placed a file on the table in front of him. He smoothed the material on his trouser leg, then focused those piercing eyes on me.

'When I was first told you were here, I can't deny you were a problem to me.'

I was hearing every word, every meaning. 'And now?'

'You're still a bloody nuisance.'

I laughed nervously. He laughed too, but he was in control. That was likely to be the case when he knew what was coming, and I was hanging on his every word.

'There are people in the eastern sectors who would love to get their hands on you.'

I shrugged. 'I've not exactly endeared myself to your chiefs.'

'There's that, but I was thinking more about General Dobrovsky, rather than Ulbricht and his cronies.'

I winced, but couldn't help notice the sarcasm. 'Forgive me, but you don't seem to be a great advocate of the leadership of DDR.'

'We'll get to that.' He sounded annoyed now. 'You've been bloody stupid, Kaymer…'

I went to interrupt, but he held up his hand. 'You've been bloody stupid, but I can understand why. I would have done the same in your position.'

For the first time in my life, I kept quiet. I felt things may be shifting in my direction. Opening my mouth might have changed that.

He leant forward and touched the file on the desk in front of him. 'In here is information which would be of use to you.'

I must have looked confused.

'*Newsweek*, isn't it?'

'*Newsweek*?'

'The publication you write for.'

'Ah…among others, yes,' I said, catching on with the speed of a sloth.

'You write the story in here and we have a deal.'

'A deal?'

'I need your word, Kaymer.'

'My word? I could agree to anything right now.'

'You could, as much as your decision making leaves a lot to be desired, I trust you.'

I smiled at that one, but I wasn't put off. 'And what do I get in return for writing the story?'

He took a deep breath and held his chin up in the air. 'You will be released… and escorted back over the border into West Berlin.'

***

In his own way, Hans Erdmann had taken Burzin's advice. He had set up his own contingency. He felt focused and in control. Dealing with Kaymer had been easy. Handing him a copy of all the reports from the border, as well as his own handwritten notes, would be enough to expose the people who had been hounding him. Those were the same people who were forcing innocents to shoot on innocents on the border. The American would always jump at the chance to pen such a story. Now, Hans had to prepare the escape route.

He was wary of Burzin's comments on Bernie's condition. He did wonder if he would be able to walk unaided. There were so many factors Hans could control, but if he had to carry Bernie over the border, that would make the task more difficult. On his office wall, Hans had a map where all the border measures were followed meticulously by him and his team. He knew what was in place in each area and he knew exactly how many troops were manning each particular section of the border. Burzin had been right about that one; it was a massive advantage.

Whilst Hans was pondering why Burzin had pinpointed the Plänterwald as the area in which to escape, there was a knock at his office door.

'Ah, Riedle, come in.'

'You asked for me, Colonel?'

Since their earlier discussion about the shootings on the border, Hans could see Riedle looked tired and drawn, his young face etched with worry. The whole project had been getting to him.

'Riedle, you should take the evening off. Get some rest. I will take charge of the border personally tonight.'

He looked surprised, even afraid. 'But, Colonel, I have to continue with the search for the Schultz woman.'

It sounded like he'd been got at again. No wonder the boy was looking tired. Marks, Dobrovsky were like a cancer, nagging away, not giving up. Hans took a deep breath.

'I will ensure the searches continue. You deserve a break.'

He still looked unconvinced, like he'd had orders, or threats, from a greater force, unbeknown to Hans.

'That's an order, Riedle.'

'Yes, Colonel.'

He sloped out of the office carrying the weight of the world on his shoulders. In normal circumstances, Hans would have spent time with him, putting an arm around his shoulder. For sure, he would have to keep an eye on Riedle, but Hans was thinking short term. He was taking charge of the border with a distinct ulterior motive. He hoped dearly it was to be his last night in the eastern sectors of Berlin.

CHAPTER 36

TUESDAY, 15th AUGUST 1961, WEST BERLIN

It took a couple of hours to organise, but Hans Erdmann had been as good as his word. I couldn't quite believe I was back on the streets of West Berlin with a story burning in the file under my arm. I couldn't comprehend my good fortune at that moment, but I suspected when I started to read the file I would learn much more about the Colonel. In the meantime, the story, and my own experience on the sector border, was far from my main priority. I grabbed a cab close to the checkpoint on Sonnenallee and headed back to the apartment to catch up with Gerd and Klaus.

I was more than surprised to find Eva's mother, Maria, at the apartment and it showed in my face.

'Yes, Jack, Klaus eventually told me everything that has happened. The *whole* story.'

She didn't look too pleased with me for a moment. I could imagine Klaus had taken a whole lot worse. It wasn't long before she was giving me a hug and enquiring after my wellbeing.

'So where have you been? We were all worried about you when Gerd told us what he'd seen. Tanja has been missing you,' she said, handing her to me.

'I had a meeting with an NVA Colonel.'

'Ah, that's what they call incarceration these days, is it?' She looked at me with raised eyebrows. 'It must be hard for you, Jack, but you can't just run off into the eastern sectors creating havoc. You've got responsibilities.'

I squeezed Tanja in a tight embrace. She squealed with delight. Maria had a very good point.

'So where's Klaus? Gerd?'

'You've missed them by about an hour. Klaus organised things with the Russian.'

'Burzin?'

She nodded, but didn't look too happy.

'Klaus has gone into East Berlin?'

'To get Eva. Burzin organised some papers for him. At least he did that.'

I think that was a swipe at me, but her heart wasn't really in it. Her face was etched with worry. She'd had enough problems of her own at the end of the war when the Russians came. Eva had told Jack the whole story. He figured she found it difficult to return here, now that she'd left for a new life in West Germany with Klaus.

'Before you think about rushing back into East Berlin, Klaus left you some instructions for tonight.'

I looked at Tanja, her cheeks bunched up in a healthy smile. I had had enough close run things in the last few days that I was loathe to take any more unnecessary risks. I was more than happy to leave bringing Eva back to the experts, or at least those with the right help. I would play my part and follow the lead given by Klaus, and more importantly, the Russian, Burzin.

It was after eight in the evening when I opened Klaus' note. I read the instructions carefully, consulting the map still laid out on the table as I did. I knew what I had to do.

I turned to Maria. 'Before the night's out, we'll have Eva back home.'

It was the only way to think now.

CHAPTER 37

TUESDAY, 15th AUGUST 1961,
EAST BERLIN

Klaus Schultz had decided to use Friedrichstrasse station to enter East Berlin. It wasn't exactly original, but, after long deliberations, he felt he was less likely to be detected at one of the busier crossing points. The station allowed passengers to pass from West to East, and vice-versa, as long as they had the all-important paperwork. Gerd would travel alone entering through the Sonnenallee checkpoint where the guards had grown used to seeing him. If either of them were stopped at the border, turned away or worse, the other could still continue with the plan.

They had been forced to discount Jack. Klaus had no idea what the man hoped to achieve by tearing off to the East like that, without help. He was amazed Jack had managed to find Eva and Gerd. He wasn't surprised he'd ended up being arrested, even if the man had shown great bravery to sacrifice himself like that. He hoped the American was coping, as he'd grown to like the man. He'd left instructions for him; he could be the final assistance on the western side of the border, if he did manage to get back to West Berlin. Klaus had taken the liberty of planning other help on the western side, if Jack didn't make it.

There were no problems getting through the border. The Grenzpolizei took one cursory look at his false West German papers and waved him down the heavily guarded stairs into East Berlin. Gerd was already waiting for him at Treptower Park.

'Everything okay?' Klaus asked.

'Easy,' Gerd beamed. Under his arm, he carried the three separate pieces of the crutch they'd made for Eva. Klaus was thankful he was with him. Not only for tonight, but for all the other things he'd done over the last few days.

Darkness was starting to close in, sooner than normal. A breeze had got up and the dark clouds threatened rain. Klaus was anxious to get to Eva now that they were so close, but still felt the need for caution.

'We have to be careful we're not followed into the park.'

Gerd pulled a face. Seemingly, this was obvious. 'Leave it to me, Herr Schultz. It'll not be a problem.'

They skirted the park on its northeastern side, careful to steer well clear of the military tents. Large spots of rain started to fall, individually and slowly at first, eventually becoming heavy and persistent. Klaus pulled up his jacket collar, feeling a slight chill on the breeze. The hot, sultry weather of the last few days had broken. They slipped into the park close to the colossal memorial to the Soviet soldiers killed in Berlin. Klaus could smell the rain on the warm stone. They followed the southern edge of the carp lake. There were people still dotted around walking dogs, anxious mothers trying any way to get young ones off to sleep. Most of them were now rushing for cover out of the gathering deluge. Klaus felt uncomfortable out in the open. Any one of the people there could have been spies on the lookout for would-be escapers, or, more particularly, for Eva and him. He would feel better once they reached cover.

The thicker trees of the Plänterwald not only provided some cover from prying eyes, but also from the rain. Klaus' jacket was already soaked through, the water dripping through to his shirt. Gerd ploughed on, not hesitating in his quest to relocate Eva's position. They heard dogs barking in the near distance, and instantly the two of them crouched down and waited. After hearing nothing further, they set off again. They were close to Eva now. Klaus couldn't wait to see her. He felt only that fatherly need to protect, to take care of her. He just hoped they weren't too late.

Gerd suddenly stopped up ahead of Klaus. He carefully peered through the leaves, then he turned back to Klaus and beckoned him forward. Gerd smiled as Klaus pushed past him, squeezing him on the shoulder as he went. As he pushed the branches apart, Eva was startled at first, but then she just looked relieved. Klaus was at her side, pulling her to him. He felt a wave of emotion flooding through his body. Tears streamed down Eva's cheeks. Neither of them spoke. The relief for both of them was palpable.

'How's the ankle?' Klaus asked eventually.

Eva wiped her face quickly. 'I've been keeping it up most of the time. I have tried to walk up and down.'

'We're here now, Eva, and we'll soon have you out of this place for good.'

'What about Jack?' she said, with a hint of hope in her voice.

Klaus pursed his lips. 'We've not heard anything.'

Her shoulders slumped.

'Jack's a big boy. He'll work a way out. In the meantime, we have to get you back to Tanja.'

'I have missed her so much. How is she?' Eva's eyes were desperate.

'She's just great. Your mother is looking after her at Jack's place.'

She exhaled deeply.

'You can't think about any of that now. As hard as it is, you've got to put it out of your mind.'

Eva seemed to come round after her father's words of comfort. 'How are we getting out?'

Klaus noticed Gerd busily putting the makeshift crutch together, slightly embarrassed at the emotion of their reunion.

'Here, try this.' Gerd passed the finished piece over. Klaus knew Gerd had tested it out himself; he and Eva were of similar height. Klaus pulled Eva up from the floor so she could put her weight on it. Gingerly, she started to test it, then she took larger, more confident steps.

'It's fine,' she said. 'I just need some practice.'

She smiled for the first time. Klaus couldn't begin to describe the relief he felt on seeing her again.

'I am so glad you're here, Dad.'

Klaus was slightly choked. He couldn't find the words even if he wanted to. He quickly changed the subject.

'I believe we have Gerd to thank for helping you last night.'

'Helping me? He saved my life at the canal.' She looked at Klaus now. 'I was stuck in the water. He dragged me free. The border police were so close to catching us...'

'It's okay now. We're here.' Klaus glanced across at Gerd, who was busily focused on something other than his burning red cheeks.

Eva was getting used to the crutch. Klaus could see her independent streak was returning.

'So, how are we getting out? You didn't answer my question.'

'We have to wait.' Klaus checked his watch. 'Another hour and there will be somebody here to guide us over. It's all arranged.'

Gerd looked slightly apprehensive, perhaps sensing the slight doubt in Klaus' voice. Once again, the fate of Klaus Schultz and his family was in Burzin's hands.

***

Hans Erdmann had spent the afternoon on the sector border. After an inspection of the main thoroughfares at the Brandenburg Gate and Friedrichstrasse, he toured the border down to Treptow in the Kübelwagen. Close to the park, he dispensed with the vehicle and continued on foot to Kiefholzstrasse. From there, using the excuse of the escapes and shootings of the previous evening, he ordered a full inspection of the fence and other border measures along the Southern Heidekampgraben. There was a very good reason for this, not only to be seen to stiffen the security measures in that area, but also to make the final, vital preparations for his own, and the others', escape. By ten p.m. he was back in the Kübelwagen, waiting next to the phone booth at Treptow S-Bahn station, as per his instructions. It would all happen from here.

Leant against the door of the jeep, the shrill ring of the phone jolted him into life. He snatched the receiver from the cradle.

'Go to Rummelsberg, Hauptstrasse, the phonebox close to the entrance to the S-Bahn. You have ten minutes.'

The line went dead. Hans slammed the receiver down, annoyed at the games. He had no time to complain. He cranked the gears, pushing the engine to its meagre limits. Very quickly he was clear of the train station and on over the Spree. He did wonder how long this game was going to last before they delivered Bernie. He forced from his mind what Burzin would want him to do for the GRU if he was ever to reach West Berlin. One step at a time, he told himself.

He spotted the yellow booth on the opposite side of the road. It was occupied. Hans cursed as he drove down to the next junction to turn around. He managed to make the u-turn and was about 150 metres from the phone when, much to his relilef, the woman who'd been using the telephone vacated the booth. He pulled up and checked his watch, not sure how long the journey had taken him. As he killed the engine, the phone was already ringing. Hans hopped out and rushed to the phone, hoping he didn't draw attention to himself. The tradecraft of espionage had been long since dispensed with.

He grabbed the receiver.

'You took your time.' It was Burzin.

'Believe it or not, I have other things to do,' Hans said, barely disguising his anger.

Burzin chuckled. 'Precautions are a necessary evil in our game.'

Hans didn't answer, knowing he was right.

'There's an old garage off Karpfenteichstrasse. Drive on past there. Your parcel will be waiting for you there, on the right hand side, just before the railway line.'

'How long?'

'Twenty-minutes. You have your instructions afterwards. I remind you that you have no time to waste. Once they realise he's gone, they'll come looking. It's reasonable to assume you will be first port of call.'

'It's all in hand,' Hans said, not entirely sure it was.

'You have transport?'

'Yes.'

'That's good. You'll need it.'

***

Eva had practiced with the crutch and was at last able to move around. Fortunately, they didn't have far to go. The difficulty would come in the vicinity of the border when they had to make their final escape. After the initial emotion, Eva was back to her old self. When her father had tried to help her when she was unsteady on her feet, she pushed him away. The independent streak ran through her. Klaus was grateful for that. He was sure she wouldn't have survived this long if it hadn't been the case.

Klaus checked his watch. It was time to move. They would need at least half an hour to get to the position close to the border.

'You both know the plan?' Klaus said, first looking at Eva, then across to Gerd.

Gerd nodded, but Eva had something to say. 'I'm not sure I like the idea of escaping with other people...'

'We've been through this. I am not happy about it either, but this is your ticket out of here, with the right help.'

She looked doubtful, but pulled herself to her feet. 'Better get moving then.' She took one last look around. She laughed. 'I'm almost sad to be leaving the place.'

Klaus was glad she was smiling. He had a feeling they'd need all the humour and strength of character they could get before the night was out.

***

Hans expected the worst. Burzin had broken the news to him Bernie wouldn't be in good shape with little subtlety. He would have the Kübelwagen to pick him up, but it was the next part of the plan that Hans was worried about. He shook his head, not wanting to think of how they could break a man physically inside such a short space of time. It made him feel sick to his stomach, the things these people were capable of.

The street to which Burzin had directed him was named after the carp lake in Treptower Park. At least it was close to the area where Hans had planned to cross the border. Hans couldn't help fretting, wondering if things were going to work out the way he had planned. It was too late to do much about it now. He would get one shot at this, and only one.

It was dark now and the road beside the park, where Hans waited, was quiet. From here he could see the opening to Karpfenteichstrasse. He'd not seen one car or van turn into the street and head towards the railway line. He could only hope Burzin delivered his part of the bargain. Hans hadn't thought much about the others who would escape with them. He could have done without the added complication, but he wasn't in any position to argue.

269

It was a minute before the agreed time. Heavy rain had started to beat down on the tarpaulin roof. Hans heard a vehicle approaching from behind him. He wanted to turn around and look, but managed to stop himself. There was a slick crackle of the tyres on the wet cobbled road as a beige delivery van passed him, then turned down the target street. Hans knew it must have been Burzin's men; it looked like the van they'd used to snatch him off the street.

He knew it could be a trap and waited as long as he dared before following on behind. He cranked the gears and manoeuvred the jeep down the street towards the railway line. Hans dimmed his lights and drove slowly past some old warehouses, then he saw the garage Burzin had mentioned on the right. There was no sign of the delivery van. Ten metres from the railway bridge, Hans stopped the jeep and grabbed his flashlight. Warily, he hopped out, switched on the light, and moved slowly in the direction of the railway line.

He did wonder how this handover was supposed to happen. There was no sign of life. He noticed a half-broken wall on his right, as he flashed his light across it. He almost walked by, then something made him return the flash light back to the wall. He could see a foot sticking out at the end. He moved more quickly now, his heart beating in his chest. He saw something wrapped in a blanket and his heart sank.

His mouth was dry as he placed the flashlight down. He carefully tugged on the blanket, not sure he wanted to reveal what was underneath. Hans could hear Burzin's words in his head. With the cover pulled away, he could see it was Bernie, but not the Bernie that could walk through the border. His eyes were swollen like two black balls. His lips were ballooned and split. His hair was matted with blood. Hans wasn't even sure he was alive.

He knelt down at Bernie's side and shook him gently. 'Bernie, can you hear me?'

Hans heard a groan. He heaved a sigh of relief. At least he was alive. He pulled back the blanket fully to see Bernie was still in his uniform. He didn't smell too good, but it was a hospital he needed before a bath. Hans tried to sit him up against the wall. He felt Bernie tense as soon as he touched him.

'It's okay, Bernie, it's me, Hans. It's going to be okay.'

'Hanf?' The word was delivered with spittle and blood.

Hans had to get him away from here quickly, then, he could decide what to do. All Hans felt was anger towards Marks for what he'd done to his comrade. He wanted to shoot him like a dog. It was all he deserved.

With great effort, Hans heaved Bernie onto his shoulder. He moaned as he did, but it was the only way Hans could get him back to the jeep. Eventually, he had Bernie in the back of the Kübelwagen. He covered him with the blanket. As Hans gunned the engine, he checked his watch. In less than fifteen minutes, Hans was due to meet his contact. With Bernie in such a bad way, there was little chance he could pull off the escape now.

***

Eva's crutch had slipped numerous times on the rain softened ground before they eventually made it to the agreed place. They were well hidden in the trees, thirty metres back from the border, close to the Heidekampgraben. These were the instructions Burzin had given Klaus, and even though he felt they were vulnerable now, he had followed Burzin's words to the letter. Eva, Gerd, and Klaus waited, partially sheltered by the trees from the incessant rain. From here, they could make out the border fence, and the guards patrolling it. Klaus had to leave the others to go and meet their contact, the person who would help them to make their final escape over the border.

Klaus made his way carefully from the area, the water trickling uncomfortably down his back as he went. The rain showed no sign of abating and the three of them were already soaked to the skin. This was the part of the operation Klaus was so nervous about. They had to rely on a stranger to escort them across the border. Fortunately, these people were to escape with them. Klaus hoped this meant the plan would be well considered. It was typical of Burzin to organise things in this way. Everything was last minute and on a need-to-know basis only. This was the cloak and dagger world of espionage in which Burzin had been operating for years. There were reasons for the secrecy, and Klaus could understand that, but when you don't have all the facts in front of you, and you have everything on the line, as he had, it made a man feel anxious in the extreme.

It took Klaus fifteen minutes to make it back to the S-Bahn stop at the Plänterwald. The place was deserted at that time of night. He'd been told to wait for a call at the booth behind the cigarette kiosk. Klaus knew full well this could have been a trap. He doubted Burzin would purposely lead him into the net, but there was always a chance the operation had been blown. He couldn't help shaking that manic smile of Dobrovsky's from his mind. It kept him on his guard. Klaus stepped back into the shelter of the rail station doorway, within earshot of the phone booth, and waited. It was moments like this he yearned for the simple life building houses in West Germany, anything but the tension and anxiety of Berlin.

The phone rang. Klaus glanced nervously up and down the street. Seeing nothing untoward, he stepped out onto the pavement, reaching the booth in a couple of seconds. He picked up the receiver. The line was dead. Sensing the worst, Klaus slammed the receiver down and turned to run, but didn't get very far.

Blocking his path was a colonel in the Volksarmee.

'Kursk,' the man said.

Klaus was only in flight mode.

The colonel repeated, with a growl this time, 'Kursk!'

Klaus' mouth was dry. His mind wouldn't work. It was the bloody password. Burzin and his games again.

'St…Stalingrad,' Klaus finally managed.

The man in the Volksarmee uniform looked more relieved than Klaus felt.

'We need to move. Follow me!' the colonel said.

Klaus went after him. 'I am sorry. It was the uniform. It threw me.'

'Burzin didn't tell you then?'

'Nothing. Only where to be.'

'Join the club.'

'Where are we going?' Klaus asked.

'Just follow me. It's best not to talk here.'

He pointed to an NVA Kübelwagen on the other side of the street. Klaus was starting to feel more confident. With an NVA truck and a uniformed colonel for help, getting across the border should be much easier. The man gestured for Klaus to get in and joined him in the front.

'Your people are in position?'

Klaus nodded.

'How many?'

'Two plus me.'

'I was told only two.'

'We need the assistance,' Klaus said awkwardly.

The colonel didn't push it. Klaus had a long list of questions about the operation, how they would cross over the border among them, but it didn't feel like the right time to ask. The man sitting next to Klaus was tense, seemingly under a lot of pressure. It didn't seem the moisture on his forehead was only due to the rain.

'I don't know who you are and I don't need to know. I only have to tell you not everything has gone to plan,' the colonel said.

'What do you mean exactly? Are we not getting out tonight?'

'For you, and your friends, it will be okay, but I have a problem.'

Klaus felt some relief, but still wanted to know what the man was talking about. Time was of the essence. The man seemed honest and straight, so Klaus decided to get to the point.

'What's the problem?'

'Somebody else was to escape with us.'

'He hasn't turned up?'

The man pointed his thumb into the back of the jeep. Klaus turned into the darkness. There was somebody in the back covered in a blanket. He looked to the colonel, who just stared out onto the street.

Klaus pulled back the blanket and winced. The man had taken a terrible beating. Klaus carefully placed the blanket back over the injured man.

'I've seen injuries like that before,' Klaus said slowly. 'There's only one place a man takes a beating like that, and they don't usually get out.'

His mind was ticking over now. 'Your uniform is genuine.'

The man nodded.

'And him?' Klaus pointed into the back.

'My sergeant. We go back a long way. Kursk, in fact.'

Klaus started to laugh. Burzin had managed his little joke in the middle of all the drama.

'You were at Stalingrad?'

Klaus nodded.

'You're a survivor then? I am impressed.'

Klaus got back to the job in hand. 'You thought he'd be able to walk over the border?'

The colonel nodded. 'It was naïve of me.'

'Everyone is naïve compared to the Stasi.'

Klaus took a deep breath. There was no other way. It was all about instinct now. He took another quick look over his shoulder. The man looked just like Ulrich when Burzin freed him from Hohenschönhausen.

'The two of us could move him together?'

The colonel was looking intently at Klaus now. 'I suppose we could.'

'I assume you've got a bloody good plan to get us over the sector border?'

He shrugged. 'It helps I am in charge of the border in this area, but we've still got to go through a hole in the fence.'

'We better get moving then,' Klaus said.

***

Hans Erdmann couldn't quite understand why the man had agreed to help him. What was his motivation? He did wonder if Burzin had thought this all through; three survivors of the Eastern Front together. Perhaps he thought that was the dynamic that would make it all work. He had no real idea, but couldn't waste energy on it now. Time was very much against them.

Hans parked the jeep behind the last house on Kiefholzstrasse and killed the engine.

'Surely we're not going through the fence here?' Klaus asked.

Hans shook his head. 'There's a passage into the woods at the side of this house. If your friends are in the right place, they should be no more than 100 metres from here.'

Hans stopped for a moment. 'You know you don't have to help me? I will make sure you get over the border regardless. That was my deal with Burzin.'

'No, I don't. But your comrade needs urgent medical attention and I am sure he's not going to get it in the eastern sectors.'

Hans nodded, thoughtful for a moment, then held out his hand. 'Hans Erdmann.'

The man took his hand. 'Klaus Schultz.'

'Schultz? With a daughter called Eva?'

The man looked at Hans suspiciously. 'Burzin told you?'

'No. Most of the NVA, and every other police and military organisation in East Berlin, is searching for her.'

275

'Well, she's sitting in the woods waiting for you to get her over the border, so it might be better if we went.'

'A KGB general called Dobrovsky is particularly interested in her.'

The man's eyes narrowed. 'He's not interested in her. He wants me.'

Hans laughed. 'Then we have a common foe, Klaus Schultz. Come on!'

***

Eva felt a tap on her shoulder. Gerd flicked his head behind him, the rain dripping off his fringe. Eva turned to see her father helping another man towards them. On the other side of the injured man, she saw the colonel from the Brandenburg Gate and immediately tensed.

'What is it?' Gerd said.

Her father noticed she had seen the uniforms. 'It's okay, Eva. This is the man Burzin sent to help us.'

The colonel nodded to Eva.

'I don't understand,' Eva said, too surprised to think of anything else to say.

'This is Hans Erdmann, and this…' Klaus carefully placed the man down.

'It's Bernie. My sergeant,' Colonel Erdmann said.

'And we're going to help him get over the border,' Klaus added.

'But he can barely walk,' Gerd hissed.

The man was conscious and able to sit up, but he appeared to be in a bad way. The colonel placed himself next to Bernie on the wet grass. Eva noted the concern he showed for his friend. It was a different person she had seen commanding troops and arguing with Dobrovsky the day the border was closed.

'Bernie, can you hear me?'

The man opened his eyes. 'I can hear you all right.' He looked around them all. 'Don't worry about me. Just get me close to the bloody fence and I'll crawl over if I have to,' he said, with some effort.

Erdmann smiled. 'Ever the old warrior, Bernie.'

'They've not finished me off yet.'

Eva looked towards her father for some explanation. She knew it wasn't the time or the place for long debates, but a colonel in the NVA was an unlikely ally at a time like this.

'Colonel Erdmann is responsible for the border guards. He will help us to get through the fence.'

Eva nodded slowly, not fully convinced. It was hard to take everything in. She shrugged, realising they had little choice in the matter. She did wonder if the man would slow them down, but Erdmann could have said the same of her injuries. She wanted to ask her father if she trusted them, but it seemed a foolish thing to ask in the circumstances. They were already close enough to the border to be arrested and the colonel was already risking everything just by being here.

Her father turned to Erdmann, 'It makes sense if Gerd and Eva go through the fence first.'

'I agree,' the colonel said.

'I will help your sergeant,' said Klaus.

Eva looked sharply at her father. 'I am not sure that's a good idea…'

Erdmann was shaking his head. 'Your daughter is right, Klaus. You've done enough already. The three of you will go ahead of us. I will help Bernie once you have escaped.'

Eva felt slightly better about that plan, even if she couldn't help feeling humbled.

'Thank you,' she said, quietly.

The colonel motioned for them to gather closer to Bernie. So close to the border they still had to be careful about noises carrying. 'All right, here's how it will work...'

***

Hans Erdmann had prepared everything he could. Earlier in the day, he'd gathered his men on the Southern Heidekampgraben and inspected the fence and coils. He'd followed his men, ensuring he was the last to check the fence. He went to the lengths of showing them the small flaws they'd overlooked. What he didn't show them were the three cuts he'd made in the fence, next to one of the fence posts.

The fence was on the back bank, behind the stream, and there was a coil of barbed wire stretched out two metres in front of the downwards bank, prior to the stream. Eva, Klaus, Gerd, and Bernie were now positioned in the trees less than five metres from the first coil. He'd pointed out the fence post adjacent to where he'd cut the wire fence. It was now Hans' job to provide the diversion for the escape.

Leaving the four of them in place, Hans doubled back and approached the border area with all the authority of a colonel in the NVA. He surprised one of his men, no more than ten metres from the coil of barbed wire.

'Gather the men, Corporal!' Hans barked.

'Er...'

'Stop dithering, man. I gave you an order.'

'Immediately, Colonel.'

The corporal relayed the instructions to his men guarding the fence along the stream. The other side of the fence was Neukölln and West Berlin. Hans was standing thirty metres further down the fence from Bernie and the others. This small gathering of his men would be the opportunity for the others to make their bid for freedom.

Whilst his corporal was rounding up the men, Hans stepped through the barbed wire and looked down into the stream. Earlier in the day, it had been dry. The persistent rain meant it was now ankle deep. The wet conditions didn't make the escape any easier. Hans peered through the fence and shivered inadvertently. It could be all over in a short space of time. Bernie and he could be in West Berlin.

'Colonel, the men are ready.'

Hans stepped back between the coils.

'Gather round,' Hans said, looking at his men. There were twelve of them. They all carried rifles or submachine guns. They looked wet and miserable. It wasn't the night for guard duty. Many of them appeared surprised to see their commanding officer at that time of night.

'Tonight is an important night,' he shouted.

***

They were huddled together, barely allowing themselves to breathe. From their final position in the trees, they were so close to the border, they could hear the guards talking. They could even hear what they were talking about. Klaus Schultz smiled to himself. Troops complaining about the shitty weather was something he knew all too well. He squeezed Eva's forearm to reassure her. It wouldn't be long now. Klaus couldn't wait for this to be finished, then he could get back to the quiet life, far from the intrigue of Berlin.

Gerd nudged him urgently. The guards were starting to move, cajoled by the corporal shouting instructions. This was it. Erdmann was pulling his men away from their positions to give them their chance. He'd told them exactly where the fence was breached; it was just a question of negotiating the barbed wire coil. Klaus looked over at Bernie. He was conscious now. Klaus couldn't help feeling sorry for the man. Like him, after many years fighting for your country, then being held captive by the Russians, they were still caught up in the aftereffects of the war.

Another minute or so passed, then they heard Erdmann's loud voice. The words weren't clear to Klaus, but Gerd heard them, because he nodded once at Klaus, slipped the wire cutters between his teeth, and slid out of the cover of the trees.

CHAPTER 38

TUESDAY, 15th AUGUST 1961, WEST/EAST BERLIN

I was dressed in dark clothes as Klaus had instructed. I was to meet a man on Sonnenallee. I parked the Karmann-Ghia a few blocks away and made the rest of my way on foot through the growing puddles. Further down the road, I could see the border crossing point where Erdmann's men had allowed me to cross only a few hours ago. It was still possible to cross into the eastern sectors, for those with the correct papers. I didn't fall into that category, but by now, I wasn't too disappointed that was the case. I was content Eva was in the best hands she could be. I knew Klaus, grumpy and uncommunicative as he was, still had her best interests at heart. I just hoped the old sod could pull it off.

It was still incredible to me I was here in West Berlin and Eva was almost within shouting distance. I could have walked to this place from my apartment. This whole situation with the border wasn't any easier to get my head around. I just hoped, after tonight, I would be through with the whole thing.

A man was at my side before I knew anything about it.

'You're a friend of Klaus Schultz?'

'Jack Kaymer.' I held out my hand.

He shook it. 'Markus,' he said. He wore black waterproof clothing. I couldn't guess his age. He was older than me, but he was slim and active looking. I guessed it was another of Klaus' old comrades. He motioned into the shadows of an old building opposite, and two men appeared from nowhere carrying medical supplies. He saw the look on my face. 'Best to be prepared, Kaymer.'

I gulped at the thought of spilled blood. 'Where are we going?'

He turned and lifted his chin in the direction of the trees over the road.

'The border is thirty metres or so that way. No more talking once we're in the trees. The guards may hear us.'

***

Eva Schultz turned one last time to look at her father. His face was set, determined. He just nodded his head. It gave Eva an amazing sense of confidence to know he was behind her, not that she would let him see it.

She'd seen Gerd go under the coil of barbed wire with consummate ease. Eva took and deep breath and slithered out, breaking the cover of the last line of trees. She could feel a dull throb in her ankle, but it was much better than before. The sodden grass had no effect on her clothes, as she was already wet through. She turned her head in the direction of the gathered guards, some way down the stream. She hoped the colonel continued to play his part.

Eva clawed at the grass, dragging herself forward, digging her elbows into the ground as she went. She reached the barbed wire coil and immediately started to inch forward, pushing the coil over her head as she went. The barbs scratched the skin on her hands as she struggled to squirm through. She felt totally exposed, not believing they couldn't see her. The top half of her body was through now. She kicked her legs free, the wire tearing at her shins as she did. The pain would come later;

now she was free and immediately dived for the cover of the stream, slithering down the bank. She landed on her backside at the bottom. The cold water ran around her waist and legs before she could get on to the other bank.

She couldn't see Gerd. She assumed he was already at the top of the bank. Not wasting a second, she scrambled onto the far bank and made her way up towards the fence. She allowed herself a glance to the left where she could see the guards, thankfully still intent on Erdmann's words.

Turning to the right, she looked for Gerd, wiping the dripping water from her face. He was at the nearest concrete post to her right, the one Erdmann had pointed out earlier. Seemingly, he couldn't find the hole Erdmann had mentioned because he was using his clippers on the wire. Eva slithered the last few metres towards him on her stomach.

Gerd seemed to be struggling to clip the taut wire. His face, covered in his soaked fringe, looked mildly concerned for once. Eva glanced anxiously back down towards the colonel and the guards. Thankfully, they'd not moved from their gathering, but it wouldn't take long for Gerd and her to be spotted in this position. Eva was willing Gerd on. He was straining his arms trying to squeeze the clippers on the thick steel wire. His face was fully concentrated on the task. The clippers slipped from his hand. Eva's nerves felt shot, but Gerd didn't lose his composure. He grabbed the clippers from the sodden ground, wiping his hands quickly on his shirt, and then started again.

Then, the first strand of wire snapped. He was quickly on to the second, and the normal, confident look reappeared on Gerd's face. As the second wire popped, the gap was probably big enough for her now, but Gerd made one more cut, probably thinking about the others to follow.

Then he turned to her with a triumphant, beaming smile, grabbed her by the scruff of her shirt, and pushed her towards the gap in the fence.

It was then they heard the dogs barking.

***

They were some way off in the distance, but there was no mistaking the sound. Hans Erdmann stopped the briefing and the whole group turned towards the noise. Anxiety started to rise in Hans' chest. He had not planned for any dog patrols to be carried out in this particular sector, for obvious reasons. He allowed himself a quick look down the border fence. He quickly turned his head back, hoping nobody had seen his anxious glance. Fortunately, all his men were focused on whoever was approaching. The barking was louder now. Hans could see troops appearing from the trees, some with dogs. He pushed his way forward to see what was going on.

It was then he saw Riedle. Following in his footsteps, looking slightly out of breath, was the unmistakable figure of General Dobrovsky.

***

Sitting in the pissing down rain at the last line of trees in West Berlin told me why I was happier doing harebrained things in the eastern sectors. I'd never been a watcher. I needed a drink. I needed some action. I was itching to do something. That was in stark contrast to Klaus' friend, Markus. He was ice cold. He didn't twitch. His eyes were fixed on the fence, totally motionless.

Then he moved his head in my direction slightly. I couldn't see what I was supposed to be looking at, then slowly but surely, my eyes started to make out a figure on the move in the darkness on the eastern side. It took me an age to spot him, working his way under the coil, but when I did, I jumped up. He had me in a vice-like grip in a flash.

'It's not the time to be drawing attention to them, Jack. Stay down.'

I looked at him wondering what breed he was, so calm under pressure. My eyes were back on Gerd. My heart was in my mouth as he freed himself from the coil. I couldn't see any guards around. They'd cleared off a few minutes before, which was very convenient.

Gerd disappeared from our view for a moment. I knew this place. This was so close to where I'd witnessed the two men escape before I was picked up by Erdmann's men. I'd also seen the guards shooting at a man and hitting him. This was unbearable to watch.

Gerd reappeared right against the fence. I felt like I could touch him now. Gerd was testing the wire close to the post with his hand. Markus still had a tight hold on me. I was tempted to break free to get to him. I wondered where Eva was. Why wasn't she there with Gerd? He was working on the fence with some clippers, struggling to make the final breakthrough. I didn't want to look, only able to imagine the worst. It wasn't the first time. I turned to Markus, pleading to him with my eyes to let me go to her. Then, he nodded towards the fence.

Eva appeared next to Gerd. I saw the wire spring open. I couldn't stop myself now, and Markus didn't hold me back this time. I made up the ground to the border in seconds, sliding the last couple of metres on my knees. As I got there, Eva scurried through and out of the other side. I held her for the briefest of moments, until I heard the dogs barking. I looked at Gerd, the wire between us. I could see he was about to turn back towards the stream, but it wasn't time for heroics. He'd done enough already.

I reached through the gap, and hauled him out. He was protesting, as he appeared on the western side. He shook me off like a sulky teenager. I grabbed Eva under her arm and within seconds Gerd was under her other arm. Together we ran for the safety of the trees.

***

Klaus Schultz felt elated. He saw Eva, Jack, and Gerd make it to safety. He knew Markus was there and he would take care of everything. Time was now running out for him and Bernie, but somehow he expected they would survive. It's what had happened before, in Stalingrad and in the camps; he wasn't about to die now.

He'd heard the dogs. He knew that's something Erdmann would not have ordered.

He turned to Bernie. 'It's our turn, now, my friend.'

Bernie shook his head. 'You go. I don't want to hold you up.'

Klaus turned and looked at the fence, then he grabbed Bernie by the collar and dragged him out of the trees in the direction of barbed wire.

'I am not leaving you to that bastard Dobrovsky.'

***

Hans had harboured deep concerns about Riedle. He knew Marks had got to him previously, so it wasn't a great surprise to see him marching through the trees with Dobrovsky. Hans closed his eyes and summoned up one last effort from his inner being. He knew if Bernie and he were to escape now, he would need one last push and a lot of luck.

Riedle was first to Hans. 'I am sorry, Colonel. I had no choice.'

His eyes told the story, full of regret and sorrow. Hans wondered what they had done, what they'd threatened Riedle, or his family, with. It was always their way. Dobrovsky eventually caught up with them. Hans was playing for time now.

'Why are your men away from their posts, Erdmann?'

'I am holding a briefing, General. The quicker we can be allowed to finish, the quicker the men can return to their posts.'

He glanced down the Graben in time to see Bernie and Klaus Schultz reach the barbed wire coil. Hans couldn't delay things any longer.

He turned to the corporal, 'Dismiss the men. Return them to their posts.'

The men seemed somewhat reluctant to disperse, sensing a confrontation and not wanting to miss out.

'It's strange you are at the border like this. In the middle of the night, I mean,' Dobrovsky said.

'I could say the same thing, General.'

Dobrovsky looked Hans in the eye. 'I am here because Bernie Schwarzer has escaped. I believe you know something about that already.'

He turned and barked orders to his men. 'Take the dogs up and down this sector. And move quickly. Something isn't right here.'

Hans followed his men down the stream, engaging them in conversation, doing his best to slow the discovery of the two men. He was waiting for the shout, just waiting for them to be spotted, then the fireworks would begin.

***

Klaus pushed the wire over his head whilst dragging Bernie with him. It took a real effort to pull the man beside him, even though he had managed to regain some of his strength. It was as if Bernie knew he had to help Klaus and he was summoning his last reserves of effort from somewhere. Perversely, the rain sodden ground was aiding their slide under the coil. It was still a painful process. Klaus was well aware the guards were moving down the stream in their direction. It would only be a matter of time before they were seen.

Klaus focused on moving the wire over their heads rather than moving themselves forward too much. He watched the boy Gerd and this was what seemed to work for him. Finally, they reached the other side of the barbed wire. Klaus dragged Bernie towards the stream. He could hear the barking of the dogs intensify. He managed to push

Bernie down the bank and then slithered after him. They were halfway there now, but it was no time to rest.

Bernie was slumped in the stream, the water flowing over his legs and feet.

'Come on, move yourself. We can't sit here.'

'You go on,' Bernie said. 'I don't think I can make it.'

Klaus snarled, 'That doesn't sound like a soldier. Now move!'

Leaning against the far bank, Klaus used all his strength to haul him up. To his credit, Bernie started to pull himself up to the level of the fence. They were close now. Klaus could smell it.

***

Eva covered her eyes. 'I can't look.'

I was getting twitchy again. I wanted to rush to the fence and help Klaus and the other man, but I knew it was too early. If I did, it would only alert the attention of the guards. Eva had quickly explained about the involvement of the colonel in their escape. In some ways, I was surprised, but deep down I suspected the man couldn't agree with sealing the border like this.

'Halt!'

The guards were within ten metres of them when they saw them. I knew time was running out and that this whole episode could end in tragedy. Then I saw him, his little legs carrying him as fast as they would go. Dobrovsky was barking instructions, shouting like a maniac.

Out of the corner of my eye, I saw Hans Erdmann slipping between the barbed wire coils further up the stream, the attention of all the others on the two escapees. I saw him drop down the bank unnoticed. He was probably twenty metres from Klaus.

Klaus was now right in front of the fence post. A gunshot echoed through the trees. The cool Markus was up in a flash, darting to the fence, with no thought for his own safety. Eva flung her head into my chest, unable to watch. I turned to Gerd and said, 'Don't even think about moving from there.'

The boy defiantly flicked the hair out of his eyes, and did as he was told for once.

Markus was at the fence and reaching through towards Klaus, who in turn was trying to haul Bernie up to his level. Another shot rang out. Eva yelped, although nobody at the fence seemed to be hit, but the guards were closing in.

Klaus turned. I could see the top of the colonel's head moving towards them. He was close to them now and he waved his arms at Klaus. 'Go!'

Markus didn't give Klaus a choice, dragging him physically through the fence. Klaus cleared the fence by pushing his foot against the concrete post, as Erdmann clambered the grass bank, dragging Bernie towards the gap. Bernie grabbed hold of the fence post and started to push himself agonisingly through. Klaus and Markus went to his aid, whilst Erdmann was still on the other side.

Dobrovsky was near them now, on the other side of the coil, his gun leveled at the men on the fence. Klaus shouted a warning. Erdmann turned and immediately pushed himself up on his knees to protect his comrade. Klaus pulled Bernie free of the fence just as the shot rang out.

Erdmann slumped forward, his arms holding the wire.

Markus had the other man on his shoulder. He shouted at Klaus, 'Move or he'll shoot you as well.'

Markus was up, his legs moving in a blur, as he carried the man to safety. I swore I saw Erdmann smile, before he slid down the fence, falling at the gap where the others had escaped. Another shot whistled close by, then another struck the fence post.

Klaus had no choice but to leave the colonel and run for the trees.

EPILOGUE

SATURDAY, 19ᵗʰ AUGUST 1961,
WEST BERLIN

My fellow countryman had finally done something. It had taken the best part of a week. It was a week in which my emotions had bounced around like a yo-yo and had finally been allowed some respite. We were all there to witness the address of Vice President Lyndon Baines Johnson on the steps of the Schöneberg Town Hall that Saturday afternoon. Even Klaus Schultz was there, grumbling that this was "too little, too late." That said, most of West Berlin was on the streets to welcome the Vice President of the United States. They needed to feel the Americans weren't going to leave them stranded, at the mercy of the Russians.

Klaus had been right. Johnson and Clay's hastily arranged visit, and the strengthening of the US garrison with a measly thousand men, wasn't anywhere near enough, but it was something. It was badly needed to prop up the morale of the West Berliners after the city had basically been sealed off.

Eva had quickly recovered from her ordeal. Her ankle was just about healed, but for the bruising. The attentions of baby Tanja and having her mother and father around clearly aided the process. I didn't want to think about the consequences if that night on the border between Treptow and Neukölln had turned out any other way. It was an episode we all wanted, and needed, to put behind us. Personally, I couldn't have been happier. My world was complete. I was one of the lucky ones.

Over that week the border had been further reinforced. In some areas of the city, Bernauer Strasse, Potsdamer Platz, barbed wire and fences had already been replaced by a concrete wall. The measures were becoming indelibly permanent. I'd been able to have my own small revenge on the regime that perpetrated the monstrosity of the wall. The only sadness to come from the night on the border was the inability of Colonel Erdmann to make good his escape. We had feared for his life when he took the bullet meant for Bernie Schwarzer, or potentially even Klaus Schultz. Curiously, the East Germans turned the shooting of Hans Erdmann into a political show. According to Neues Deutschland, the regime mouthpiece, Erdmann had been shot by escapees at the border. He was awarded the Medal for Exemplary Border Service. I did wonder how Hans Erdmann might feel about that. At least, his sergeant, Bernie, was recovering well from his injuries in a West Berlin hospital.

The articles I wrote about the "Schiessbefehl," the order to shoot on the border, were the first realisation of just how big a humanitarian scandal the border in Berlin, and the inner German border, was to become. The supporting articles about Xavier Marks led to some changes in the East German government. It was quietly done, but it was there, deep in the newspaper, more focused on the visit of Lyndon Baines Johnson. Burzin confirmed Marks' disappearance from the political scene. He also confirmed Dobrovsky's recall to Moscow. Perhaps life for Colonel Erdmann may have been bearable in East Berlin after all.

Gerd joined us as we cheered the words of General Lucius Clay, better known for keeping Berlin fed during the blockade of 1948. Gerd was living with an uncle in Spandau. Our little family was grateful for what he did for us during that week. It would never be forgotten.

I squeezed Eva's hand. She dropped her head to my free shoulder. Tanja was bright and happy on my other arm. I wondered what more in the world a man could want.

Thank you for reading

I would like to thank you for taking the time to read *Berlin: Caught in the Mousetrap*. Further books about the Schultz family and Berlin will be available very soon. For further information, please visit my website blog below.

I hope you enjoyed it and if so, I would be grateful if you would leave a review.

The second in the Schultz family series, BERLIN: Reaping the Whirlwind is now available.

You can find more information about the author online:
www.paulgrant-author.com

E-mail:
info@paulgrant.com

About the Author
Paul Grant is from Leeds, UK, and continues to live in West Yorkshire, England. His first degree was in History, specialising in Germany between the wars, during the period of the Third Reich and the Cold War.

Acknowledgements and comments

I have read a number of excellent books whilst researching this novel, and it is important to acknowledge them here. Probably the most used reference was Curtis Cate's *The Ides of August: The Berlin Wall Crisis 1961.* This is a book I will never tire of reading and continue to refer to on a regular basis.

Frederick Taylor's book, *The Berlin Wall,* is a must read for anybody interested in the subject. There are a number of excellent books about the history of Berlin, such as David Clay Large's *Berlin – A Modern History*

There are a number of wonderful museums to visit in Berlin on topics dealt with by the book. It is impossible to name them all here, but the visits I particularly enjoyed were the Stasi prison museum at Hohenschönhausen (http://www.stiftung-hsh.de/homepage-2) and the Refugee Centre museum at Marienfelde (http://www.notaufnahmelager-berlin.de/en/), and an area also well worth a visit, where Klaus and Burzin meet, is the Berlin Wall memorial on Bernauer Strasse. (http://www.berliner-mauer-gedenkstaette.de/en/)

Berlin: Caught in the Mousetrap is a work of fiction based closely on historical fact. Any mistakes contained in it are solely my own. In writing the book, I wanted to explore the social effects of the Cold War, in this case upon the Schultz family. There will be more to come on the family and how the Second World War and the Cold War affected them and many other normal people like them. Personally, I find the recent history of Berlin to be fascinating. The history of Berlin, and history in general, is something we must continue to learn from; otherwise, the same mistakes will be made all over again.

Printed in Great Britain
by Amazon

17280234R00173